"Let me up, you m

a…" Isobel flailed wildly

"Now, sweetheart," mock severity, "is that any way for a lady to speak to her husband?"

Wedging one leg between her thighs, he used the weight of his left arm across her stomach to keep her pinned beneath him. With his other hand he caught hold of her wrists and brought them both up above her head. The action drew the fine fabric of her undershift taut across her breasts, and Dominic eyed the result appreciatively.

"Are you ready to concede yet, madam?" he asked pleasantly. "We could negotiate terms—you never know, I might be prepared to be generous…"

Isobel glared up at him defiantly.

"You may take your terms and stuff them up your…"

She gave a muffled gasp as his mouth closed over hers, and Dominic was instantly and painfully aware that what had begun in all innocence as a game between them had suddenly become something entirely different and infinitely more dangerous.

A Necessary Risk

by

Emily Ross

This is a work of fiction. Names, characters, places, and incidents are either the product of the author's imagination or are used fictitiously, and any resemblance to actual persons living or dead, business establishments, events, or locales, is entirely coincidental.

A Necessary Risk

Contact Information: info@thewildrosepress.com

Cover Art by *Debbie Taylor*

The Wild Rose Press, Inc.
PO Box 708
Adams Basin, NY 14410-0708
Visit us at www.thewildrosepress.com

Publishing History
First Tea Rose Edition, 2015
Print ISBN 978-1-62830-886-0
Digital ISBN 978-1-62830-887-7

Published in the United States of America

Dedication

In memory of Enfys,
who taught me to believe in dreams and never give up;
and for all the wonderful girls I have worked with
at MR/RKL
over the last twelve years.
Thank you for putting up with me, ladies—
you know who you are, especially Paula!!

Acknowledgments

A huge thank you to the Team at The Wild Rose Press for their support, help, and encouragement in making my storytelling dreams come true. Most especially thanks to my wonderful editor, Nan Swanson, without whom Dominic and Isobel would never have made it!

Prologue

Waterford, Ireland, August 1170

Richard de Clare, nicknamed "Strongbow" for his prowess with that fearsome weapon, pushed back his mail coif and raised his clenched fist in a gesture of triumph to the inhabitants of Waterford. Behind him the cathedral bells pealed in celebration of his marriage, and at his side rode his wife, Aoife, and his father-in-law, Dermot MacMurrough, King of Leinster.

De Clare glanced sidelong at the not-unpleasing profile of his bride and congratulated himself once again on having had the foresight to respond to MacMurrough's call to arms. An advanced army of his Welsh vassals and an expedient marriage seemed a small price to pay for the chance of dominion over Ireland.

On receiving the news of de Clare's triumph, the reaction of Henry, King of England, was not nearly so sanguine. He snatched at the thin roll of vellum hesitantly proffered for his inspection by the dusty, travel-stained herald and scanned it. His thick sandy brows drew together ominously.

Anticipating the onset of one of Henry's famous Angevin rages, Robert Fitz-Harding, the king's close friend and current companion, bestowed a look of pity on the young messenger. He indicated with a slight nod of his head that the boy should leave.

Henry swung round with a furious bellow.

“Who in God’s name does de Clare think he is?” he roared. He crumpled the missive and hurled it at the door in the wake of the departing messenger. “See this?” He thrust his hand under Fitz-Harding’s nose so he could not fail to see the great emerald thereon. “This is on *my* hand, not de Clare’s. *I* have the Holy Father’s authority to rule in Ireland, not him!”

Fitz-Harding inclined his head in diplomatic acknowledgment of Henry’s waggling fingers before bending to retrieve the abused document. He smoothed it out and studied the contents for himself.

“Calm yourself, Sire,” he advised.

It was a testimony to his position as wealthy merchant, money lender, and acknowledged royal favourite that he dared to address the king thus. Henry snorted incredulously. One of the qualities he had most admired in Fitz-Harding from the early days of their acquaintance had been his remarkable intellect. He could not believe it to be so lacking now.

“Cannot you see the danger here?” he roared. “I gave him dispensation to subdue the Irish, not to make himself their king!”

Fitz-Harding crossed to a small table by the window and poured a generous measure of wine from the flagon it held. He handed it to his liege lord.

“Marriage to a princess does not necessarily make a man a king.”

Henry spat a mouthful of wine into the rushes, perversely enjoying Fitz-Harding’s frown of disapproval.

“And would you have me believe that the potential

of the situation has never crossed his mind?" He rounded on Fitz-Harding. "This is your fault, Robert!" he accused. "You were the one who bade me favour his cause when he came begging my approval for this venture!"

"Yes, Sire."

Fitz-Harding bowed his head in apparent contrition. He deemed it prudent not to enlighten his sovereign that it had been to himself that the King of Leinster had first applied for assistance against his fellow countrymen. Nor did he choose to disclose the fact that the erstwhile de Clare was heavily in his debt, and that his recommendation had been made with the sole intention of providing the debtor with an opportunity to pay his dues.

"MacMurrough cannot live forever," Henry continued furiously as he paced restlessly about the chamber, "and Strongbow has at least two hundred men at arms and a thousand archers to enforce his claim to Leinster when the time comes."

"Yes, Sire," Fitz-Harding agreed again, "and *when* that time comes, we will be ready for him." He raised his goblet in Henry's direction, his expression innocently bland.

The king's eyes narrowed in speculative appreciation. "And you commended de Clare to me as a friend," he mused. "By God, Robert, I would not want to be your enemy!"

Outwardly Fitz-Harding smiled, but his mind was already working furiously.

Chapter One

Late February 1171

Isobel de Lescaux allowed herself to be distracted by the sight of her father approaching across the bailey and immediately paid for her loss of concentration by scraping her knuckles against the whetstone upon which she had been honing her eating knife. She gritted her teeth and forced back the oath that sprang to her lips, having no wish for a repeat of the occasion last week when Lord William had seen fit to upbraid her in public for her "unsuitable language and unseemly behaviour." His scathing attack had come as something of a surprise to everyone, since for the past fifteen years William de Lescaux had scarcely even bothered to acknowledge the existence of his daughter, let alone take any interest in her.

Although confused by her father's outburst, Isobel had duly taken note of his criticism, vowing to herself that she would strive to conform—if only in the vain hope of at last gaining some measure of approbation from the man who had sired her. Today, however, it seemed she need not have bothered, since he proceeded to storm up the stone steps to the keep without so much as a backward glance. Isobel exhaled and allowed herself the oath after all, much to the amusement of two off-duty men at arms who were lounging idly against the wall at the bottom of the stairs. She scowled at them and sucked at the grazes on her hand.

Lord William had, in fact, seen Isobel but in his present mood much preferred to pretend that he had not. The last of the six surviving children born to him and his adored wife, she'd been unwelcome in his home since the day she had drawn her first breath. Weakened by seven pregnancies in quick succession, the sixth of which had resulted in twins, his beloved Anwen had not lived long after the delivery of her only daughter, leaving a distraught and bewildered William to oversee the upbringing of their extensive brood. So great had been his love for her that he had never remarried, nor had he taken solace from any other quarter. His desire had died with his wife, and he had resisted all urging from his sister, Rohese, to provide his children with a stepmother.

It was Rohese's latest missive that was responsible for his current ill temper. Christ, didn't the woman ever give up? William pulled out the crumpled sheet of vellum and scanned the familiar detested script, which, like its author, was inevitably neat and precise. He bellowed at a passing servant to fetch him some wine, then slumped into his favourite chair, running a hand through his over-long iron grey hair. It was all Isobel's fault, he told himself, knowing even as he did so that he was being unfair. The wretched girl hadn't even had the grace to follow her mother to the grave, growing instead into a daily reminder of all that he had lost—a living thorn in his flesh.

Never expecting the infant to survive, William had promised his dying wife not to part with their daughter to his childless sister, nor to banish her to a convent. So when the tiny baby had perversely continued to grow and thrive, he had conscientiously maintained his wife's Welsh dower lands as their daughter's marriage portion, in accordance with her mother's wishes. Thus he consoled himself that he had done his duty by the girl, conveniently ignoring the fact that Isobel's upbringing in this almost exclusively male household was entirely unsuited to her station in life.

William swallowed a generous measure of rich Anjou and glared mutinously at the fire. He could not be blamed, he reasoned, for not knowing what to do with a girl-child. He had always done his best—no one could accuse him of stinting in the education and training of his sons. A smile of pride and satisfaction lifted his mouth. To have raised five boys to handsome maturity was a formidable achievement, and he knew without conceit that the name of Lescaux was deemed a force to be reckoned with.

He conjured their faces in the flames. First his eldest and namesake, Will, knighted three years since, and, at the age of three-and-twenty, recently married very advantageously to the eminently suitable Alais de Beauvoir, daughter of a neighbouring landowner. In due course the Lescaux and Beauvoir estates would be joined, and their combined holdings would make a fitting inheritance for his grandchildren.

Next came twenty-two-year-old Henry, who had also already gained his spurs. Henry's future was assured. He had fortuitously been named heir to his uncle's estates, where the widowed Rohese currently dwelt. It crossed William's mind that Rohese might expect to move into Lescaux with him when Henry married. He shuddered at the prospect, consoling himself with the hope that she would remain on her former husband's property to torment whatever unfortunate woman would become her niece by marriage.

William's craggy brows drew together in a slight frown. His next son, Adam, would be twenty-one this year. By rights, the boy should have been destined for the church, but by the time he had reached his seventh year-day it was abundantly clear that Adam's nature would never be suited to life in the cloister. Undeterred by his lack of inheritance, at sixteen he had announced his intention to make his own way in the world. To William's enormous gratification, his third son had proceeded to demonstrate remarkable prowess on the tourney field and had earned himself a position as lieutenant to the noted mercenary commander Dominic du Bois. From Adam's infrequent correspondence William surmised that the past year had been spent in Ireland, most recently fighting under the banner of Richard de Clare. His last communication, however, hinted that the king was growing alarmed at de Clare's rapid advancement. It was rumoured that Strongbow would soon be ordered to curtail his activities, and Adam seemed to think he would be back in England for Easter.

A stillborn infant and a miscarriage had followed Adam's birth, before the twins, Robert and Stephen, were born. Now nearing eighteen, they were serving as squires in the household of William's old friend Hubert le Vaillant—a mutually beneficial arrangement, since Hubert's son, Alain, had boarded at Lescaux since beginning his page's training. It had originally been William's intention to send one of his own boys to

Vaillant at that time, but the twins had fiercely resisted all attempts to separate them, and William had, in truth, been loath to let them go. Even now he missed the boisterous and irrepressible nature of his youngest sons. Lescaux seemed unnaturally quiet without them.

He looked up, his expression changing abruptly.

“Come here!”

Isobel turned away from the stairs leading to the upper chambers and came back to stand before him, surreptitiously pushing her bruised knuckles into the folds of her skirt.

“What have you done to your hand?”

She bit her lip, silently cursing her ill fortune. “Nothing, Papa.”

“Don’t lie to me!”

William reached out, gripped her arm, and pulled her towards him. Forcibly he uncurled her fingers and turned her hand over. There was an uncomfortable silence, followed by his forbidding tones telling her she was no longer permitted to use the whetstone.

She should have known better but, this being simply the latest in a growing list of restrictions he had imposed on her in recent weeks, Isobel unwisely sought an explanation. In answer, William jerked her hands upwards and forced her to look at them.

“Do those look like the hands of a lady to you?” His throat worked convulsively. “Before God, I tell you your mother would be ashamed of you.”

Isobel’s mouth dropped open in surprise. Never, in all her fifteen years, could she remember her father mentioning her mother in her presence.

“Get out!” he growled at her.

She hastened at once in the direction of the stairs,

needing no second bidding, and upon reaching the sanctuary of her bedchamber she flung herself down on the straw-stuffed mattress, refusing to shed the tears that stung her eyes. At length she arose, splashed her face with cold water, and considered her position. She could not remain in her room forever, and she had a duty to at least attempt to oversee the preparations for the evening meal. She sighed and headed for the kitchens.

Lescaux's keep boasted few female servants, and fewer still who could lay any claim to respectability; thus there had ever been little opportunity for Isobel to learn the day-to-day skills of domestic management. Hildred Leval, the widow of a long-departed steward, had been more perceptive than most. She had seen the gaps in the child's education and had tried her best to ensure that she learned something about the running of her father's household, but Hildred had died of the spotted fever three winters ago, and Isobel's source of knowledge had died with her. As a consequence, although the cook treated her with the deference due to her status, Isobel suspected he frequently took advantage of her lack of expertise and did not overly exert himself in the performance of his duties. Tonight was no exception and, as she prodded experimentally at the very ordinary pottage simmering above the fire, she found herself wishing that Mistress Leval were here to tell her what she should do.

With the steward's wife still very much on her mind, she returned to her chamber and rummaged in the bottom of her clothing coffer for a pot of rosewater unguent Hildred had once helped her make. Pulling the wooden stopper from the jar, she sniffed dubiously at the contents. Being over three years old, the salve was probably well past being any use, Isobel guessed, but she rubbed some into the backs of her hands anyway, in the hope their condition might improve before her father had cause to notice them again. Once she'd replaced the stopper in the jar with a decisive snap, she made her way down to the hall.

As Isobel had feared, the meal was even more indifferent than usual, and William de Lescaux's mood had not improved. His brooding gaze frequently came to rest on his daughter, and the pages waiting at table cast speaking glances at one another.

Performing his accustomed duties as William's body servant brought Alain le Vaillant closer to Isobel than most. He leant over her shoulder and hissed in her ear, "*Jesu*, Bel! What have you done this time?"

Isobel gave an infinitesimal shake of her head. She did not dare reply, for fear of drawing further attention to herself, but she was grateful for the fleeting smile of sympathy Alain bestowed on her. Of an age with her youngest brothers and often a childhood playmate, he was, she supposed, the closest thing she had to a friend. She sighed inwardly, reflecting how incredibly difficult her life seemed to have become since the twins left for Vaillant. Whilst they had remained at home, seldom a day passed when they had not done something to incur their father's ire. Now they were gone, leaving her to bear the brunt of his displeasure.

Lord William crooked his finger at his squire, and Isobel's heart rate increased, thinking he might, after all, have overheard their brief exchange, but he merely signalled for Alain to pour him more wine before turning to address her.

"Your Aunt Rohese has written me again," he informed her bitingly. "Have you been complaining to her behind my back?"

Isobel was genuinely astonished. She had little liking for her father's sister, who, on the rare occasions they spent any time together, criticised her constantly for everything from her table manners to her wardrobe.

"No, Papa. What opportunity have I had, even had I wished to do so?"

William sniffed derisively. "You've spent enough time with Father Padraig to have learned to pen a missive for yourself. Did you, or did you not, write to your aunt?"

Colour surged into Isobel's cheeks as her temper snapped.

"Whatever I say, it seems you will come to your own conclusion—and invariably find me lacking!"

She registered Alain's swiftly indrawn breath behind her as Lord William rammed his wine cup down onto the trestle with such force that its delicately wrought metal stem twisted. Isobel stood up and pushed her chair back from the table. Conscious that all eyes followed her progress, she drew herself up and, head high, made for the stairs which led from the hall to the family's private apartments.

Not one of the men present would have had the effrontery to treat William de Lescaux so, and even his sons might have thought twice about deliberately inciting his rage with such a display of disrespect. His face suffused with wrath, William leaped to his feet, unlatching the broad leather belt from his waist as he did so. There was little doubt in anyone's mind as to what he intended to do with it; nor was there anyone who would try to stop him. It was, after all, a man's right to discipline the women in his household.

Isobel heard her father's footsteps as he came after her, but she altered neither her course nor her speed. He caught up with her as she set her foot on the bottom stair, seized hold of her wrist, reversing their positions, and hauled her up the stairs. As he dragged her towards her room, she found herself distantly wondering what it would be like to be beaten. She knew her brothers had all been punished thus for various misdemeanours during the course of their childhood, but until now her father had never laid a finger upon her. William kicked the heavy oak door shut and loosed his hold.

"Bare your back, madam," he ordered.

Isobel tried not to let him see how hard she was trembling. She faced him squarely, chin raised, arms folded determinedly across her chest.

"And help you punish me when I do not even know what it is I am being punished for? I think not!"

In a corner of William's mind, grudging admiration dawned. He throttled it down mercilessly. Catching hold of her wrists again, he attempted to pin them behind her back, but Hildred's rosewater cream had made the skin greasy, and Isobel managed to twist away, ducking beneath his arm. He let out a bellow of rage.

"I should have taken my belt to you years ago!" he thundered. "Were it not for your mother's memory…" He broke off, staring at the young woman who stood before him, seeing not his daughter but his beloved wife as she had looked in the early days of their marriage, fresh and youthful.

"Anwen," he whispered, taking an involuntary step

towards his vision. He reached out and cupped her chin in his fingers, his face just inches from her own.

"Papa…please!"

Isobel's voice was no more than a whisper, but it was enough to break the spell. William looked down at the belt still clenched in his fist, then thrust her away from him with an exclamation of disgust. The resounding thud of the closing door echoed round the room, and Isobel sank to the floor, her whole body shaking. She wanted to vomit. The years of seeming indifference, changing more latterly into unmistakable dislike, now made perfect sense to her. The logical part of her mind reasoned that it was not her fault she had grown so closely to resemble her mother, but there was another part of her that understood her father's behaviour. Her very existence was enough to remind him daily of all that he had lost—like grinding salt into an open wound.

Why hadn't he sent her away? She knew her Aunt Rohese had repeatedly asked to be given charge of her, and Father Padraig had advocated her despatch to the Convent of Our Lady at least twice, first when Adam had left and again when Robert and Stephen had gone. For the second time that day, Isobel found herself on the verge of tears, and this time she allowed herself the luxury of letting them fall. Finally, exhausted by the unaccustomed bout of self-pity, she crept under the coverlet and slept.

Chapter Two

Alain le Vaillant balanced a ewer of water precariously in the crook of his elbow and gripped a tankard of ale with the fingers of one hand whilst using his other to knock on the door. He lifted the latch, put his shoulder against the iron-studded oak, and pushed. Once over the threshold, Alain hovered on the edge of the chamber, mindful of the fact that neither Lescaux's lord nor his daughter had returned to the hall last night—and consequently uncertain of his reception this morning.

"Come in, boy, I won't bite!" William de Lescaux snapped from within the shadow of his bed hangings.

"My lord." His squire was dutifully respectful and bowed before setting down the water pitcher and ale tankard on a side table.

William eyed him thoughtfully. "Your father has written to me, Alain. He is interested to know how you are progressing. He is holding a tourney as part of the Easter celebrations and has suggested that I bring you home for a visit. What think you?"

Alain swallowed nervously, for he was unused to his lord seeking his opinion on anything.

"I should be pleased to see my father and my lady mother, my lord," he offered carefully.

William nodded approvingly. "And you'd like even more to see your brother, Dominic, I'll warrant?"

"Dom is coming home?" Alain was unable to keep the excitement from his voice.

Dominic du Bois was, in fact only a half-sibling to Alain, being the bastard offspring of their mutual father, but the difference in their respective ages was sufficient to ensure there was no resentment on either side. Indeed, there was more than an element of hero worship in Alain's regard for Dominic.

William smiled. "Aye—and that means Adam will be with him. What's more, your father tells me he has invited William and Henry, too."

He sat up in the bed, his mood considerably improved by the thought of having all five of his sons together again. The de Lescaux family would be a formidable force on the tourney field.

Alain laid out fresh garments for his lord and served the bread and ale that would break his fast. He waited until William indicated that he required nothing further from him for the time being, then bowed and quitted the room.

Preoccupied with thoughts of the imminent visit home, he failed to see Isobel coming towards him and almost collided with her in the doorway to the hall. To his surprise, he saw she was dressed to go riding, and he found himself considering the unlikely possibility that Lord William had not beaten her after all, since his own experience told him she'd not be so eager to sit a horse today if he had. Glancing round to ensure that no one was observing them, Alain hesitantly placed a hand on her sleeve.

"Bel, are you all right? Last night, I mean, he didn't..." He broke off, embarrassed, and looked away.

Isobel managed a wan smile. "No, Alain, he didn't,

but in a way, I almost wish he had—it might have been easier to cope with the pain of a physical beating."

Alain shot her a curious look, which she chose to ignore.

"Bel," he began awkwardly, "I know you don't intend it, but everything you do seems to anger him at the moment." He flicked a finger at her riding dress. "Wouldn't it be better to keep to the solar today?"

Isobel sighed. Now that she understood the reason for her father's antagonism towards her, she doubted that there was anything she could do that would improve matters between them—except to keep out of his way as much as possible, hence her decision to spend the better part of the day away from the keep.

"You've seen my sewing, Alain. Do you not recall the day Robert tore his shirt climbing that oak in the meadow and insisted that I mend it before Papa found out?"

Alain's answering smile told her he remembered the occasion well.

"It was not a pretty sight, was it?" she continued. "Believe me, I'm a much better horsewoman than I am needlewoman!"

"All the more reason why you should confine yourself to the bower and practise," Alain called after her, as she continued on her way.

She turned and made a childish face at him. With a despairing shake of his head he watched her across the bailey until she disappeared into the stables, recalling the way in which she had joined unhesitatingly in the games of war he had played with her twin brothers—and how quickly and competently she had mastered the rudiments of sword and dagger fighting. Adam had presented her with a small hunting bow for her tenth birthday, and she had shown remarkable skill with that, too. Indeed, Alain found himself thinking Isobel might have made an excellent squire, but for the fact she had been born a girl. On the other hand, he acknowledged with a rueful grin, he supposed he should be grateful for small mercies, for doubtless she would have excelled at everything she was asked to do and put all others—including himself—to shame.

It was after midday when Isobel returned, cheeks glowing and tendrils of hair escaping from her wayward braid. The outing had served its purpose, and she had succeeded in temporarily banishing her unhappy situation from her mind. She patted her mount's glossy neck and slid to the ground, oblivious of the admiring look on the face of the groom's apprentice. He made no move to take the animal from her, but then, she did not expect him to. Isobel, like her brothers, had learnt from an early age to take care of her own horse.

Looping the reins over the mare's head, she led her into an empty stall, pausing briefly to rub the nose of her father's stallion. The horse had a reputation for his uncertain temper, and his master's daughter was amongst the few human beings he was prepared to tolerate. Dropping the bar across the opening, she proceeded to remove the mare's harness and was so involved in her task she did not realise her father was behind her until he spoke her name. Isobel jumped in surprise.

"Papa," she acknowledged warily, the unwelcome memory of last night's confrontation returning.

Ducking under the bar, she thrust a straw wisp at the loitering apprentice.

"See to my horse, if you please—and make sure you do it properly, for I will check on her later."

As the lad bowed and hastened to obey, William once again felt a reluctant stirring of pride warring with his other emotions. Like it or not, he could not deny that his daughter was any less a de Lescaux than his sons. The shock of having to acknowledge just how like her mother she had become had been a painful awakening. Now he faced the undeniable truth that she could no longer be treated like her brothers, nor could he continue to ignore her. He must do his duty and see that she learned to behave as befitted a lady of her birth and rank. His face resumed its habitual frown.

"Go and change," he ordered brusquely. "Then come to me in the solar. I wish to speak to you."

Resigning herself to yet another unpleasant interview, Isobel curtsied and turned away.

A short time later, clad in one of only two passably decent gowns she possessed, hair combed and neatly re-braided, Isobel entered the solar to find her father sitting in the window embrasure. On the floor beside him his favourite hound was stretched full length, nose on paws. The dog's tail thumped as Isobel approached, and she bent down to scratch its neck, smiling at the blissful expression that appeared on its face as she did so. She looked up to find her father's eyes on her.

"You have a way with animals," he murmured reminiscently. "Your mother had it, too."

William reached for his daughter's hand and drew her down on the velvet cushion beside him, frowning as he smoothed his thumb over the roughened skin.

"I have neglected you," he said, half to himself. "Despite my promise, I have not done my duty by you."

"What promise, Papa?" Isobel's voice shook a little, for, truth to tell, she found this new William de Lescaux even more unnerving. Lost in his memories, her father's eyes dwelt on her without focussing.

"She made me promise I would not shut you away in a convent, nor allow Rohese to have governance of you." He sighed and lifted one weathered brown hand to touch her cheek. "But she would have wanted me to raise you as a lady. To see that you were equipped to make a good marriage."

Isobel's eyes widened. When Will had married Alais last summer, she had fleetingly imagined standing before the church door, gazing up at some faceless stranger with hopeless adoration in her eyes, but she had dismissed the notion almost as quickly, for she and Alais de Beauvoir were about as dissimilar as the proverbial chalk and cheese. Alais was diminutive and delicate, whereas Isobel had fallen only a couple of inches short of the twins at their last reckoning. Alais spoke in a breathy whisper, and she deferred to her husband over almost everything—indeed, Isobel would not have been surprised to hear that Alais even sought Will's permission to breathe! She tried to ignore the uncomfortable feeling that her eldest brother had seemed delighted with his bride, and that, in all probability, this was what men desired of their wives.

"…my mind is made up, daughter, and in this I will not be gainsaid."

Isobel realised with a start that her father had continued speaking, and that she had not heard a word. Belatedly she cast around for an excuse.

"I am sorry, Papa, I…"

"There's no need to look so stricken, girl. I won't

be breaking my vow to your mother. I simply need to ask Rohese's advice—she is bound to know what you will need in the way of fashionable clothes and other such nonsense."

"Fashionable clothes?" Isobel repeated the words as if they were part of some foreign language.

"You must have several new gowns, of course," William acknowledged, "and doubtless there will be other things…"

Isobel's sense of unease grew.

"New gowns?" she echoed.

William uttered an impatient oath. "Father Padraig led me to believe you were more intelligent than Robert and Stephen put together, yet here you stand before me like the veriest simpleton! You. Will. Need. New. Clothes," he enunciated carefully, with a disparaging look at the dress she was wearing.

"What for?" she demanded suspiciously.

William stood up and ran an exasperated hand through his still vigorous hair.

"It is my intention to see you wed and settled, as your mother would have wished; however, I have realised of late that perhaps the education you have received has not been, er, entirely adequate for that purpose. Therefore, I have decided that you will accompany me to Vaillant, where I will hand you over to your sister-by-marriage. If Father Padraig has the right of it, I am sure that it will not take you many months under her tutelage to learn what you need to know about managing a household, and in the meantime I will begin to search for a suitable match for you. There, are you not pleased?"

He expected her to be, Isobel realised. She

struggled to find something to say, but no words came. Only moments ago she had been trying—and failing spectacularly—to envisage herself cast in her sister-in-law's mould; now it appeared she was to be forced into it. Her father was frowning again.

"Yes, well, it is perhaps rather sudden, but you are very nearly a woman grown, Isobel. You cannot continue to behave as you did when you were a child, running free with your brothers. Surely you can see that?"

"But Papa…"

William raised his hand to signify that he would hear no more and turned away from her. Isobel clenched her fists impotently. Was this what her father had been waiting for all her life—for her to reach an age where she could legitimately be palmed off on some other man so that he could rid himself of her mother's ghost, whilst still being able to salve his conscience with the knowledge that he had not broken his promise? Had he still been looking in her direction, Lord William would have seen his daughter's lips set in an all too recognisable de Lescaux expression and known that she considered the matter far from settled.

Chapter Three

As they came in sight of the whitewashed square keep rising majestically above a bend in the river, Alain le Vaillant turned in his saddle and smiled with unconcealed delight at his lord's daughter.

"There it is, Bel—there is Vaillant."

There was an unmistakable note of pride in the young man's voice, for Alain held his home in very real affection, and Isobel supposed he would one day make a good master for its people. On this particular day, however, she was feeling decidedly uncharitable.

"After twelve months of Robert and Stephen in residence, I'm surprised it's still standing," she remarked acerbically. Alain grinned at her, refusing to be intimidated by her waspish manner.

"At Vaillant they won't have had time to ferment the sort of mischief they indulged in at Lescaux," he boasted confidently. Isobel rewarded him with a withering look.

"If you truly believe that, then you do not know the twins at all."

Alain ignored her. "My father said that Dominic would be bringing his troop to fight on our side in the jousts," he mused. "I wonder whether they will have arrived yet?"

Isobel sniffed. "Mercenaries!" she said, scathingly.

She had heard plenty from Alain about the exploits

of his half-brother, the great Dominic du Bois, and she was heartily sick of the man already. Alain considered reminding her that her own brother was amongst those she had just dismissed so disparagingly, but on seeing the look upon her face, decided against it. He cast a covert glance at Lord William and realised he was scowling at his daughter. Alain returned his gaze to Isobel and gave her careful scrutiny, trying to see where she could be found wanting. She was richly clad in what Rohese Pascale had decreed to be the height of fashion when she had descended on Lescaux some weeks since, attended by a veritable army of cloth merchants, seamstresses, and sundry other acolytes. Isobel had been less than grateful, as she had been confined to the bower for several days. In a rare moment of freedom she had encountered Alain in the kitchen gardens. She had sworn him to secrecy and then proceeded to complain at length. At the time he had, of course, tendered sympathy, but looking at her now, he could not help thinking her new clothes had made her look very fine. He could see nothing in her appearance or behaviour to merit her father's censure, save perhaps her rather tart conversation, and he found himself wondering anew at the cause of the almost tangible friction between Lord William and his daughter.

When Isobel had told Alain of her father's plans for her future, he had seen nothing amiss, excepting, of course, their suddenness. He had been at pains to point out that she was the daughter of a noble house, and that it was the duty of all daughters to make advantageous matches, as his own half-sisters had already done. Isobel's answer had been to hurl a clod of earth at him. He grimaced. Unfortunately her aim was rather good.

Alain risked a further glance in Isobel's direction, then spurred his horse forward, judging her best left to herself whilst she was so out of temper.

****

In the great hall of Vaillant's keep, Dominic du Bois was feeling uncharacteristically relaxed. This was one of the few places where he felt able to lower his guard, and he stretched his long legs comfortably towards the fire that burned hospitably in the huge canopied hearth.

"Good to be home, my lord?" His lieutenant, near-constant companion, and closest friend, Adam de Lescaux, flashed an understanding smile.

Both men were above average height and boasted the well-honed physique that proclaimed a lifetime spent in training for war. They were a contrasting study in good looks—Dominic ebony-dark and blue-eyed, Adam tawny gold, like a lion's pelt, with eyes of clear hazel.

Dominic shrugged carelessly by way of response. "I have not counted Vaillant my home for a good many years," he said laconically.

"You know what I mean," Adam countered. He ran tanned fingers appreciatively over the fine carving on the arm of his box chair, idly tracing the pattern. "It will be good not to have to look over our shoulders all the time."

Dominic snorted. "I'd advise you to be looking hard enough tomorrow," he said darkly. "There may not be any Irish to worry about, but there will be enemies a-plenty."

Adam nodded. "Yes, Piers de Bracy, for one," he said, naming a fellow mercenary from the recent Irish campaign. He slanted a glance at Dominic, knowing that he and de Bracy were old rivals from their early days on the tourney circuit, when both had been out to make a name for themselves. There was little love lost between them. "Why do you think he is here?"

"Why are you here?"

Adam grinned at him. "The order from Henry was quite clear. Anyone who was not back in England by Easter would forfeit everything to the crown. I may not have anything to call my own, but I hardly think my father and two elder brothers would welcome me with open arms if they lost their lands and position on account of my folly. I am not so lackwitted as to think Henry's avenging arm would not strike at them as a way of punishing my disobedience."

"Exactly so," Dominic agreed. "The word is that de Bracy has got his eye on a tidy inheritance—a distant cousin on his mother's side. The present incumbent is in poor health, and his only issue is a fourteen-year-old girl to whom, God help her, de Bracy has managed to get himself betrothed."

Adam's breath whistled between his teeth. "I'd not give a dunghill cur into his keeping, never mind an innocent child. What can her father be thinking of?"

Dominic regarded him cynically. "Oh, I'd say our friend Piers can be very persuasive when it suits him—and if the charm offensive fails, well, that's quite an army he's got to his name these days, in case you hadn't noticed."

"So," Adam surmised, "he would not want to be seen doing anything now which might jeopardise his claim when the time comes. Mind you, de Bracy's been a sight closer to de Clare than ever we were." He paused, his eyes on the fire, as one of the logs cracked open and a shower of sparks danced upwards. "Do you think Strongbow really means to challenge the king?"

Dominic shook his head. "He's a fool if he does. His prospects are by no means promising. There is not one square mile of Irish soil he could call his own, and I would not trust the adherents of Dermot MacMurrough further than I could spit. Added to that, Henry's embargo on trade with Ireland effectively means that de Clare's now got the problem of provisioning those who have stayed with him. You know as well as I do that an army without food is no army at all."

"Even so," Adam continued to probe, "we could have gone elsewhere from Ireland. Why did you suddenly choose to accept your father's invitation to spend Easter at Vaillant, if it were not for the chance to come home?"

Dominic cast a look round the hall to check that there was no danger of their conversation being overheard.

"Put it down to my insatiable curiosity. I know better than anyone that my father is a wily old fox. I want to know what he's up to. He claims to be hosting this joust at the king's instigation, ostensibly in honour of the queen. Now, on the face of it, it's a plausible enough explanation—it's no secret Henry and Eleanor have been at odds again recently and she's threatened to take herself off to her own court at Poitiers. Her fondness for such entertainments is well known, and mayhap Henry really does believe that the thought of all these chivalric clashes being performed in her name will go some way towards appeasing her—but you take a good look around at who's here. I'd wager you a month's pay my father has instructions from Henry to do just that, and to make a careful note of the absentees. It's my belief my father's been charged with assessing who from this part of the world could be counted to stand with the king in the event of a serious challenge from de Clare."

"And you want to be seen declaring yourself for the Angevins, especially as we have been allied with de Clare until now?" Adam concluded.

"Up until now," Dominic reminded him, "de Clare's endeavours are supposed to have been with Henry's blessing…"

He paused as a commotion in the doorway heralded the entry of more guests, effectively bringing their conversation to an end. Dominic turned, smiling indulgently as he discerned the identity of the latest arrivals. He rose and embraced his half-brother, then set him at arm's length, looking him over like a man gauging the mettle of an untried horse.

"You've grown," he conceded.

Alain rolled his eyes at this predictable greeting, but before he could open his mouth to reply he was almost knocked off his feet by two young men dressed in Vaillant livery. Dominic regarded the newcomers with genuine astonishment. Adam de Lescaux had spoken often of his twin brothers and their exploits, but nothing could have prepared a man for their combined impact. Clothed identically as they were, it was quite impossible to tell them apart.

Dominic had not reached the heights of his chosen profession without developing certain skills. Intrigue was part of his stock in trade, and he was therefore quick to see the potential of having a man who could, quite literally, appear in two places at the same time. He determined to approach his father as soon as possible with a request that the two youngest de Lescauxs be permitted to continue their training under his direction. Like Adam, they would need to make their own way in the world, and Dominic was confident they would find the prospect of working for him far more appealing than becoming hearth knights for either of their two older brothers. With an amiable nod in the direction of the boys, he sauntered away toward the other side of the hall.

Alain frowned, minutely examining one face and then the other, trying to decide whether the twins were telling the truth. It was a game they had played many times before, and it appeared he was no better at it now than in the days of their shared childhood.

"I suppose I'll just have to take your word for it," he said grudgingly, "though I'll wager you wouldn't fool Bel."

"We never could," admitted the twin who had declared himself to be Stephen. "Even when we dressed the same, or changed clothes halfway through the day, Bel always seemed to know."

"I've told you before," his double pronounced disgustedly, "it's because she's a witch! But seeing as our little baby sister isn't here to spoil the fun…"

Alain allowed himself a superior smile. "Much you know. Isobel travelled with us, and she's to go home with Will and Alais."

"Whatever for?" Robert was plainly surprised.

"She'll hate it," Stephen warned with certainty.

"Very likely," Alain concurred, "but my lord your father has decided she must learn the necessary skills to equip her to make a good marriage—and even you must see that Lescaux is not the place for her to do so."

Robert exploded with laughter. "The old man's finally lost his wits! Who in their right mind would consider marrying Bel?"

Stephen's face showed clearly that he was in complete agreement, and Alain shook his head at them reprovingly.

"It's no wonder poor Isobel has grown up the way she has."

"What's that supposed to mean?" Stephen asked, still struggling to control his mirth.

"It means you cannot see what is right under your noses." Alain coloured slightly. "Your sister is not a child any more. Indeed, some would consider her quite beautiful."

"You amongst them, obviously," said Robert, his eyes narrowing. "Just how much time *have* you been spending in Bel's company of late, Alain?"

The implication was unmistakeable. Alain lunged towards his aggressor, ready to do battle, both for Isobel's honour and for his own, only to find himself restrained by a firm hand on his shoulder.

"*Pax*, you two." Adam placed himself between the would-be combatants. "I'm sure Alain would never do anything to harm Isobel. As Father's squire, her honour is as much his to protect as it is ours."

"Where is she?" Robert demanded, not in the least appeased. "I want to see her."

"I've not seen her myself yet," Adam admitted. "I imagine she is with Lady Marguerite and the other women in the solar, and mayhap you owe Alain an apology, Robert, for I think he has the right of it."

"Alain said she is to go home with Will and Alais?" Stephen challenged.

Adam nodded assent. "So I've heard."

Robert and Stephen pulled identical faces at the thought of their slightly pompous older brother and his fussy little wife, and Adam struggled to hide a smile.

"Isobel is almost sixteen," he reminded them, "and Father has realised he must make arrangements for her future."

"Marriage!" The twins uttered this exclamation and shuddered in unison, as they were sometimes wont to do, and this time Adam could not help smiling.

"It's what girls do," Alain pronounced sagely.

"Has anyone tried telling Bel that?" Stephen wondered.

"I did," said Alain, grinning at the memory. "We were in the kitchen garden at the time, and she assaulted me with a clod of earth."

Adam grimaced, and the twins shouted with laughter.

"How welcome do you think we would be in the solar right now?" Stephen asked.

"Not as welcome as you would be in the armoury," Adam assured him dryly, "unless your singing has improved beyond all measure. There's plenty of work to be done before tomorrow, so I suggest you take yourselves off there immediately—you too, Alain, before Robert and Stephen lead you into mischief."

"What is it about older brothers?" Robert grumbled as they departed the hall.

"And why did we have to get three of them?" his twin added, in the same aggrieved tone.

"I think you'll find you've got four," Robert

corrected him smugly. "I was born first, remember."

"So what?" Stephen retorted, distinctly unimpressed. "You needn't think that entitles you to start lording it over me too."

"Oh, for heaven's sake, you two…" Alain's voice cut across their argument.

"What it is to be young," Dominic remarked lightly as Adam turned away, still smiling. "Mind, I was forgetting—*you* still are!"

"Am I? Being their age seems a lifetime ago."

Dominic, settling back into his chair, inclined his head in tacit acknowledgement. Adam had grown up quickly under his command—any man who did not was likely to end up dead and, worse still, might take others with him. He signalled a page to bring some wine.

"I've need of a new squire since Huw gained his spurs," he commented, glancing up at his companion, who had remained standing. "Would your father be prepared to transfer one of your brothers to my service?"

"Your reputation speaks for itself, my lord," Adam replied with a mocking bow.

"Hmm," Dominic nodded. "The question is, which of the boys it should be?"

Adam snorted. "They're pretty much alike, as well you must have noticed; however Robert would never forgive me if I failed to apprise you of the fact that he is the elder, albeit by less than a full candle notch."

"Of course," Dominic speculated, "if you were to earn your spurs at this tourney, you'd have need of a squire, too. It could be arranged, you know. Fitz-Harding is here as the king's representative, and he and my father are great friends."

Adam's expression was shrewd.

"You want both of them," he surmised. "The puzzle lies in why, for you've seen neither in training."

Dominic shrugged dismissively.

"I know you well enough, and I've seen Will and Henry fight. You all come of the same stock; you share the same physique and—I assume—enjoy the same rude health. It's unlikely your younger brothers will not become equally skilled, given the right instruction."

Still Adam was not deceived. "You have some purpose in mind for them," he stated with conviction.

Dominic studied his face and was not displeased. Adam de Lescaux had a quick mind and an uncanny ability to see situations the way Dominic himself saw them. He tended to know instinctively what was expected of him, and it had saved both their lives on more than one occasion. He watched with satisfaction as comprehension dawned.

"You realise, of course, that their bond is both a blessing and a curse?"

Dominic nodded. "I have heard before that twins can share more than looks. But think, Adam, how useful it could be."

Adam looked thoughtful. "One of them always seems to know when the other is in trouble," he admitted.

"Exactly," Dominic pursued, "and how advantageous could it be for us to have a man who can be in two places at the same time?" He raised his cup in salute and gave his young lieutenant a satisfied smile. "To knighthood, my friend—and to your need for a squire of your own."

Chapter Four

On arrival at Vaillant, Isobel had thought about feigning illness simply to escape another afternoon in the company of her Aunt Rohese; now Father Padraig would have said it was just punishment for such wickedness that her head was beginning to ache in earnest. As the pain in her temples steadily worsened, pretending an interest in the proper distillation of lavender water became nigh on impossible, and she concentrated instead on keeping her spine upright and maintaining the rigid posture that her aunt demanded. Consequently, it was a moment or two before she realised she was being addressed. With an effort she forced herself to focus on Alain's mother, Lady Marguerite.

"I crave your pardon, madam; I fear I have the headache."

Isobel saw her aunt exchange a look with her brother's wife.

"But of course, you are tired from your journey." Lady Marguerite nodded sympathetically, and she beckoned to her maid. "You must retire at once, my dear, so that you may be rested for this evening's festivities."

Rohese Pascale viewed her niece with definite suspicion, for it was her considered opinion that the ride from Lescaux was unlikely to have exhausted a young woman who, by all accounts, often spent the better part of each day on horseback. What she did not know, however, was that since the onset of her courses Isobel occasionally found herself beset by headaches so severe they rendered her almost insensible until they passed, and this was one such. Now she mouthed clumsily the appropriate words to excuse herself. Gratefully seeking the solitude of her allotted chamber and sinking down on the bed, Isobel miserably resigned herself to missing the feast planned to mark the start of the tourney and, with considerably more regret, the opportunity of seeing her beloved brothers before morning.

"Poor Isobel." Lady Marguerite sighed guilelessly, her eyes on the girl's retreating figure. "I do hope she will be recovered sufficiently to attend the entertainments tonight. She really is remarkably lovely, and I was rather looking forward to seeing what effect she would have on our younger knights."

Isobel's aunt, by nature something of a prude, stiffened and coloured uncomfortably, but Marguerite affected not to notice.

"Five boys and only one girl!" She tapped her flustered companion lightly on the arm. "Now your nephews, Lady Rohese, they are a handsome brood."

"Indeed, madam," stammered Rohese, "but it is her mother Isobel takes after, not the de Lescauxs."

"Ah, yes." Marguerite nodded. "The fabled Anwen of Pyr."

"You are well-informed, my lady." Rohese was unable to conceal her surprise, and Marguerite smiled disarmingly.

"My husband and your brother are old friends," she offered by way of explanation, "and I have a weakness for romantic tales, which Hubert has always indulged. If he is to be believed, your brother's was a true love match. Tell me, did he really defy your father and risk disinheritance in order to wed his love?"

Rohese's face flamed at the reminder of what she still privately considered to be her brother's scandalous behaviour.

"It is true, yes," she admitted grudgingly. "William was very much in love with his wife, and she with him. When she died, he was distraught. Indeed, I do not believe that he has ever truly recovered."

"Such fidelity is a rare quality in a man." Marguerite sighed mournfully. "Hubert mentioned an estate, the lady Anwen's home. Does your brother ever go there?"

"I do not think William has visited Pyr for many years," Rohese confided. "The management of the estate is left almost entirely to his steward."

"Of course." Lady Marguerite nodded sensibly. "This estate is profitable, Lady Rohese?"

"I believe it is good and productive land." There was a touch of pride in the response. "The revenues are not inconsiderable, and William has done his duty, you may be sure. Pyr has been maintained as Isobel's dowry, and it will pass to her husband on her marriage." Rohese sniffed. "It is my belief that William will think himself well rid of it."

Still maintaining nothing more than an air of casual interest, Marguerite le Vaillant prepared to strike, homing in on her unsuspecting victim with all the natural instinct of one of her husband's prized hunting birds.

"And where exactly is this manor?" she purred.

"Wales." Rohese gave a delicate shudder at the very thought of such an uncivilised place. "It is quite close to the sea, I think."

Marguerite smiled and patted her hand. "Well, then, we shall have to see what can be done to ensure a good match for little Isobel, won't we, Lady Rohese? Men can be so insensitive in these situations, don't you think?"

She drifted away towards the window, concealing her satisfaction at having so easily garnered the information she had been directed to seek. Hubert would be delighted to receive confirmation of the intelligence already provided by Fitz-Harding's agent—that Isobel de Lescaux's dower estates did indeed lie in close proximity to the disputed Earldom of Pembroke, stronghold of the irksome Richard de Clare.

****

In another of Vaillant's private chambers, William de Lescaux had just received a somewhat surprising, but far from displeasing, request that his youngest sons be permitted to join their brother under the command of Dominic du Bois. Prompted by Dominic, Hubert had already announced his intention to approach Fitz-Harding with the suggestion that Adam be knighted on the field, and judging his continued advancement to be recommendation enough, William had readily given his consent.

With the matter of the twins' future settled, the conversation had turned not unnaturally to the situation in Ireland, and to Dominic's way of thinking, his father seemed extraordinarily keen to know the details of de Clare's activities. Recalling his conversation with Adam earlier in the day, he was more certain than ever that he had been right to suspect the motive behind this Easter gathering.

"Of course, Henry's been on edge ever since Strongbow went and married MacMurrough's daughter," Hubert remarked, watching his son's face for reaction. "All it would take is MacMurrough's death and he could have an independent Norman kingdom on his western seaboard."

Dominic smiled. "Yes, I imagine his spies have been working overtime all winter. He must think he knows enough to be really worried by now, else he would not have ordered de Clare to cease his activities and return immediately."

"But de Clare has chosen to ignore the order?"

Hubert was openly probing now, but Dominic merely shrugged, refusing to be drawn.

"Raymond le Gros was sent with despatches to reassure the king."

His father snorted. "But de Clare's not seen fit to take ship for England himself?"

"I'm not privy to his thoughts, my lord, or his future plans." Dominic parried the question with ease.

"You've been serving him." William de Lescaux joined the attack.

"I've been serving a variety of masters," Dominic corrected. "I'm a mercenary—a hired sword. I go where I am paid."

Hubert eyed his son speculatively. "And where does that put you, if it comes down to a fight between de Clare and the king?"

Dominic decided the time was ripe for a strategic retreat.

"Well, now, I suppose that would depend on who

has the deeper pay chest," he offered amiably as he made for the door. "Until later, my lords."

****

When that later arrived, William de Lescaux was, for once, feeling well pleased with the world. Lounging comfortably in his chair, he surveyed each of his five sons in turn, ranged around the room according to their current stations in life. The similarity of their strongly chiselled features proclaimed their shared blood, and William was assailed by a surge of pride. The twins, already informed of their changed circumstances, were to commence squiring duties for their new masters on the morrow. It had been agreed that Robert, as the elder, would serve Dominic, with Stephen going to attend Adam. The latter was an unorthodox arrangement, but William had no qualms about it proving entirely satisfactory. As a consequence, the boys' spirits were even higher than usual, and he watched indulgently as they both instigated and joined in some vigorous horseplay with their peers.

Others, however, were less pleased to see the de Lescaux star in the ascendant. Alain le Vaillant, unhappily aware that his feelings of jealousy were not honourable, was doing his best to drown them in his father's excellent claret, but Louis Montierre could not lay claim to so noble a disposition. At eighteen years of age he boasted an impressive physique, and he already had a reputation amongst his fellow squires as a determined fighter whose technique made up in ferocity what it lacked in finesse. Well aware that Dominic du Bois' last squire had recently progressed to knighthood, and seeking similar promotion for himself in due course, Louis had already decided who was going to replace him—and Robert de Lescaux had not figured in his reckoning.

"It is only because their older brother is so much in favour with du Bois," Louis whispered venomously in Alain's ear. "We've all heard the rumours—maybe they are true, and that's why he wants the little whelps, as well!"

Whilst Alain himself suspected that Adam's presence in Dominic's troop had been a significant factor in the twins' preferment, he was not so drunk as to misunderstand Montierre's vile insinuation and, by virtue of his blood tie with Dominic, felt bound to defend him.

"Have you ever seen the de Lescauxs in combat?" he asked morosely, his pleasant voice slurred by the effect of too much wine. "Take my advice—make sure you're fighting on their side tomorrow."

But Louis was not paying attention. His eyes focussed on the twin objects of his discontent as his mind explored various options for removing them from his path. It was widely accepted amongst Vaillant's junior retainers that Robert and Stephen de Lescaux shared more than their identical looks. Generally they were well-liked, and few had ever attempted to challenge either of them. Those unwise enough to do so had soon discovered that to harm one brought double the retribution down on the head of the offender. To succeed in his aim, therefore, Louis reasoned that he must strike at both simultaneously, at the same time taking steps to ensure that whatever misfortune befell them could not be traced back to him.

Unlike Alain and many of their fellows, the twins were being careful to limit the amount of wine they were consuming, well aware that if they wished to impress Dominic du Bois in the morning they would need clear heads and ready wits. Louis scowled at them before being distracted by the presence of a serving girl who leaned over him to refill his own cup. He leered appreciatively at her and pinched her behind. In return she gave him an inviting smile, and as he watched her move away, he realised he had found the means to further his ambitions. He crooked his finger imperiously, and she came back to him with a deliberate sway of her hips. Louis was certain no one who had witnessed the exchange of looks between himself and the girl would be in any doubt as to why the two of them left the hall together, and that suited his purpose admirably.

Her name was Megan. Like her mother before her, she had been in the service of Vaillant for as long as she could remember, and she had been a whore from the day she became old enough to understand what it was that men wanted from her. Louis pulled her skirts down and refastened his braies.

"It is by way of a jest," he purred cajolingly. "No lasting harm will come to them. I merely wish to prick their pride a little."

Megan hesitated. Like most of Lord Hubert's female servants, she was attracted to the handsome de Lescaux twins; on the other hand, they had never once so much as looked her way, and Louis had. He ran his finger suggestively along her cheek and trailed it downwards to her breast. She made up her mind to do as he asked.

Slipping easily through the shadows, Louis disappeared in the direction of the squires' quarters. He returned with a small glass vial which he pressed into her hand, along with a silver penny. Megan's eyes widened at the sight of the coin.

"For services rendered," Louis said, with a smile. "Just a drop, now—I want them unconscious, not dead."

Bestowing a last lingering kiss on her eager lips, he left her to rejoin the feast. Megan tucked the vial into a fold of her skirt and waited a few minutes before following him.

Once back in the hall, she resumed her serving duties, careful not to look in Louis' direction. It was an easy matter for her to pause unnoticed amid the revelry and dispense a small measure of the white poppy juice into each of the cups being used by the de Lescaux twins. Then she watched with a smile of satisfaction as the boisterous youths seemed to drink themselves rapidly into oblivion before the entire company.

Louis had already selected his accomplices, all of them the worse for drink and sworn to secrecy. With much laughter, stumbling, and muffled curses, they assisted him in carrying the insensible de Lescaux brothers from the hall and depositing them in a conveniently empty cellar. Louis checked their breathing and assured himself they would not stir until well after the castle had been deserted for the tourney the next day. He dropped the wooden bar across the outside of the door.

"Sweet dreams, boys!"

****

Morning brought Adam to the armoury in a sour mood. His normally equable temper, already somewhat strained by the ritual cold bath and night of prayer he had been forced to endure as a precursor to impending knighthood, was stretched to breaking point by a fruitless search for his younger brothers.

"I'll bloody kill them when I catch up with them," he snarled. "Where the hell can they be?"

Many of the squires, including Alain le Vaillant, were reaping the rewards of their overindulgence the previous evening, and several visibly winced. Adam glared at them witheringly whilst Alain fought to marshal his disordered wits, racking his fuddled brain in an effort to recollect the events of the previous night. Nothing was clear, but he could not help a nagging suspicion that his exchange with the disaffected Louis Montierre might have some bearing on the disappearance of the twins.

Having delivered a concise and blistering assessment of the assembled young men, Adam spun on his heel and strode out. No one spoke, each concentrating on his allotted tasks and offering silent thanks to God that it was not he who would have to face the combined wrath of Adam de Lescaux and Dominic du Bois.

Louis glanced in turn at the faces of those who had been with him last night. He was fairly certain most of them had been too drunk to remember anything of note. His gaze rested thoughtfully on Vaillant's heir. The boy clearly had his own problems this morning, not least a head like a blacksmith's anvil. Louis smiled to himself. Even if Alain did, by chance, recall the words that had passed between them, he was unlikely to connect those whispered remarks with the disappearance of his lord's precious sons.

But Louis was wrong. Alain had been covertly

watching him ever since Adam's departure, more convinced than ever that Montierre's discontent had translated itself into some nefarious deed linked to the missing twins. On the pretext of fetching a forgotten item from his lord's chamber, Alain hurriedly left the armoury, intent on finding Adam and confiding his suspicions.

His search led him by way of the hall, where he chanced upon Isobel, seated at one of the many trestles set up around the room. Her face was pale, and she was picking without interest at the slice of fine white bread in front of her. Alain hesitated for a moment, then headed over to her.

"Bel," he greeted courteously, "have you seen Adam?"

She shook her head slightly and winced.

"No, not yet. Why?"

Realising somewhat belatedly that Isobel was very likely unaware of all that had transpired since their arrival, Alain leant across the board and gave her a brief account of the events leading up to the disappearance of her twin brothers. She listened, her expression one of growing dismay.

"Oh, Alain, I am sure you are right. Having been presented with such an opportunity, I cannot see Robert and Stephen doing anything that might risk it being withdrawn."

Alain nodded worriedly. "I know, that's why…" He broke off, seeing that Adam had arrived in the hall. Before he could stop her, Isobel was out of her seat and running towards him. With a strangled oath, Alain hastened after her.

Adam de Lescaux was a man accustomed to

attracting attention from the opposite sex, but even he was forced to admit that it was unusual for a woman to fling herself at him quite so early in the day—particularly with such embarrassing enthusiasm. He glanced down with a vague sense of irritation, intent upon detaching the clinging vine, and his jaw dropped in astonishment.

"Bel?"

He returned her embrace automatically, his mind wrestling to reconcile the image of this undeniably beautiful young woman with that of the engaging child he remembered. With a pang Adam realised that Alain had not been exaggerating—Isobel had truly grown up, and she had become quite enchantingly lovely in the process.

"Adam, we must find Robert and Stephen," she said without preamble. "Something must have happened to them."

"*Something* will certainly happen to them when I catch up with them," Adam vowed, recalling himself to the matter in hand and setting Isobel away. "I cannot believe they have chosen today of all days to indulge in one of their irresponsible escapades!"

Discerning that Adam's temper had not improved since his departure from the armoury, Alain spoke somewhat hesitantly.

"My lord," he said, deciding it was wise to address Adam thus, in view of his impending elevation to knighthood. "If I might speak with you?"

Adam regarded him severely. "I take it this has to do with the twins, Alain? If you know aught, you had best tell me."

Isobel saw Alain grimace and guessed that his head

felt as tender as did hers, although she imagined it was from an entirely different cause. She placed her fingers over Adam's much larger hand, immediately struck by the contrast between his tanned flesh and her own. It seemed that the regular application of Hildred Laval's rosewater cream had been of some benefit after all.

"We should go somewhere a little less public." She glanced meaningfully at the interested faces around them.

"We?" Adam's eyes narrowed as he looked between his sister and his father's squire, wondering if there had perhaps, after all, been some merit in Robert's asking how much time Alain had been spending with her.

"Adam," Isobel admonished, "according to Alain, you have been charging about Vaillant like an enraged bear this morning. There will already be enough gossip circulating to send Papa into an apoplexy, should he come to hear of it. For goodness' sake, be sensible."

She moved towards the turret stairs, indicating with a slight motion of her head that Adam and Alain should follow. Isobel counted herself fortunate to have been given a modest chamber to herself in the overcrowded domain of Vaillant, its walls swelled to bursting by the arrival of so many guests. She sat down on the lid of her travelling chest and motioned to Adam to make similar use of the bed. He did so, with ill-disguised impatience. Since there was no help for it, Alain remained standing as he haltingly voiced his suspicions.

Adam forgot about Isobel's presence and uttered an oath that made his father's squire wince. He flicked an apologetic glance at his sister, but she was frowning thoughtfully and seemed not to have noticed.

"As I see it, since we cannot prove the involvement of this Louis Montierre at present, we really have no alternative but to continue looking for the twins. Alain, this is your home—you know it better than anyone else. Think of all the places it might be possible to conceal someone." She turned to Adam. "Does Dominic du Bois know that there is anything amiss, as yet?"

Adam shook his head. "I had hoped I might find them, sober them up if necessary, before he got to hear of it. I thought that if even one of them was in a fit state to attend him…"

"Get Will and Henry," Isobel interrupted. "Tell them what you suspect, and enlist their help. God knows, it's not normally difficult to locate Robert and Stephen. You should let Papa know, too. Better that he should hear the truth of the matter from you rather than a fraction of it from someone else…" She stopped, seeing that Adam was regarding her with a dazed expression. "Well, what is it?"

Her brother shook his head admiringly. "Bel, you give orders like a seasoned general."

Arranging to meet Alain by the stairs to the gatehouse once he had located the older members of the de Lescaux family, Adam flourished his sister a mock salute and quitted the room, his naturally cheerful disposition much restored.

Isobel turned to Alain. "Í need to borrow some of your clothes," she told him peremptorily.

He gaped at her in open disbelief.

"You need to do what?" He backed away, hands raised defensively. "No, Isobel," he said firmly. "No, no, no! Don't you think we're in enough trouble as it is, without you embarking on one of your hare-brained schemes?"

"It is not hare-brained at all," Isobel soothed cajolingly. "You know I can perform most of the duties expected of a squire. I'll simply tell your esteemed half-brother that there is some sickness amongst us and we've all been redeployed for the nonce."

"No," said Alain again, with every intention of meaning it. "I'll go and attend Dominic myself. Your story about the sickness will serve just as well to explain my being there."

Seeing his determined expression, Isobel decided it was time to try a new tactic. Affecting a fair imitation of the sort of pout she had seen Alais use to great effect on her brother Will last Christmas, she looked up at him through her lashes.

"Please, Alain. I agree it would be much better for you to go and attend Dominic, but Adam needs your help. No one knows Vaillant like you," she added, flattering him mercilessly.

Alain groaned. He knew exactly what she was doing, but, already fancying himself half in love with William de Lescaux's daughter, he was rapidly discovering he was not proof against her when she chose to employ her hitherto untested feminine wiles.

"You're not playing fair, Bel," he gritted.

"Since when has that bothered you?" Isobel shot back at him, referring to their childhood games.

Alain could feel himself weakening.

"Oh, God, Bel! If anyone ever finds out, we'll both be dead."

"In which case, it won't matter, will it?" she quipped with some asperity, rewarding him with a bewitching smile and an impulsive kiss on the cheek.

"Hurry up, now, before anyone comes."

"You mean before I have a chance to change my mind," said Alain, absently touching his fingertips to the place where her lips had briefly rested. "Christ, I must be out of my wits even to think about doing this."

"Then don't think," Isobel advised him cheerfully.

Chapter Five

A short time later, clad in Alain's outgrown garments, which he had assured her would not be recognised by his half-brother, and her hair concealed beneath a drab brown woollen hood, Isobel approached the temporary pavilion erected to house Dominic du Bois and his lieutenant for the duration of the tourney.

As he loaded her arms with Dominic's equipment, Alain had uttered numerous and dire warnings about the consequences should she be discovered, having refused point blank to allow her to go to the armoury to fetch his half-brother's accoutrements herself. Staggering slightly under the weight, and wondering how on earth Dominic du Bois ever managed to keep himself upright, never mind land a blow, Isobel pushed her way through the tent flap.

"Well, it's about bloody time! Where the hell have you been?"

Alain's hero rose from a cross-legged folding stool, the sword belt he had been inspecting dangling loosely from his fingers. *And good morning to you, too.* Isobel's thought was sour as she studied his face surreptitiously. She set down her burden, alarmed to see his eyes narrow. Her heart beat faster, and she wondered dizzily if he had seen straight through her pretence.

"You're not Robert de Lescaux," he said abruptly.

"Who are you, and what are you doing here?"

Isobel took a deep breath to steady her nerves and repeated the story which she had agreed with Alain. Du Bois continued to regard her with his piercing blue gaze.

"And Robert de Lescaux is among the sick?"

"I believe so, my lord," Isobel offered a slight bow.

"And his brother?"

"They are twins, my lord. I believe that when one is ill, the other is often similarly afflicted." In this at least she was answering truthfully.

Dominic sighed with frustration. "And you are?"

She gulped nervously and cast wildly in her imagination for a suitable name. "Walt, my lord."

Du Bois quirked one eyebrow in sardonic amusement. "Just Walt?"

"It's short for Walter, my lord." Isobel busied herself with laying out the equipment.

Dominic's expression changed. "Are you trying to be funny, boy?"

"Oh, no, my lord." Isobel shook her head emphatically. "That is to say, my surname is Laval, my lord." She offered a silent prayer for forgiveness to the departed soul of the steward's wife.

Dominic frowned. The lad before him looked overly young and delicate for the kind of duties expected of a squire during a bout in the lists. The boy's tunic hung slack on his spare frame, and he wondered what his father could have been thinking of to send him such a lad. The sickness among the squires must be more serious than he had at first thought.

"How old are you, Walt?"

There was a pause whilst the boy seemed to

consider this question, and Dominic imagined him to be doing some arduous mental arithmetic. He added being painfully slow to Walt's already considerable list of deficiencies. Isobel, wondering frantically how best to answer him, eventually decided to take a couple of years off her own age.

"I am thirteen, sir—but I'll be fourteen come Michaelmas," she offered with a nervous smile, hoping he would surmise from this that "Walt" had only recently been promoted from page to squire, which would serve nicely to account for any mistakes she might make.

Dominic gave the boy another searching look, then enquired acidly, "Well, now you're here, perhaps we could get started?"

"Yes, my lord, of course."

Isobel inclined her head dutifully and reached for his padded and quilted gambeson. This at least she could handle with competence, having at various times assisted all five of her brothers with such garments. He shrugged himself into it, and she reached up to lace the neck opening, registering with some surprise that he was fractionally taller even than Adam, for she needed to stand on tiptoe. Her eyes fixed on the pulse beating in Dominic's throat, and Isobel was suddenly conscious of a nervousness she had never experienced when performing this task for her brothers. Her normally deft fingers fumbled, and she looked up to find him watching her with evident dissatisfaction.

Dominic stared down at the boy's hands. Bitten nails aside, they were almost effeminate. He was relieved when the job was done and Walt stepped away.

The riveted iron rings of du Bois' hauberk winked

at her in the dim sunlight filtering through the half-open tent flap, as if sharing a jest. Isobel bent to pick it up, but it was heavier than she anticipated and slithered out of her grasp. With barely concealed impatience, Dominic snatched it up, gesturing at various other items strewn about the tent.

"See if you can make yourself useful by tidying some of this stuff away," he said, making it obvious that it was all he thought "Walt" good for.

Isobel felt a spark of resentment flare, but she said nothing, simply inclining her head. Dominic's mouth thinned, and he turned away, resigned to attending his own needs.

****

Hastening to his appointed meeting with Adam at the gatehouse stairs, Alain was trying hard to banish all thoughts of Isobel's potential difficulties from his mind, concentrating instead on how the geography of Vaillant might lend itself to the disappearance of two ebullient teenage boys. As he passed the stables, he saw a brassy-haired girl flirting with one of the lanky adolescents employed to tend his father's horses. He recognised her as Megan, the serving wench who had briefly left the hall with Louis Montierre last night and recalled that, although she had left with Montierre, they had returned separately. Without really knowing why, Alain called out to the girl, commanding her attention. She turned towards him, eyes widening, and hurriedly smoothed her hair with one hand, using the other to dust down her dress. Vaillant's heir was an infinitely better proposition than a mere stable hand.

"My lord." She dropped him a curtsey, knowing the movement displayed her natural assets to their best advantage—something Alain tried hard to ignore.

Wisely deciding that Adam de Lescaux would surely be a far better person than himself to find out what, if anything, the girl knew, Alain took hold of her hand and began to lead her towards the gatehouse. Expecting a rapid fumble in the usual dark corner favoured by her clients, Megan was somewhat bemused. Sensing that all might not be as it had at first seemed, she began to hang back a little, forcing Alain to tighten his hold until he was all but dragging her behind him. The sight of four members of the formidable de Lescaux family gathered at the entrance to the gatehouse was enough to scare the hapless girl out of the few wits she possessed, and she dug her heels more firmly into the trampled earth floor of the outer bailey.

"Sweet *Jesu*, I swear I meant no harm," she babbled. "I only used a drop, just like he said…"

"Alain!" William de Lescaux covered the ground in great strides. "What in God's name do you think you are doing?"

"Ask her," said Alain, scarlet faced and panting slightly. He flung the terrified girl towards the assembled de Lescauxs. "Go on, ask her."

"Please, my lord!" Megan fell to her knees. "I meant no harm. Truly, I only did what he said."

"Who?" Adam interrupted, seizing her by her shoulders and hauling her to her feet.

"Louis!" she almost screamed at him in her haste to get the words out. "Louis Montierre."

Adam's face darkened with fury.

"Where are my brothers, you idiot girl?"

Megan was sobbing in earnest now.

"I don't know, my lord, I swear it! All I did was to

put a little bit in their drink. Not to harm them, he said, just to make them sleep a while."

Grim-faced, Adam began to march Megan back across the courtyard.

"Adam, wait." His brother Henry chased after him. "Where are you going?"

"Montierre serves with Piers de Bracy, our opponent in the combat today," Adam informed him curtly. "Unfortunately, we're going to need Dominic's help to unravel this mess."

"What about the twins?" Henry kept pace with him.

"Keep looking," Adam advised tautly. "Ask Father to go to Hubert le Vaillant—and pray God he and Alain know their keep as well as they ought to."

"I think he's already gone," said Henry, glancing behind him. He clasped Adam's shoulder. "I'll catch up with you at the pavilion."

Adam nodded assent. "Henry?"

His brother paused. "Yes?"

"Make sure someone is sent to tell Isobel when Robert and Stephen are found."

Henry looked surprised. Like his father and his eldest brother, he rarely spared much thought for the sister his mother had died bearing.

"I saw her this morning," Adam offered by way of explanation. "She was anxious about them." With the still-wailing Megan firmly in hand, he set off for the tourney field.

****

Robert de Lescaux forced his eyes open. Someone was standing over him with a horn lantern, and a booted foot was prodding his ribs none too gently. He struggled to sit up, and the disembodied face of his eldest brother swam into focus. Robert slumped back with a barely audible groan.

"Sod off, Will. It's still dark!" The boot prodded again, with greater force.

"It's dark because you're in a cellar, lackwit."

Will put down the lantern and grasped Robert's tunic with both hands, pulling him into a sitting position. His brother's shoulders heaved with unmistakable intent, and Will just managed to step back in time. Mindful of the twins' propensity for identical behaviour, he shouted a warning to Henry, who was crouched over Stephen administering similar assistance. True to form, Stephen followed suit.

Henry waited for him to finish vomiting into the mouldering straw and then proffered a drink from the leather water bottle at his belt. Stephen took a couple of sips, and Henry wiped the mouth of the flask on the hem of his tunic before passing it to Will.

"Think you can stand up?" he asked.

Stephen nodded, wincing. "Not sure about walking, though," he jested weakly. Seeing Alain hovering in the doorway he added, "Your father keeps a bloody awful vintage, le Vaillant."

"Might have been better for you if he had," Henry remarked sagely. "I suspect the poppy syrup might have been easier to detect in a rough wine."

"Poppy syrup?" Robert had recovered enough to participate in the conversation. "Why in God's name would anyone want to dose us with that?" he choked, his voice hoarse from retching.

Will tutted impatiently. "Well, you and Stephen weren't exactly reticent about your sudden good fortune, were you? A sound, old-fashioned desire to teach you a lesson in humility looks to have been the most obvious cause."

"I'll kill them," Robert promised, touching a hand to his pounding temple. "When I find out who is responsible, I'll kill them!" His eyes met Stephen's, and an unspoken vow passed between them.

"Yes, well, time enough for that later," Henry said. He had never been at ease with the ability of his twin brothers to communicate without words. "Our priority now is to get you two where you were supposed to be at first light this morning."

"My priority is to get hold of a willow-bark tisane," Stephen muttered. "My skull is splitting asunder. I'm sure I must have half of Robert's head, too."

"If what I am left with is anything to go by, you may keep it," his twin assured him.

Henry slapped Stephen bracingly on the back, ignoring the ensuing moan of anguish.

"You'll live," he said, then added as an afterthought, "at least until Adam catches up with you."

Amid further protestations from Robert and Stephen, they emerged into the bright sunlight and headed towards the flat ground between the castle and the river, where the tourney bouts were destined to take place. Suddenly Henry swore and clutched at his forehead.

"Damn it, I completely forgot! Adam told me to let Isobel know when you'd been found."

Alain, who had been trailing somewhat miserably in their wake, brightened visibly.

"I'll go," he said, at once thinking he might have a

chance to slip through the postern gate and warn Isobel to make herself scarce before her entire family arrived at Dominic's tent, but to his dismay Henry declined the offer.

"No," he decided. "Better I go myself. "You'll be needed to corroborate whatever that little trollop is saying. Adam's already taken her off to see Dominic because Montierre is with Piers de Bracy's rabble."

Alain paled. "Adam's already gone to Dominic?"

"Well, of course," said Henry, looking somewhat surprised. "Where else did you think he'd gone?" He turned away and headed in the direction of the keep.

Alain refrained from saying that he would have preferred at this moment to take Isobel's flippant advice and not have to think at all. He shook his head dumbly, unhappily facing the inevitable, for having only just renewed his acquaintance with her that very morning, there was no way on God's earth Adam de Lescaux could fail to recognise his own sister. The game, such as it had been, was well and truly up.

Chapter Six

Adam pulled aside the canvas flap and thrust the whimpering Megan through the gap. Dominic, in the process of buckling on his sword belt, gave the girl a cursory glance.

"Not your usual style, Adam," he commented with a wry grin. "Nor, in so far as I recollect, do they normally snivel in response to your attentions. Has Vaillant become so crowded that you needs must bring her here?"

At the sound of her brother's name, Isobel stifled a gasp and attempted to move further into the shadows. She cursed herself for not considering the possibility that Adam would be sharing Dominic's accommodation and might chance upon her here.

"Tell my lord du Bois why Robert de Lescaux failed to report for his duties this morning," Adam commanded, pushing Megan forwards.

Dominic frowned. "I already know," he said. He gestured towards the silent figure in the corner. The lad had his back to them. "My father sent Walt here to assist me in his stead, and the boy told me about the sickness. I trust it is not serious?"

"Sickness?" Adam laughed mirthlessly. "I've no doubt they'll be sick enough when they wake, and if your father knows aught about any of this I will be very surprised indeed." He closed the distance between

Dominic's replacement squire and himself and placed a hand on the boy's shoulder, forcing him into the light.

Had the situation not been quite so desperate, Isobel might have laughed at the expression on Adam's face.

"Bel!" He uttered incredulously. "What in God's name do you think you are doing?"

He gave his sister's shoulder a less-than-gentle shake, and she twitched to throw off his hand, annoyed at being treated thus.

Dominic was not slow to realise Adam addressed "Walt" by another name, and he recalled the boy's hesitation on the subject earlier.

"I take it you are acquainted with our young friend here," he said, fixing Isobel with a cool stare. To his not inconsiderable amusement, a flush darkened his lieutenant's cheekbones.

"In a manner of speaking," Adam gritted. "Our 'young friend here' happens to be my sister—and whilst at the moment her presence here is something of a mystery, you may rest assured that I mean to have the truth of the matter very shortly."

"Your *sister*!" Dominic was unable to conceal his astonishment. He studied Isobel hard, as if seeking a resemblance. "I cannot recall you ever having mentioned a sister." His tone was distinctly suspicious.

"Am I surprised, or just disappointed?" Isobel wondered aloud.

The interruption earned her a glare from both men, but she merely returned their lowering stares with interest, refusing to be cowed.

"She favours our mother," Adam tendered grudgingly, in response to Dominic's continued scrutiny of his sister's face.

"Could we perhaps discuss family likenesses some other time, please?" Isobel enquired acidly. "Have you found Robert and Stephen? Why will they be sick?"

Before Adam could reply, the interior of Dominic's pavilion was filled by what, in that confined space, felt like half an army. Seeing her chance, little Megan slipped away, and by the time Adam realised she had gone it was already too late. He ground one clenched hand into the palm of the other and silently cursed his family.

First inside were Robert and Stephen, much restored and clearly anxious to set matters right, but the ready words of apology died on their lips and their eyes widened as they took in their sister's appearance.

"Holy Mother Mary, Bel!" Stephen's exclamation was accompanied by a low whistle.

Robert looked her up and down and grinned at his twin.

"I must say, Papa has some novel ideas about what it takes to equip a lady for marriage."

Isobel shot him a quelling look.

"You'd better have a good excuse for all this," she hissed, spreading her arm to encompass the resultant chaos, which now included Will and Henry, mouths similarly agape, together with a wretched-looking Alain.

"Not half as good as the one you're going to need when Papa gets to hear what you've been up to," Stephen assured her.

"He doesn't needs to hear anything…" Isobel broke off in horror as the tent flap parted once more, this time to admit her father, accompanied by Hubert le

Vaillant.

“Adam.” Lord William’s voice was tight with suppressed fury.

“Sir?”

“You will escort your sister back to the keep immediately.” He unfastened his cloak and thrust it at his daughter. “Cover yourself, madam. I’ll deal with you later.”

From his expression, Isobel was quite certain that this time he meant to deliver the beating she had so narrowly escaped at Lescaux. She saw identical expressions of sympathy on the faces of her youngest brothers and, with heightened consciousness, the slightly scornful amusement with which Dominic du Bois was regarding her. She lifted her chin a notch and met his gaze unflinchingly as she swept the concealing garment around her shoulders. Then, her head high, she followed Adam’s lead and made the best exit she could.

Dominic watched the girl leave with a mixture of irritation and amusement. The irritation he blamed on his failure to see through her shallow deception from the outset; his amusement was born of the sneaking suspicion that he had just met by far and away the most dangerous of William de Lescaux’s undeniably remarkable offspring. He permitted himself a slight smile at the varying degrees of shock and horror on the faces of her brothers. At twenty-seven years of age Dominic could hardly be unaware of the reputation that attached to his name. Many of the tales were fanciful in the extreme, but he had never troubled to deny them, seeing them all as useful armour against those who sought to undermine his hard-won position. The simple fact that Isobel de Lescaux had been discovered alone with him in his private quarters would be enough to tarnish her good name irrevocably, should the tale be touted to the outside world.

Remembering the look on Lord William's face, Dominic frowned. The chit had undoubtedly earned herself a beating, at the very least, and for some reason he found the notion disturbed him greatly. With an impatient shake of his head he dismissed her from his mind to concentrate on the more serious business of the day.

Chapter Seven

Adam did not speak as he escorted Isobel back to the keep. It was a sure sign he could not trust himself, and he did not want to draw attention to their progress. Once they had gained the privacy of her chamber, however, he had no such hesitation and rounded on her.

"You total fool!"

Isobel put a hand to her temples, where yesterday's headache threatened renewal, but Adam was in no mood to be sympathetic and ignored the gesture.

"I suppose you browbeat young Alain into helping you?" he continued, flicking a contemptuous finger at her borrowed clothes. "I find it hard to imagine that even *you* would have thought to pack these particular items in the hope of just such an opportunity."

Isobel sighed. "I did not browbeat him," she defended, feeling a twinge of guilt, for she knew she had not been entirely fair in her dealings with Alain. "I thought…"

Adam did not allow her to finish. "You did not think at all, Bel! Christ, if I had possessed the slightest idea of the stupidity of which you were capable, I would have given orders that you be confined to your chamber, which, incidentally, is exactly what I am going to do now."

"Oh, do what you will," she responded wearily.

Adam took hold of her arm and swung her round to

face him. "You do realise what this means—for all of us?"

Isobel shrugged. "I don't know why you're so surprised," she returned coolly. "It seems to be the expectation where I am concerned—in so far as any of you have any expectations of me at all."

Adam winced, recollecting Dominic's remark about not knowing he had a sister. Guilt and compassion stirred uncomfortably within him.

"Bel," he said more gently, settling his hands on her slender shoulders, "that girl who was with me when I arrived at Dominic's pavilion, she's a wh—she works in the kitchens," he amended hastily, "and last night, Louis Montierre—he's a squire in de Bracy's retinue—convinced her to lace the twins' cups with white poppy, because he wanted them senseless and unable to attend on Dominic and myself today. I think he intended to offer himself in their place."

Isobel stared at Adam aghast. Hildred Laval had introduced her to the properties of poppy syrup, with strict instructions as to the correct dosage and dire warnings as to the consequences of its misuse.

"*Jesu*, they were lucky to wake up at all," she whispered.

Adam could not disagree.

"The point is, she heard me tell Dominic that you were my sister. Now she'll trade that information for whatever she thinks it might be worth, and before long all Vaillant will have the story of how William de Lescaux's daughter was caught attempting to pass herself off as a boy so that she might consort privately with a notorious mercenary. Your reputation is ruined, Bel. There is little chance of Papa securing an advantageous marriage for you now, with the name of de Lescaux being sniggered at the length and breadth of England."

"And which of those is more important to you, I wonder," Isobel mused softly, "your sister's virtue, or the precious de Lescaux name?"

Adam's complexion darkened angrily.

"The two are inextricably bound, Bel, and you know it." He pushed a hand through his disordered hair. "For God's sake, what did you think to achieve by acting thus?"

Isobel sighed. "I sought only to gain a little time," she confessed miserably. "If you and Alain had been able to find the twins, then Dominic du Bois need never have known there was anything amiss. I did not want him to think them unreliable and rescind his offer to train them. God knows I've heard enough about how wonderful *he* is."

Through the unshuttered window the heralds could be heard calling the start of the bouts.

"I have to go," said Adam distractedly. "You are not to stir outside this room, do you understand?"

She nodded.

"I want your word of honour, Bel."

She laughed derisively. "Is that your idea of a jest, Adam? After what you have just been at pains to tell me, might I not be forgiven for thinking that I have no honour?"

Adam's lips tightened ominously, and he took a step towards her. She raised her arm as if to ward off a blow.

"Peace, brother, no more. I will give you my word."

He nodded, seemingly satisfied, and she watched as the door closed firmly behind him. Had there been a key, she was in no doubt he would have turned it.

****

Adam returned to the lists feeling both angry and frustrated. Years of disciplined training meant that he knew what he must do, and he immediately set about channelling the destructive emotions into his performance on the field, proceeding to demonstrate his impressive skill to devastating effect. In partnership with Dominic and his older brothers, he was instrumental in taking several prestigious ransoms, thus making a significant contribution to the victory eventually pronounced in their favour.

Dominic unhelmed and stripped off his thick leather gauntlets to watch with approval as Adam bent his knee before Robert Fitz-Harding and swore the oath of fealty that gained him his knighthood. Without warning, the fine short-cut hair at the nape of his neck suddenly prickled, and he turned his head to see Piers de Bracy approaching, his squire in close attendance. In the same instant he realised he was not the only one to have marked de Bracy's progress. Robert and Stephen de Lescaux stood silently side by side, but beneath their identically blank expressions Dominic felt certain they were somehow communicating with one another, and his interest was piqued. His determination to explore and utilise their unique abilities intensified.

Evidently Piers had come, as custom demanded, to acknowledge his defeat and to yield formally to his opponent. Dominic glanced at Adam and received an answering grimace in return. Both knew it was not de Bracy's nature to be gracious on such occasions, and from the expression on his opponent's face Dominic saw no reason to think that this day would be different from any other. Slanting a sideways look at Dominic and Adam, as if daring them to do anything, de Bracy halted before William de Lescaux with a smooth courtier's bow.

"You will allow me to present my compliments on your family's prowess, my lord," he said in a carrying voice. "What a pity your fair daughter was not present to witness their triumph."

The words were innocent enough, but the calculated manner in which they dropped from de Bracy's tongue, coupled with the knowing smirk on Louis Montierre's face, made it obvious Adam had been right when he told Isobel that Megan would lose no time in selling her tale to the highest bidder, and it was impossible for the de Lescauxs not to recognise the intended insult for what it was.

William de Lescaux, still a worthy jouster in his own right, coloured angrily. His fingers tensed around the hilt of his sword, and immediately his two eldest sons stepped forward to stand with him. Dominic saw Adam move to do the same and instinctively checked him with a swift negative shake of his head. His own eyes were on Fitz-Harding, who seemed to be viewing the unfolding tableau with only moderate interest, but beneath that impassive gaze Dominic knew the man's mind would be working with breathtaking rapidity, seizing and discarding possibilities until it arrived at a satisfactory conclusion. He felt a gut-wrenching twist of apprehension as he realised that the narrow, assessing stare of the king's representative had settled on him, and he watched with a growing sense of unease as Fitz-

Harding leant forward to whisper in the ear of Hubert le Vaillant. Hubert looked surprised, but he nodded. Fitz-Harding beckoned William de Lescaux to approach. He spoke again, and Dominic watched as a startled expression spread across Lord William's face, but then he too nodded agreement.

In the same moment he became aware that Alain's mother was looking at him with undisguised interest, and he knew immediately that whatever Fitz-Harding had suggested to his father and William de Lescaux undoubtedly involved him. He gnawed pensively at the inside of his lower lip, trying to gauge what mischief the sly old buzzard was working this time.

Apparently satisfied, the king's representative sat back and motioned for the leaders of the two opposing sides to approach, indicating that de Bracy should make his declaration. Relieved to have the formalities of tourney etiquette completed without further incident, if nothing else, Dominic turned to make his way back to the camp, deciding that the need to rid himself of his mail and avail himself of a drink was for the nonce more pressing than his desire to know what his father and Fitz-Harding were up to. He scanned the field for the twins, intending to call one, if not both of them, to assist him.

"Dominic!"

Hubert had left the dais almost immediately and was now at his son's side. "A word, if you please. Away from here would be best, I think."

Dominic lifted his shoulders in a resigned shrug. It would seem that he was about to be made privy to the plot whether he wished it or no. He gestured with a self-deprecating hand.

"I take it that whatever you have to say is so urgent it cannot wait until I have had a chance to rid myself of the day's dust?"

"It is a matter of some importance, yes," Hubert confirmed. "Shall we go?"

As was his habit, Dominic turned aside to advise Adam of his intention to leave the field.

All six of the de Lescauxs were engaged in what appeared to be a heated family discussion, and as Adam glanced up Dominic saw wariness and uncertainty war with something very like hostility in his eyes. He looked away again hurriedly, seeming to rejoin the conversation with renewed vigour, evidently remonstrating with his father.

"I think," said Dominic ominously, "that the sooner you tell me what is going on, the better. I have never had Adam de Lescaux look at me like that before, and I'd as lief not repeat the experience."

The smile on Hubert's face put Dominic in mind of a hungry fox that had just found its way into an unguarded henhouse. It was not at all reassuring.

****

Will de Lescaux planted his feet slightly apart and folded his arms.

"I agree with Papa," he pronounced. "It is an excellent solution. Marriage to Dominic du Bois will see Isobel well settled, and it will silence any gossip about the impropriety of her conduct."

"*The impropriety of her conduct,*" Adam mimicked scornfully. "Will you listen to yourself, you pompous ass? Isobel is not yet sixteen, for God's sake. Dominic is more than a decade her senior—and undoubtedly double that again in experience," he added feelingly. "I cannot believe you are even considering this, sir."

His father regarded him frostily. "I am not considering it, boy. The decision is made, and you may think yourself fortunate that I am doing you the courtesy of telling you what has been decided. Hubert and I have agreed with Fitz-Harding's suggestion—this is the best possible outcome for both families."

"And does du Bois agree with you?" Henry asked neutrally.

"I am sure he will see the sense in it," William stated firmly. "Isobel has your mother's lands as her marriage portion, and I am confident a man like Dominic du Bois will be quick to see the advantages of marrying her."

A man like Dominic du Bois. Adam contemplated his father's carelessly chosen words. Dominic's parentage was common knowledge—no attempt had ever been made to hide it—and it was virtually unheard of for such a man to find himself offered an heiress of good birth in marriage. Conscious of the fickle nature of the tourney circuit and the daily hardships of survival in a mercenary troop, Adam, for one, was certain Dominic would not pass up the opportunity to exchange that hazardous existence for one so much more secure.

Having served Dominic closely for the last four years, however, Adam could not be unaware that his friend possessed something of a reputation where women were concerned. Like most men of normal persuasion, he enjoyed their company frequently enough, but Adam had never known him to show partiality for any one in particular, and he gave every indication he regarded such liaisons as nothing more than a pleasurable interlude. Common courtesy dictated that he would treat a wife with more consideration than he might show for a whore, but Adam was uneasy in the knowledge that Isobel already felt betrayed by her family. How much worse would she feel now, hastily wed and packed off to a strange place as the wife of a man she barely knew?

Henry was nodding thoughtfully. "I have to agree with Papa and Will on this matter, Adam, unless, of course, you feel Isobel might prefer to take the veil?"

"No!"

Robert and Stephen spoke as one, which was not unusual, but to their single combined voice, perhaps more surprisingly, was added their father's.

"I made a promise to your mother," he said awkwardly. "I swore I would never send your sister to a convent, and I will not break that vow. I had already decided to seek a suitable match for her, and I believe I have found one. It is perhaps not quite in the manner I would have wished, but this marriage will take place."

Robert and Stephen directed identical angry glares at Henry.

"Bel would never be happy locked away in a convent," Robert spoke vehemently. "You don't know her, Henry. She…"

"She's wild and undisciplined, just like you two," Will interrupted cuttingly. "Alais and I had already decided…"

"Enough!" bellowed William de Lescaux. "Stop it, all of you. There is no more to be said on the subject."

His growing sense of failure where Isobel was concerned had swollen to almost intolerable proportions. Were it not for his lack of care, he was certain it would never have occurred to the girl to behave as she had done today. With a muffled oath, he turned on his heel and stalked in the direction of Vaillant's keep.

"Of course, there is always a chance that du Bois might refuse," Henry suggested mildly.

Adam shot him a look sour enough to turn milk. "What I can't understand is Fitz-Harding's interest in all this," he said bitterly. "What could he possibly have to gain by…oh, *Jesu*, of course!" He broke off as realisation dawned.

His brothers waited expectantly.

"Mama's estate," Adam enunciated carefully. "Where does it lie?"

They continued to regard him with blank expressions, and he clutched at his hair in exasperation.

"Pembroke, you dolts!" he all but shouted it at them. "This is all to do with Richard de Clare."

Will shrugged. "What of it? Du Bois is your friend—I would have thought you at least should be pleased for him."

"Oh, yes," Adam retorted angrily, his voice dripping with sarcasm. "I shall gain great pleasure from watching my friend stick his head in a noose of Fitz-Harding's making—not to mention the kick I will get from seeing our innocent sister thrust into a marriage for which she is far from ready—and all to ensure that Henry of Anjou keeps his royal arse on the throne!" He swore and ground viciously at a divot of turf beneath his boot. "Jesus bloody Christ, Fitz-Harding's a scheming bastard."

"Takes one to know one," Will muttered, turning to follow their father.

Adam snarled and lunged after his eldest brother's

retreating figure, only to be brought up short by Henry's restraining arm. He jerked his head significantly in the direction of the white-faced twins.

"Let it be, Adam," he advised.

****

Dominic accepted his half-brother's presence without question and similarly his offer of assistance. He shrugged himself out of his gambeson and wrinkled his nose with distaste. "*Jesu*! See if you can hang that on a pole outside for a while, Alain."

Indicating that his father should have the only proper chair, Dominic sat down on the lid of his clothing coffer. He picked up a flagon and poured wine into two horn beakers, proffering one to Hubert and raising the other to his lips, whilst steadily regarding over the rim the man who had sired him. He drank deeply before setting down his cup.

"You'll forgive me, I hope, for not donning a fresh shirt until after I've washed?"

Le Vaillant allowed his gaze to roam over the familiar features of his firstborn son. The candid eyes of his former mistress looked back at him, patiently waiting. Hubert considered himself a fortunate man. His first wife had born him two daughters, both now grown and married, with households of their own. That first wedding had been the customary arranged marriage of convenience, but it had been happy enough, and he had been suitably grieved when she died giving birth to a stillborn son.

Dominic's mother, Marie du Bois, was the widow of a moderately profitable cloth merchant. An uncomplicated woman with a generous nature, she had entered Hubert's life at a time when he was vulnerable.

It had been simply comfort at first, but she won her way into his affections when she bore him the son he so desperately desired. His daughters had welcomed Marie's motherly presence in their lives and doted on their small half-brother, but duty had dictated that Hubert marry again, and in no way could Marie be considered a suitable match. She accepted this without rancour, but her innate sense of honour precluded any continuation of their relationship once he had wed Lady Marguerite, and thus she retired to the convent of St. Therese, where Hubert, through Dominic, believed her to be content.

Marguerite had given Hubert the legitimate heir he needed, together with three more children, and genuine affection and respect had grown between them, but there were still times when he wondered what his life might have been like had he followed his heart. He swirled the wine in his cup reflectively, and a few ruby-red drops bounced out to bead on the back of his hand.

"Fitz-Harding has suggested that there should be a marriage between you and Isobel de Lescaux," he said abruptly, "and her father is amenable to the idea."

Dominic raised his brows. "I assume it would be in my interests to be 'amenable' too?"

"You were party to the girl's dishonour, albeit unwittingly," Hubert reminded him.

Dominic laughed.

"Any blame for the demoiselle's loss of reputation may be laid squarely at her own door," he said coolly. "It was none of my doing, I assure you."

Alain shifted uncomfortably, and Hubert shrugged.

"You heard what de Bracy said. I think we may safely infer that by now everyone knows the girl was found in a compromising situation with you, and by tomorrow the tale will be all over the county—doubtless embroidered to your detriment."

Dominic gave a derisive snort. "I doubt there's much that de Bracy could say about me that has not already been said a dozen times before. You'll have to do better than that, Father."

"Think of the girl, then."

Dominic found himself remembering a pair of remarkable green eyes.

"Tempting," he allowed. "If one's taste runs to wilful redheaded wenches with a tendency to masquerade as boys. Which, I feel compelled to inform you, my lord, mine does not."

"There's a dowry," Hubert said cunningly.

Dominic looked shrewdly at his father. "And just how much is William de Lescaux prepared to pay me to take his daughter off his hands?"

Alain all but choked. "You really are a bastard, aren't you?" he accused wildly. "All the things people say about you are true!"

Hubert automatically opened his mouth to rebuke his heir, but Dominic forestalled him with a negative shake of his head. His lips twisted mockingly.

"I think you are looking at the wrong son, my lord. Perhaps you should be negotiating for Alain to wed the lady—in truth, he seems far more eager than I."

"I would not object," Alain admitted, with a sidelong glance at their father.

Hubert waved his hand dismissively. "You're far too young to be thinking about marriage."

"I'm older than Isobel," the youth retorted sulkily.

Dominic was smiling openly now. "She'd run rings

around you, little brother," he promised.

"What do you know?" Alain challenged, flinging caution to the winds. "You know nothing about her. She's…"

"Going to be my wife," Dominic finished for him repressively. He turned back to his father. "We were discussing the dowry, I believe?"

With a muffled oath, Alain spun on his heel and quitted the tent. Hubert rose as if to follow, but Dominic stopped him.

"Let him go," he advised. "Give him time to cool down."

Inwardly he was cursing himself for having underestimated the strength of his half-brother's feelings. He seemed to be making errors of judgement hand over fist today—and Isobel de Lescaux was the cause of them all. *Jesu*, the girl was a veritable menace!

Hubert sighed ruefully. "Aye. You have the right of it, and that is the very reason I would not consider allying him to young Isobel. He needs time to mature before he considers settling down—and she will need a firm hand."

Dominic nodded. On the strength of this morning's escapade, he could not disagree. A sudden thought occurred.

"Just how old *is* the girl, my lord? She said she would be fourteen come Michaelmas, but given the ease with which lies seem to trip from her tongue, I suppose that may not be the case?"

"If you are having doubts on that score, then you need have none," Hubert responded quickly. "She is almost sixteen, and perfectly marriageable. Of course, it will be for you to decide whether or not you bed her."

Dominic made no comment, but at the back of his mind lay the dangerous and irrefutable knowledge that an unconsummated marriage was one that could be set aside.

"I take it you are willing?" Hubert probed. His son smiled wolfishly.

"Why not? I'd be a fool to turn down such an opportunity. But then we both know that, do we not?"

Le Vaillant got to his feet with a relieved smile. He'd been half expecting Dominic to refuse for some perverse reason of his own, thereby ruining his own chance to see his bastard son advance to a level beyond anything he could ever have hoped for.

"I will see to the details." As he turned to leave, Dominic called him back, a thoughtful frown creasing his brow.

"You said that it was Fitz-Harding who proposed this match, yet he would not have done so without good reason. What does he expect from me in return?"

"Why, your undying gratitude, of course," Hubert answered smoothly. "What else?"

Dominic watched his father cross the now-deserted tourney field until he was lost from view. Whatever Hubert might think, he was not deceived. There was decidedly more to this matter than met the eye, and Dominic was in no doubt he would at some point be called upon to recompense Fitz-Harding handsomely for such a hoist up fortune's ladder.

Lacing the tent flap against the chill April wind, he poured water for himself from a leather jug into a wooden bowl, reflecting with wry amusement that he once again appeared to be squire-less. He stripped off his soiled shirt and pondered his unexpectedly changed circumstances. After so many years of following the tourneys and seeking a mercenary's wage, might it not be good to dwell within the security of stone walls, where wind and water could not penetrate? Dominic embroidered the vision a little, imbuing it with a bathtub wreathed in herb-scented steam, and an attentive woman to see to his comfort. His involuntary gasp was due not to the coldness of the water as it hit his skin but to the realisation that the woman of his imagination had worn the face of Isobel de Lescaux.

"Christ," he muttered to himself, "indebted for life in the name of four walls and a bed to call my own—not to mention the dubious reputation of a redheaded vixen. I must be insane!"

Fitz-Harding had known his measure, he acknowledged ruefully. He hoped Adam would not despise him too much for seizing the opportunity, but he was not optimistic. If he'd had a sixteen-year-old sister, the last man in the world on whom he would have considered bestowing her would be a bastard mercenary almost twelve years her senior. His last thought on the matter was that perhaps there was not so great a difference between himself and Piers de Bracy after all.

Chapter Eight

Hubert le Vaillant raised his cup to William de Lescaux and toasted the union between their families, whilst at a small writing desk in a corner of the room his scribe, head bent in diligence, busied himself setting down the terms of the agreement under the benevolent eye of Robert Fitz-Harding. William grunted and beckoned a page to replenish his own goblet. Since coming from the meeting with his sons, he had downed enough wine to convince himself that Dominic du Bois was an excellent match for his daughter. He was persuaded that he had fulfilled his promise to Anwen whilst at the same time gaining a son-in-law whose reputation for martial prowess made him more than equal to dealing with Isobel and her dower estates.

Latterly William had been vexed by the matter of finding a suitable steward to replace the current holder of that office, whose advancing years must soon render him unable to perform his duties. He had toyed with recalling Adam for the purpose but now congratulated himself that Dominic du Bois would make an admirable alternative, coming as he did complete with Adam and an entire troop of soldiers into the bargain.

He was under no illusions, knowing it was the lure of Isobel's dowry that had ensured the mercenary's willingness. Whatever the gossips might make of her presence in Dominic's private quarters, William did not think for a moment that Hubert's son had behaved improperly towards his daughter. For one thing, there had barely been time amidst his preparations for the joust before her deception had been discovered, and for another, Dominic had been under the impression that Isobel was a boy, and William gave no credence to the rumours which circulated about Adam's closeness to his commander, confident in his certainty that his son's appetites were healthy enough.

He crooked his finger once more at the hovering page. Isobel had yet to be advised of her good fortune, and William, for all his courage on the battlefield, had elected to abdicate this responsibility. Let Will's wife be the one to tell her. Women were supposed to be good at handling situations like this, and it was time that Alais did something to earn her keep.

****

Alais de Lescaux viewed her sister-in-law's panic-stricken look with mounting irritation.

"If I were you," she said, adopting a tone of censorious seniority, "I would be down on my knees thanking God instead of standing there with that petrified expression on your face. Dominic du Bois may have been born on the wrong side of the blanket, but he's still the son of a nobleman—and with his reputation, you're lucky he didn't just laugh and discard you along with all the rest."

"But nothing happened," Isobel protested. "Why must I marry him—and what do you mean 'all the rest'?"

" 'Nothing happened,' " Alais mimicked. "You mean, aside from the fact that you were found alone with him, in his private quarters on the tourney field, no less? Not forgetting the fact that you were dressed in boy's clothing at the time!" She shook her head. "You surely cannot be that naïve, Isobel. What really happened is irrelevant. People will believe the worst, whatever the truth of the matter."

"I do not care what people believe," Isobel said firmly. "I will not marry him. I do not like him—and I am quite sure that he does not like me."

Alais threw up her hands in exasperation.

"Are you some sort of simpleton that you do not understand what I have been saying? Your likes and dislikes are of no consequence. There is no element of choice in this for you, Isobel. It is arranged between your father and his, and he has agreed."

She picked fussily at a loose thread on the heavily embroidered bedcover. "I don't know what you've got to complain about, anyhow. He's not too old, and he's handsome enough. From what they say about him, you should be thankful he has sufficient sense of honour to care about the damage to your reputation and is prepared to do what he can to redeem it."

Isobel was no longer listening. She had flung open the door and was already halfway through it. Alais leapt off the bed in alarm.

"Where are you going? Isobel! Come back here at once!" With an oath she would never have uttered in her husband's presence, Alais hastened in pursuit of her errant sister-in-law.

Isobel was careless of all but a desperate need to see her father. What little she knew about Dominic du Bois convinced her that she could not contemplate being bound to him for the rest of her life, whatever he might or might not have agreed to. Intent on her purpose, she rounded the corner blindly and ran full tilt into a solid wall of muscle.

Adam's arms closed around his sister, and he braced himself to absorb the impact of her body. He had found time to bathe since the joust and was now wearing a fine russet wool tunic that creased beneath Isobel's fingers as she grabbed hold of him to steady herself.

"Easy now, Bel," he soothed over the torrent of words that tumbled from her lips.

Sliding the palms of his hands up her arms, he brought them to rest on her shoulders, exerting subtle downward pressure until she was forced to pause for breath. Taking in her dishevelled state and tearstained face, he guessed immediately the cause of her distress, and the arrival of his eldest brother's wife only served to confirm his suspicions.

"Really, Isobel," Alais admonished somewhat breathlessly. "As if you had not caused enough trouble already today!"

"It's all right, Alais." Adam smiled conspiratorially. "As you can see, there is no harm done."

Alais sniffed. "Perhaps not," she conceded. "Since it's only you."

Adam struggled not to laugh. Evidently tact was not Alais' greatest virtue—a pity, really, since neither was it Will's.

"I am on my way to see Papa myself, so I will escort Isobel to him," he soothed his disgruntled sister-in-law. "She will be safe enough with me, I think." He flourished her his best courtier's bow. "No doubt we shall see you again later, Alais."

She glared at him for a moment, her face stiff with disapproval. Then, with a curt nod, she turned away.

"*Jesu*, she's almost as bad as Aunt Rohese," Adam said feelingly as they halted before the door to William de Lescaux's chamber. At the sound of her father's voice, Isobel tensed, and Adam squeezed her arm sympathetically.

"Come on, Bel. Best get it over with."

She took a deep breath, bit her lip, and followed him.

William regarded her frostily. "Well, madam?" His tone was decidedly lacking in warmth. "What do you here? I do not recall sending for you."

Isobel clasped her hands in front of her determinedly and fixed her eyes on the rush-strewn floor.

"I'm sorry, Papa. It was not my intention to…"

"Intention or otherwise, what's done is done," he forestalled her abruptly. "The outcome is better than we could have hoped. There was always a chance that du Bois would refuse to have you."

"It is that about which I had hoped to speak to you, Papa." Isobel swallowed nervously. "Is it not a little drastic to rush into such an alliance?" She risked a glance at his face and wished she had not.

"By what right do you question the arrangements I have made for your future?" William demanded silkily.

Isobel lifted her head bravely. "For the very reason that it is *my* future, and I do not wish to wed Dominic du Bois."

"I see." Lord William steepled his fingers and rested his chin on their tips, with every appearance of a rational and tolerant man. Adam winced. "Perhaps you would be so good as to tell me why *your* wishes should have any bearing on what *I* deem to be best for you? Your conduct today is hardly conducive to my believing you are fit to determine your own course."

His words cut her as they were meant to, but still Isobel refused to be cowed.

"Because I had thought that you might have *some* care for my happiness," she said quietly. "I see now that I was wrong."

A muscle tightened in William's throat.

"You will wed Dominic du Bois," he said inexorably.

Defiant to the last, his daughter stood her ground. "I want to enter the novitiate."

William snorted contemptuously. "I'll not dower you to spend the rest of your life behind convent walls." His eyes met briefly with Adam's, then slid away. "Besides," he said disparagingly, "I doubt any respectable house would take you. You have not the demeanour of a nun. Adam?"

"Sir?"

William handed over a roll of vellum.

"Take this to your lord." He glanced significantly at Isobel. "It is the marriage contract, and I would have his agreement to it. The ceremony will take place tomorrow."

"Tomorrow!" Isobel gasped and swayed. Her face paled to the colour of newly bleached linen, and Adam instinctively reached out to steady her.

"An announcement will be made tonight," her father informed her with a finality that brooked no further argument. "In the meantime, I suggest that you take yourself to the chapel and ask for the Blessed

Virgin's help in being a dutiful and obedient daughter for once."

Adam felt Isobel recoil as though she had been slapped. With a furious look at the unrepentant William, he led her from the room. Outside in the passageway, he locked his arms around her once more as agonised sobs shook her slender frame.

"I cannot help that I remind him of her," she wept brokenly. "I did not ask to be born. Indeed, I wish to God that I had died when she did!"

Adam knew there was naught he could do but continue to hold her close against him and offer her meaningless words of comfort. It put him in mind of the day, not long after her fifth birthday, when he had come upon her crying her heart out in a corner of the bailey because their head groom had just drowned the stable cat's latest litter of kittens. The fact that Lescaux had at the time been in serious danger of being overrun with feral felines had not been any consolation to a weeping child, and now as then he could think of little to say which might ease her pain.

"It would seem it is your day for distressed damsels, Adam. Dare I hope this one is more promising than the last?"

Adam stepped hurriedly away from Isobel, trying in vain to position himself so her identity was hidden by his body, but he could see from the expression on his friend's face that it was already too late. Dominic did not stop to question the disproportionate surge of rage that coursed through him at the sight of Isobel de Lescaux locked in another man's embrace. The memory of young Alain's outburst still fresh in his mind, he fixed her with a look of disgust and said the first thing that came into his head.

"Is no man safe from you?" he asked cuttingly. "*Jesu*, woman, this one's your own brother!"

Isobel simply stared back at him in bewilderment, but Adam's face was a mask of compounded fury and shock.

"Dear God, Dominic, what are you implying?" he gasped. "Who can have led you to think such a thing?"

Comprehension dawned, and Isobel shot Dominic a look of pure contempt.

"Oh, I'm sure my lord du Bois has an imagination quite vile enough without having to rely on others to feed it, Adam."

Dominic's gaze narrowed dangerously.

"I warn you, madam, I will not tolerate such conduct after we are wed. If necessary, I will confine you to our own manor, where you will be unable to practise your tricks."

Buoyed by indignation as much on Adam's part as on her own, Isobel drew herself up to her full height. Her green eyes blazed.

"I think you mean *my* manor, do you not, my lord? That is, after all, the only reason you are prepared to marry me. Or perhaps that is no longer the case?" Her brows arched with the question. "Mayhap your lily-white conscience is too troubled by what you think you have just witnessed?"

She had the satisfaction of seeing him gape like a landed trout and imagined with some pleasure that it was not often anyone rendered the great Dominic du Bois speechless.

Adam's voice was tight with anger. "If you can truly think such a thing of me, I will resign my commission with you."

Dominic shrugged negligently. "That is your prerogative. At least I would not have to trouble myself thinking up reasons to keep you out of your sister's company once she is my wife." He looked scornfully at Isobel. "Perhaps I am beginning to understand why no one in your family ever cared to mention her existence."

Adam swore viciously and started towards him, but Isobel stepped quickly between them and placed a restraining hand on her brother's chest. Dominic's watchful eyes followed the path of those slender fingers which had so unsettled him when they laced his gambeson just hours ago.

"Adam, no," she implored. "What purpose would it serve? Do not make matters any worse than they already are."

Prising the marriage contract from his taut fingers, she thrust it at Dominic, her tone hardening.

"Here, my lord, take it. I am sure it will make interesting reading. Be sure to tally everything your alliance with me will bring you before you quite make up your mind whether or not I am worth the trouble!"

She spun round, and the setting sun caught the ends of her braid where it hung below her wimple, striking sparks of gold amidst the chestnut strands. Dominic watched her walk away, his fingers clenched round the scrolled vellum. With every fibre of his being he longed to tear the document into a hundred tiny pieces, but he knew with equal certainty that he would not do it, and for that reason he was as close to hating himself as he had ever been.

Adam broke the silence.

"You are wrong about what you think you saw. She was distressed and I was comforting her. That is all. Whosoever has given you reason to think otherwise, I would swear on my life it is not so."

Dominic schooled his face to neutrality. "When we are wed, you may be sure that I will treat your sister as she deserves," he responded, fully conscious of the ambiguity of his words and knowing Adam was not fooled either.

Adam shook his head in disgust. "*Jesu*, has she not suffered enough? It should be us on our knees in the chapel begging forgiveness, not her." He gestured at the contract. "Well, you'd best do as she says and read it. I am to wait for your reply."

He propped himself against the wall, arms folded across his chest and one knee bent so the sole of his boot rested on the stonework. Dominic frowned askance at him but broke the seal, unrolled the parchment, and read.

"Christ *Jesu*!"

Adam smiled mirthlessly.

"The proverbial poisoned chalice," he mocked. "Welcome to the family, *brother*—if you're still willing to make contract, that is?"

Dominic, still struggling to assimilate the geography of his wife's dower lands, swore again.

"I'd say that about sums it up," Adam agreed. "De Clare won't even be able to piss in his own garderobe without you being expected to report it to Henry or his minions. Clever of Fitz-Harding, don't you think?"

"Damn him to hell!" Dominic responded. He joined Adam in using the wall for support and stared unseeingly into middle distance.

"Are you still going to wed my sister?"

Dominic turned his head and their eyes met. "Should I expect to lose my second in command, and a trusted friend, if I say yes?"

Adam regarded him with a steady hazel gaze. "What you saw was not what you imagined. Can you accept that?"

Dominic held the contact for a moment, then nodded.

Adam shrugged. "Then it is forgotten. Sign the contract. I will bear witness and return it to my father."

He accompanied Dominic to the steward's office and waited with him whilst quill, ink, and sand were found. Dominic hesitated.

"Adam, there is something else you should know, before you agree to stay with me. Your sister's estates—I cannot be certain, but I think there is a possibility they share a border with the lands de Bracy stands to inherit on his marriage."

Adam paused in the act of sprinkling sand on the wet ink and looked up. He whistled softly through his teeth, and his expression was pitying.

"I'd say you've been sewn up tighter than a sailor's shroud, my lord." He tipped the document, and a shower of loose grains pattered against the rushes. "Rest easy, Dominic. I'll continue to serve under your command, and gladly. But just you remember that my little sister is an innocent child, and if you hurt her, then I swear to God I will kill you myself."

Eyes on Adam's retreating figure, Dominic's mouth tightened. His father had implied that Isobel de Lescaux had been allowed to run wild for much of her life, and for himself he found it difficult to believe that any female who had spent so much of her time in the company of boys verging on manhood could possibly remain innocent. He wondered idly how many men she might have caught in her snare. Certainly his half-brother was besotted, although he did not think the boy had dared further thus far than to dream.

She was a shrewd little witch, too, he acknowledged, thinking back to their heated exchange. She had known he would not turn his back on the material advantages that marriage to her would bring, and she had mocked him with her knowledge. A humourless smile twisted his lips. A few words spoken before a priest need not commit him to sharing her bed for eternity, but, he vowed silently, once those words had been spoken, he'd make damn sure no other man shared it.

Chapter Nine

Belatedly, Isobel did as her father had bidden her and sought the solace of Vaillant's chapel, although it was for her own comfort rather than out of any deference to his wishes. When she left Dominic du Bois and her brother, she had been borne along on a high tide of anger and indignation, and consequently she had walked without conscious thought and in no particular direction. Now she realised she was hopelessly lost in a part of Vaillant she did not recognise at all. Why had she never realised Alain's home was so extensive?

She turned decisively towards a shaft of light that beckoned invitingly through the stone-arched opening in the wall to her left, certain that if she could only gain the inner courtyard she would surely find her bearings again. To her dismay, she found herself not in the courtyard, as she had hoped, but in a small, secluded pleasaunce. Realising upon what she had unwittingly stumbled, Isobel coloured and murmured an apology to the occupants, intending at once to withdraw, only to discover her path blocked by a powerfully built man of middling height.

He looked her up and down with insolent appraisal and made a remark to his companions which caused her blush to deepen still further. Evidently this amused him, for he threw back his head and laughed. She angled her chin with icy hauteur.

"An you will step aside, sir, I shall overlook your impertinence."

Piers de Bracy, still smarting from the afternoon's defeat, and further irritated by his subsequent failure to incite the de Lescauxs to an undignified public brawl, was more than ready for a little sport, and if his victim was unwilling, then so much the better. He bent towards the imperious little madam and took hold of her wrist, drawing her closer.

"Softly now, *doucette*," he purred. "I can see I will need to teach you better manners."

She lunged at him. Taken completely unawares, the knight could do no more than grunt as his shoulders hit the ground, and Isobel made a mental note to thank the twins for having demonstrated the technique so effectively on their last visit home. Panting slightly with the effort of having overcome an assailant significantly heavier than herself, she turned to make good her escape, only to find that two of her tormentor's comrades now stood between her and the doorway. As they advanced, she was forced to retreat.

De Bracy, having gained his feet again, attempted to close his arms about her from behind, but Isobel twisted out of his grasp, relieving him of the fine jewel-hilted dagger that hung from his belt in the process. He laughed and nodded approvingly.

"Very good, *petite*. I will own that I am impressed. Let us not be foolish, however. The first time you had the element of surprise, I grant you—but a second time? I think not."

"Are you willing to take the risk?" Isobel challenged. She tightened her grip on the stolen dagger, wishing desperately she was not so encumbered by the skirts that wrapped themselves about her ankles.

"If the prize is worth it," de Bracy assured her, "and in your case, *demoiselle*, I rather think it is."

He stepped forward confidently, only to draw back again with a yelp of outrage as the tip of his own dagger inscribed a thin red line across the back of his hand.

"You bitch!" he swore, this time reaching for her in earnest.

Isobel ducked his avenging arm and ran, but the odds were heavily stacked against her, and very soon she found herself caught and held hard against another unyielding male body. She gave a little sob of frustration as strong fingers closed around her own, increasing the pressure until she was forced to let go of the dagger haft. In a last attempt to win free of her new captor's hold, she aimed a hefty kick at his shins, but it availed her nothing. In short order her arms were pinned behind her back and she was held immobile.

"Bravo, du Bois—a worthy contest," de Bracy applauded mockingly. "Now, if you would be so kind as to hand the *lady* over, I believe she and I have a little matter to settle." He glanced meaningfully at his blood-smeared cuff.

Dominic's lips tightened. "I regret that I am unable to oblige you, my lord. I'm afraid I have a prior claim on the *lady*." He imbued the word with the same sarcasm as de Bracy himself had used.

"Do you, indeed?" De Bracy's eyes lingered on Isobel with renewed interest. "Well, well, well! Am I to take it this is the little de Lescaux? God's nails, du Bois, I had not realised you were quite so desperate."

"No more so than you, from what I hear," Dominic replied neutrally, alluding to de Bracy's own betrothal, and with scant regard for Isobel's indignation. He glanced cursorily in the direction of the knight's hand. "Shall I send a surgeon to attend you?"

De Bracy laughed dismissively. "A scratch, no more."

"Very well, if you will excuse us?"

Dominic tightened his hold on Isobel's arm and all but dragged her away. He could not remember when he had last felt such anger. En route for the stables to check a slight injury sustained by his destrier during the joust, the last thing he had expected to encounter was the woman he had just contracted to marry engaged in yet more dalliance, let alone conducting a knife fight, and with Piers de Bracy, of all people. He spoke only to elicit directions to Isobel's chamber. Once there, he flung open the door and thrust her inside.

"You dare bleat to me about propriety, madam?" he asked icily, ignoring her protests as he bundled her maidservant from the room with an obvious gesture of dismissal. He forced Isobel down onto the cushioned window seat. "Before God, I begin to think your family will be well rid of you."

She would have argued with him, but he forestalled her with a peremptory wave of his hand.

"Spare me your protestations of innocence," he scorned. "When we are wed—and wed we shall be whether you wish it or no—I promise you, you will conduct yourself like the lady your brother claims you to be."

It was too much. Isobel bounced off the window seat, eyes blazing, and retaliated with the greatest insult she could think of.

"You are evidently determined to prove yourself a

bastard by more than just birth, Dominic du Bois. I hardly think *you* are in a position to lecture *me* on the proper conduct of ladies."

His sharp intake of breath told her she had scored a definite hit, and the knowledge afforded her no little pleasure. Dominic struggled to curb his mounting fury, once again assailed by the certainty that, in her own inimitable way, Isobel de Lescaux could be as lethal as any of her brothers. Despite his anger, he could not help but admire her spirit. Hard on the heels of that admiration followed a sharper sensation which, with some surprise, he recognised as desire.

Intrigued, he made himself study her objectively. She was tall for a woman, and certainly not in the current fashion of cool madonna-like beauty. Not the kind of female to whom he was usually drawn at all, but Dominic was experienced enough to recognise the attraction for what it was, and honest enough to admit it, even if only to himself. A feral smile twisted his mouth. Perhaps marriage to his friend's little sister might not be so bad after all.

"Rest assured, madam," he murmured provocatively, "I know all about *ladies,* and I have been in their company oft enough to know *exactly* how they behave. I also know how to treat them. Would you like me to demonstrate?"

Green eyes clashed with blue, and to her chagrin Isobel was the first to break the contact. A point to him, Dominic registered with satisfaction. His mocking gaze slid to the rapid rise and fall of her chest, and he knew he had rattled her. He took a step towards her, his smile widening at her involuntary retreat. Sensing he had regained the upper hand, Dominic judged it time to deliver the *coup de grace.*

"Then again, perhaps I should wait until you show some signs of being one." He turned away from her with a mocking bow. "Until later, *ma* Bel."

Had he been a split second slower, Isobel's missile would have hit its intended target. As it was, the hastily flung pewter goblet merely rebounded off the door before crashing to the floor and rolling to a standstill at her feet. She buried her face in her hands and wept tears of pure frustration.

****

"Bel?" Adam spoke hesitantly. "Bel, it's me."

There was no answer. The door opened to his tentative touch, and he entered the room cautiously, but as he turned to close it again behind him, he heard his sister's voice.

"You'd best leave it, Adam," Isobel said without looking round. She was sitting in the window embrasure, gazing out at the wide sweep of meadow that sloped down towards the river. "You would not want to do anything that might fuel your lord and master's disgusting suspicions."

Adam crossed the room on silent feet and came to join her. The colourful pennants attached to the pavilions were tossing angrily in the rising wind, and a storm was now brewing to equal the one that raged in Isobel herself. She flinched as a bolt of lightning leapt from ground to cloud, and in the distance a rumble of thunder sounded, as if in answer to the challenge.

"'Tis not so bad as it seems, Bel," Adam offered tentatively. "Truly, there are many things about Dominic that may be admired. Once you become accustomed to one another, and he realises he was mistaken…"

He tailed off hopelessly, for she did not respond, her stare remaining fixed on the horizon. Adam ran a hand through his hair in frustration.

"Christ *Jesu*, what a bloody mess!" he exploded.

"Send for Alais and Aunt Rohese, Adam," Isobel responded in a tired voice. He looked at her questioningly, and she sighed. "Would you have the de Lescaux name dragged further through the mire? If I do not appear in the hall tonight, the gossip will only grow tenfold."

Adam opened his mouth, intending to offer some comforting platitude, but closed it without making a single utterance when he realised that, once again, he could think of nothing appropriate to say. Instead he bowed and turned abruptly on his heel. Isobel listened to the sound of his retreating footsteps and reluctantly forced herself to admit that her determination to be present when Hubert le Vaillant announced her betrothal to his bastard son had less to do with her family's honour than with her overwhelming need to show Dominic du Bois she was not afraid of him.

****

Vaillant's great hall was more crowded than it had ever been. On a raised dais at one end, its lord presided like a complacent spider at the heart of its web. As befitted his status as the king's representative, Robert Fitz-Harding had been granted a place of honour at Hubert's right hand; to his left sat William de Lescaux. Hubert glanced further down the table and nodded approvingly in the direction of his wife, who had seated herself next to Dominic. Although Hubert had never taken any pains to conceal Dominic's paternity, neither had he ever flaunted it quite so blatantly, and the presence of his illegitimate son at the high table raised a few eyebrows. For himself, Dominic was aware of their scrutiny, and to his consternation he realised he had communicated his unease to Lady Marguerite. She leant a little closer and whispered in his ear.

"Pay them no heed. It will do them good to wonder."

"You are very generous, madam." He inclined his head slightly and was surprised when she smiled conspiratorially at him.

"Your mother and I never met, Dominic—and many would say I should be grateful for her tact and sensitivity—but I have often imagined that in other circumstances we might have been friends. As for yourself, you had good cause to resent me, yet you have shown me nothing but respect and courtesy, and you have ever been kind and patient with Alain and the younger boys. It behooves me to be equally gracious to you. That aside," she continued, looking artfully up at him, "I really am quite genuinely fond of you, and what woman of my years would not be flattered to find herself entitled to claim the attention of so handsome a man?"

Dominic's lips twitched. "Are you flirting with me, madam?"

"Of course!" She laughed delightedly. "With you, I know I am safe."

He responded with a slight quirk of his brows, and Marguerite laughed again.

"Oh, your reputation may be legendary, my dear," she assured him, "but sadly, a woman of my years knows the difference between what is plausible and what is simply fanciful. If only half the tales told of you were true—oh…"

Dominic ceased wondering exactly what his father's wife had heard about him and looked up to see what had caused her to break off in mid-sentence. Isobel de Lescaux stood on the threshold of the hall, surrounded by her brothers. She was clad in an overdress of green velvet, the shade of which Dominic knew instinctively would enhance her startling emerald eyes. Its side seams had been left open to show an under-tunic of fine cream silk, and a girdle of gold links interspersed with amber lozenges encircled her narrow waist. The rich chestnut hair he had glimpsed earlier was once again decorously covered by a plain wimple, secured with a simple circlet of twisted gold wire. Against the overt masculinity of her escort she looked so undeniably fragile and feminine Dominic was forced to wonder anew at his failure to see through her earlier pretence. Briefly her eyes connected with his. Panic flared in their depths, and he found himself willing her to master it. He saw her fingers tighten almost imperceptibly on Adam's arm, and then her chin lifted defiantly. Dominic realised he was holding his breath. He exhaled abruptly.

The de Lescauxs advanced with slow deliberation, proceeding with almost military precision to the high table. Adam remained at his sister's side; Will and Henry flanked the couple, and the twins followed close behind. It was an unmistakable declaration of family unity. Dominic watched as his father exchanged greetings with the two eldest de Lescauxs, who then bowed and withdrew to their allotted places.

Hubert stepped down from the dais and came to

stand before Isobel and Adam. Placing his hands on the girl's shoulders, he drew her away from her brother and into his embrace, kissing her formally on both cheeks. "I bid you welcome, daughter," he said in a voice deliberately loud enough to carry round the hall.

Relishing the murmur of surprise that greeted his words, Hubert led Isobel towards the raised platform.

"Come, we will drink a toast to the alliance between our families."

The ripple escalated to tidal-wave proportions as the significance of the empty seat beside Dominic du Bois became apparent. Adam studied Isobel intently as she was handed to her place. Her face was still pale, but she seemed to have regained the composure that had so nearly deserted her a moment ago. Concern for her warred with his loyalty and respect for the man who would soon become her husband, and with a curt nod he sent Robert to take up his position behind Dominic. His duty done for the nonce, Adam beckoned Stephen to follow him to the table where the remainder of their family waited.

In the time it took the de Lescauxs to settle, Hubert le Vaillant planned his next move. Earlier he had assured Fitz-Harding that it would be an easy matter for him to convey that the match between Isobel and Dominic was an arrangement of long standing between William de Lescaux and himself, and now the time had come to prove that boast. He cleared his throat, positioned himself the better to play to his audience, and proceeded to address his friend.

"William, when you sired five sons in quick succession, I will own that I despaired of ever realising my dream to unite our blood."

Hubert paused to allow the laughter which greeted this sally to abate whilst bestowing an indulgent smile on the girl at his side. “But at last, you had the good sense to beget a daughter, and although I have had a long wait for her to become a woman grown, I do not believe there is anyone here who would question the wisdom of my waiting.”

He glanced expectantly at Dominic, who responded exactly as he had hoped, allowing his eyes to roam lazily over Isobel with an unmistakable air of possession. A delicate flush stained the girl’s cheeks, and with a satisfied smile Hubert raised his cup.

“A toast!” he cried. “A toast to Isobel and Dominic. On the morrow they will make their vows, and I invite you all to bear witness.”

Isobel became aware of Dominic’s fingers closing round her own as he raised her hand to his lips. He bent his head close and whispered against her ear: “Smile, sweeting. Who knows, if you appear suitably besotted, our enemies might even be charitable enough to put this morning’s little escapade down to your eagerness to be alone with me.”

She could not be sure whether the roaring in her ears came from the pounding of her own blood or the rising swell of voices toasting her betrothal. Swallowing hastily over the lump in her throat, Isobel rallied instinctively.

“Your enemies,” she hissed, “not mine.”

Appreciative laughter coursed through him. He lowered her hand but did not release it, and when she twisted her fingers in an effort to free them, he merely increased the pressure of his grip. As she drew breath to protest, Dominic casually raised his other hand to run his index finger lightly across the fullness of her lower lip.

"Be very careful, *ma* Bel," he warned. "You would not want people to think that this was a match made anywhere but in heaven."

Isobel shivered. Until today only Alain or her brothers had ever used the diminutive version of her name, and never had she heard it imbued with such menace or uttered with such unmistakable accents of possession. At a loss to know how she should respond, she looked away hurriedly and caught her father watching her. Outwardly he was smiling, but the underlying hint of steel in his gaze warned her to do nothing that might shatter the illusion so skilfully wrought by Hubert le Vaillant. Her two eldest brothers, meanwhile, wore such identical expressions of forced gaiety that anyone looking at them might be forgiven for thinking that they, rather than Robert and Stephen, were the twins in the family.

Fighting to suppress the tide of hysteria rising within her, Isobel looked to Adam for reassurance. He dipped his head in silent acknowledgement and raised his cup to her. She bit her lip and surreptitiously dashed away threatening tears with the back of her hand. The movement, small as it was, caught Dominic's attention, and he frowned, struggling against the surge of jealousy that coursed through him. Forcibly reminded of his suspicions concerning his betrothed and the men of her acquaintance, he twisted round, seeking his half-brother, but the boy stood close behind William de Lescaux, supervising the pages attending to his lord's needs, and his face was an expressionless mask.

At Dominic's own back, Robert de Lescaux was

performing a similar function. Like Alain's, his face revealed nothing, but when Dominic's gaze strayed across the hall to his squire's mirror image, some sixth sense told him the twins were once again communicating privately across the space that presently separated them, and his inability to intercept their wordless exchanges disturbed him far more than he would have thought possible.

Irritated, he returned his attention to Isobel. Her eyes were downcast in what might, by those unacquainted with her, be construed as maidenly modesty; to Dominic it seemed far more likely she was simply preoccupied with searching for a way to avoid their imminent marriage. He toyed with telling her she was no match for men like Fitz-Harding and his father but decided she would not thank him for the advice. Instead, he contented himself with vowing that no matter what excuses she sought to contrive, he would, with equal determination, ensure that she stood beside him in Vaillant's chapel come the appointed hour tomorrow. He concentrated on persuading himself it was her dowry and his own potential loss of face that motivated him rather than an insidious desire to see her inextricably bound to him.

When Hubert's musicians struck up an estampie, Isobel raised her head to watch the dancers, but to her dismay the twisting patterns woven by their feet quickly made her eyes ache. The familiar and dreaded spots of colour pulsed behind her lids. With a panicked gasp she pushed back her seat, almost running in her haste to escape from the hall.

Dominic half-rose, intending to fetch her back, but Robert de Lescaux had recognised the telltale signs on his sister's face, and he leant forward hurriedly on the pretext of refilling his lord's cup.

"My sister suffers from megrims," he murmured in hushed tones. "They make her most grievously sick, and I do not think she would appreciate you standing over her while she loses the contents of her stomach. Do you remain seated, my lord. I will ask Adam to send Stephen after her."

Reluctantly Dominic nodded assent. He subsided into his seat and watched as his squire crossed the hall, noting how adroitly the young man avoided the efforts of the many women participants to draw him into the dance. Adam acknowledged Robert's appearance with a genial nod, shifting slightly along the bench to make room for him, but Robert responded with a negative shake of his head, and Dominic saw him lean closer to Adam and whisper urgently in his ear. A frown creased Adam's forehead, and he twisted round to speak with Stephen.

Neither they nor Dominic saw Louis Montierre nudge his lord's shoulder and draw his attention to Isobel's departure. De Bracy grinned appreciatively and slapped his squire on the shoulder. Extricating himself from his companions with the most innocent and plausible of excuses, he slipped unobtrusively from the hall.

Isobel staggered weakly against the wall of the garderobe, gaining brief comfort from the press of cold stone against her forehead, before sliding to the floor with a whimper of pain. This was far worse than yesterday, and had come upon her more suddenly than ever before. Oblivion beckoned invitingly, and she welcomed it.

Piers de Bracy, happening on her just moments later, viewed his quarry with mild irritation. His intention had been to waylay the little de Lescaux for his own amusement, and to find her in such a state did not suit his purpose at all. He was half-inclined to leave her where she was, until it dawned on him that if *she* went missing, as her twin brothers had done the previous evening, the implications would be a great deal more serious. He imagined with some delight the expression on Dominic du Bois' face when the man heard where his betrothed had spent the night—and with whom. Even the combined efforts of Vaillant and Lescaux would not be able to bury the resultant scandal. It would, he decided, be a fitting revenge for his inglorious defeat on the field today, together with all the other slights, real or imagined, that he deemed himself to have suffered at the hands of Dominic du Bois and Adam de Lescaux.

Piers bent down and seized the girl's shoulders, dragging her upright and ignoring her faint cry of protest at his less than gentle handling. He grinned to himself. She had not seemed to consume overmuch wine at the feast; obviously she did not have the family head for drink.

"Up you come, poppet," he murmured cajolingly, heaving her to her feet and getting one shoulder under her arm in order to support her.

"Please…" she whispered, words tumbling incoherently from her lips.

"You are flatteringly eager, *doucette*," de Bracy mocked approvingly.

A shred of memory set alarm bells ringing in her head, vying with the other noises already clamouring there. Instinct alone guiding her, Isobel sought to pull away from the imprisoning arms, but Piers merely tightened his grip, enjoying the way his body hardened in appreciation of its proximity to hers. She stumbled, throwing them both off balance, and he cursed roundly.

"Bel?"

This voice was reassuringly familiar, and Isobel half turned towards the illusion of safety, slipping through de Bracy's hands. With the enviably swift reflexes of youth, Stephen de Lescaux reached out to catch his sister before she hit the stone-flagged floor, registering with surprise as he did so that she seemed considerably more fragile than he remembered. He glared suspiciously at De Bracy, who raised both hands in a placatory gesture.

"Don't look at me like that, stripling," he admonished, with an air of tolerant amusement. "This is naught of my doing, I assure you. Your precious sister appears to be suffering from a surfeit of drink. Then again, perhaps that is no more than one might expect, given her general immodesty—du Bois is welcome to her."

Although well aware of the insult, Stephen was sensible enough to realise he would be wasting his breath in addressing de Bracy's retreating back. Instead, he pushed Isobel's sweat-dampened hair back from her forehead and spoke gently to her.

"Bel, sweetheart, we need to get you to your chamber."

Her lips moved in an effort to respond, but the words when they emerged were slurred and disjointed, and Stephen wryly acknowledged that de Bracy could hardly be blamed for concluding she was drunk. He heaved an exasperated sigh and resigned himself to carrying her back to her room. She was light enough, but her height would make her an awkward burden. He bent over her recumbent form again, considering the best way to accomplish the task. He heard footsteps and swung round, thinking perhaps de Bracy had been smitten by an uncharacteristic bolt of compassion and was returning to help.

Dominic was unable to prevent himself from voicing the expletive that formed in his throat as he came upon yet another of his intended's brothers handling her in what could only be viewed as an intimate manner.

"God's blood," he muttered, "not you, as well!"

Stephen stared at him in some confusion. "My lord…" he began, as Dominic pushed past him.

"Get up," he ordered, his annoyance escalating as his betrothed apparently ignored him.

Stephen bent over his sister again. "She can't," he said matter-of-factly. "Sometimes it takes her this way, but usually only when she has suffered some *great* distress."

This last was spoken in such an accusatory tone that Dominic bristled. Already angry with Isobel for once again having wrong-footed his normally sound judgement, he swept one arm beneath her legs and lifted her against his length. Her moan of pain told him she was still semi-conscious and earned him a reproachful look from her youngest brother.

For the second time that day Dominic shouldered his way into Isobel's chamber. He laid his burden down on the bed and reached out to draw one finger down her pale cheek from brow bone to chin. A shaft of pain lanced through her at his touch, and she cried out. Dominic withdrew his hand immediately.

Having sought out the maid assigned to care for his sister and sent the girl in search of something that might ease her, Stephen de Lescaux returned to the room. He regarded Dominic with a troubled frown.

"It is not fitting that you should be here, my lord," Stephen addressed him stiffly. "You should go."

Dominic looked at the young man and was once again assailed by his doubts. He forced himself to be objective and to admit that the girl on the bed was in no state to indulge in an incestuous dalliance at present, yet still he lingered, unwilling to leave her to her brother's care.

"How often does this happen?"

Stephen shrugged, searching in Isobel's coffer for a piece of linen from which to fold a pad. Pouring some water on the wad of cloth, he applied it gently to her forehead.

"Not often. Not like this, anyway."

Dominic's frown intensified.

"She cannot help it, my lord!" Stephen defended hotly. "Surely you do not imagine that anyone would seek this sort of torment?"

"Will she be recovered by morning?"

Stephen's mouth thinned. "I expect so, my lord."

He did not add that such was their father's determination to see Isobel married to this man that he would probably have her carried to the chapel if she proved unfit to walk. The door opened to admit the maid, and Stephen relinquished his self-appointed task.

With one final glance for the girl he had foolishly committed himself to wed, Dominic followed his lead and quitted the room, but he did not go back to the hall. The hour was still sufficiently early for him to ride the short distance to the convent of St. Therese, and Dominic wished to inform his mother of his impending marriage.

Chapter Ten

It took him a little over half an hour to reach the neat white stone walls that surrounded the convent. Not an infrequent visitor, Dominic was well known to the diminutive sister whose job it was to keep the gate, and she welcomed him within, urging him to gain the shelter of the Abbey's guest rooms and rid himself of his storm-soaked outer garments. He handed his reins to the elderly man charged with caring for the abbey's own mounts and pressed a coin into his palm. By the time he reached the small but comfortable room set aside for receiving guests, his mother was already there, waiting for him.

"What I would not give for an intelligence network like the one that operates within these walls," Dominic teased admiringly, giving himself up to her embrace.

Marie regarded her son critically, studying his face and the way he moved for signs of recent injury. Finding none, she motioned him towards a low wooden bench and, folding her hands within the sleeves of her pristine black habit, sat down beside him.

"So, my son, what brings you here at this late hour?" A shadow crossed her face. "It is not Hu…your father?" she amended hastily, a faint flush of colour mantling her cheeks.

Dominic shook his head reassuringly. "No, *Maman*. He is well, and in good spirits."

"Then it is yourself," Marie surmised.

"In a manner of speaking," said Dominic, unsure now that he was here how best to begin.

Haltingly he outlined the events that had culminated in his betrothal to Isobel de Lescaux, and Marie listened uncritically, and without interruption, until he came to the end.

"I can see why your father thinks he has turned this situation to his advantage," she acknowledged thoughtfully. "This marriage will bring you that which he has never been able to give you himself—but what of you, Dominic? Is this what you want?"

Unable to meet his mother's eyes, Dominic got to his feet and wandered distractedly to the window. He could hear the nuns chanting in their chapel.

"I am keeping you from your devotions," he prevaricated.

"I think God will forgive me, just this once," Marie assured him dryly. "I will ask you again, Dominic, are you content?"

He sighed and sat down. "With the estate and the titles, yes. Never in my wildest dreams could I have hoped to attain such wealth and status."

"It is the girl herself, then?"

Dominic was silent, thinking of Isobel de Lescaux as she had appeared in the hall earlier. His face seemed to soften slightly, and Marie waited, struggling to hide the small smile that lifted the corners of her mouth.

"No." The admission was forced from him, yet still he felt unable to confess his suspicions concerning Isobel and the men of her acquaintance, especially her brothers. "She has taken me in dislike," he offered at last, looking down at the floor and kicking moodily at the edge of an uneven flagstone.

Marie quirked her brows at him, and he coloured defensively.

"*Maman*, you must remember that I thought her a boy at first. I confess my manner was not altogether…kind."

"And later, when you realised your error, and had the opportunity to mend matters?"

Dominic shifted uncomfortably. "The next time I saw her, she was wrapped in her brother's arms." He broke off, experiencing again the now familiar surge of anger that ripped through him whenever he thought about Isobel and Adam.

It was Marie's turn to sigh.

"Dominic, I know it is difficult for you, but try to put yourself in her place. To begin with, how old is this girl?"

"I believe she is almost sixteen."

"*Almost* sixteen! The object of everyone's censure, and hastily betrothed to a man she has scarce laid eyes on. A man, I might add, about whom she is sure to have heard certain things—and I would not be surprised to learn she's had a beating from her father, into the bargain."

Dominic did not want to think about William de Lescaux using the buckle end of his belt to chastise his wayward daughter. He concentrated instead on his mother's gentle voice, allowing it to draw him back to the present.

"You have the opportunity to do great things through this marriage, Dominic. I am sure you and your Isobel can deal well enough together, but you must remember she is very young, and you will need to make allowances for her. You will need to be gentle and patient—as gentle and patient as you were with that colt your father once gifted you."

Dominic smiled at the memory. The colt had been a golden creature, full of courage and fire. The secret had been to train him to accept mastery without destroying the spirit that had made him unique. He wondered how his mother had known to liken Isobel to the horse.

"The hour is late," she observed mildly. "You should be on your way."

He kissed her smooth cheek.

"Dominic…"

"Yes, *Maman*?"

"With all my heart I wish that I could be there for you tomorrow, but you know I cannot. Be happy, my son. I should like to meet your wife. I hope you will bring her to see me when you can."

Dominic inclined his head. "Of course."

Marie listened to the sound of his retreating footsteps, and love for this one child she had borne threatened to overwhelm her. She allowed herself to weep a little for the boy she had lost, and the man he had become. A good marriage might just be his salvation. She would pray for him.

Chapter Eleven

Isobel woke to the sound of rain beating against the closed wooden shutters. Her head was thick with residual pain, and for a moment she lay still, wondering whether this alone should be enough to make her feel so heavyhearted. Then she remembered today was to be her wedding day. It was also her sixteenth birthday.

She swung her legs to the floor, shivering at the chill which the light strewing of rushes was unable to disguise. Her struggle to open the shutters eventually revealed a dun-coloured sky, laden with the promise of further rain. Isobel sank onto the window seat and wondered dully whether things could get any worse.

She was still sitting there when her aunt and her sister-in-law bustled into the room, full of their own importance. Neither wished her good morning nor offered felicitations. Instead they pushed and pulled her about, thrusting her behind a screen to bathe in rose-scented water, then dragging her forth again and towelling her so vigorously that she cried out. This prompted such a torrent of scolding and recrimination that Isobel clamped her mouth firmly shut, resolved not to utter another sound.

Aunt Rohese bundled her into her shift whilst Alais rummaged through the clothing coffer in search of a gown sufficiently grand to serve as a wedding dress, eventually settling upon a sapphire-blue silk. Fine hose and a pair of delicate doeskin slippers were added. Isobel's still-damp hair was brushed and left to hang in a shining fall that reached to her hips, and Alais produced a circlet of fresh flowers which she pinned into place. The two women stood back to admire their handiwork.

"For heaven's sake, what is the matter with you, Isobel?" Rohese Pascale demanded. "You're as stiff as a mammet—and you have about as much conversation! Have you naught to say for yourself?"

"I will?" her niece retorted sarcastically, with a fleeting return of her old spirit.

Alais tittered behind her hand as Rohese delivered a lecture on the perils of impertinence, especially towards one's husband. Isobel gritted her teeth and stared over their heads, willing them to leave. Alas, by the time they pronounced themselves satisfied, Adam was already standing at the door waiting to escort her to Vaillant's chapel. She felt a frisson of panic as his warm fingers closed over her own cold, stiff ones. Her eyes stung with tears, and her throat ached with the effort of holding them back. Adam squeezed her hand gently.

"You are very beautiful, Bel," he told her seriously, drawing her unresisting towards the door. "Dominic is a lucky man."

Isobel essayed a tremulous smile in response but still could not trust herself to speak. The walk to the chapel was too short, and her composure too precarious. All eyes turned to watch her as she approached, but her own gaze remained fixed unseeingly on the milky green glass in the small circular window above the altar. Adam released her fingers, placing her hand in their father's, and she felt William's grip tighten, as if he feared she might try to break away.

The priest's voice intoned the words, and Isobel's lips formed the appropriate responses almost without being aware that she was doing so. She seemed startled to find her hand transferred from her father's to Dominic's and looked down uncomprehendingly at the slender plain gold band now encircling her heart finger.

Struggling to conceal his mounting frustration at his bride's seeming indifference to the whole business, Dominic angled her body towards his and bestowed the customary chaste kiss sanctioned by the priest. So cold and unresponsive was she that he fancied he might almost have touched his lips to one of the carved marble effigies of his Vaillant ancestors, whose noble images filled the niches cut into the chapel walls.

Isobel heard her father release his breath and vaguely wondered how long he had been holding it. Still in her trancelike state, she swallowed the host and wet her lips with the sweet, dark wine, sure that at some point she would wake up, and that with waking would come the attendant relief that this nightmare was over. But slowly, painfully, feeling began to return. She noticed that Robert and Stephen were looking unnaturally clean and tidy and that her two eldest brothers were once again wearing their benign smiles, whilst Alais was prettily accepting compliments on the appearance of the bride. She risked a fleeting glance at Adam but looked away again hurriedly when she saw Dominic's eyes narrow upon her brother's face.

Realising that his father was speaking to him, Dominic turned to respond, and in doing so he released his grip on Isobel's hand for the first time since the priest had bound them together. She flexed her cramped fingers and, moments later, found they were being taken and raised to another's lips.

"I suppose that I must call you sister now," Alain said ruefully.

"She'll only plague you all the more if you do," Robert warned, catching Isobel around the waist in a hug that all but drove the breath from her body. Stephen had been quick to tell him how changed their sister was, and he was disconcerted to discover his twin had not been exaggerating. He frowned.

"You're nothing but skin and bone, Bel," he admonished. "What have you been doing to yourself? I'll wager you would not last even a quarter of a candle notch against me now."

"It would be most unwise of you to make such a wager, however," Dominic interjected smoothly, "since now that your sister is become my wife, and you are my squire, there will be no more of this unseemly brawling between you."

Isobel felt a spark of anger kindle and begin to melt the ice that seemed to have set in her veins. "There is a great deal of difference, my lord, between 'unseemly brawling,' as you put it, and a brotherly embrace."

Daring him to contradict her she moved out of Robert's arms and recklessly leaned towards Alain to bestow a kiss on his rapidly colouring cheeks. She saw him shoot a wary look at his half-brother and felt a strange thrill of excitement as she witnessed the tightening of Dominic's jaw. Well and good! Other well-wishers claimed her attention, and she turned away, determined to play the part of the radiant bride, since it appeared to be all that anyone required of her.

Dominic responded automatically to the congratulations showered on him, but his eyes never left the figure of his bride as she moved about the hall, receiving kisses and compliments from the many guests his father had invited to remain for the wedding. So marked was his attention that some of those watching idly began to speculate as to whether this really was a love match after all, at least on the part of the groom. Alain, still at Dominic's side, followed the direction of his brooding stare.

"You had best not do anything to hurt her."

His half-brother raised one brow sardonically. "Are you threatening me?"

Alain shook his head. "Not at all. I'm merely offering you some good advice. You cannot fail to have noticed there is no shortage of men who would gladly lay down their lives for her."

Dominic's lips thinned. "Yourself included, no doubt? If you are harbouring any romantic notions towards my wife, you had best forget them, Alain. I will have both her duty and her obedience."

The boy sniffed contemptuously. "I'm pleased that your sense of honour extends to fidelity. I hope it is not just on the part of your wife."

He bowed formally to Isobel, who chose that moment to return to Dominic's side, then abruptly quitted the chapel, leaving her staring after him in open-mouthed surprise.

"It's not like Alain to be so out of sorts," she observed thoughtfully. "Did you say something to upset him?"

Dominic bit back the urge to tell her he knew exactly what ailed his half-brother.

"Even if I did, it is no concern of yours," he said coolly. "I suggest that we rejoin our guests before we occasion comment."

Isobel gave him a curious look but did as he commanded, placing her fingers lightly in his outstretched hand. An inexplicable current of excitement coursed through her. She shivered and glanced apprehensively at Dominic. He returned her look with one of fleeting irritation, quickly masked as he flashed the expected witty response to yet another of the ribald jests being heaped upon them. Isobel blushed uncomfortably and averted her eyes.

Some little distance away she could see her father standing beside Dominic's. The look of undisguised relief on his face at seeing her safely wed was such blatant confirmation of his desire to be rid of her that it hurt. Isobel found the smile she had worked so hard to maintain was suddenly in danger of faltering. She bit down hard on the inside of her lower lip to prevent the betraying tremble.

Hubert le Vaillant, meanwhile, was surveying the scene with evident satisfaction. He had spared no expense with this wedding feast, and in so doing had been able to make more open acknowledgement of his illegitimate son than ever before. He nodded and smiled in the direction of his wife, knowing that without her generosity and understanding such a gesture would have been impossible. He saw that Marguerite had drawn Isobel to one side and now appeared to be engaged in animated conversation with her. Privately Hubert hoped she was giving the girl the benefit of some womanly advice.

Had he been privy to his son's suspicions, Hubert

would have laughed. He had little doubt that Isobel de Lescaux—or du Bois, as she now was—was entirely ignorant of what would be expected of her this night. Whatever unusual talents his friend's daughter was rumoured to possess, he'd wager his own keep that the skills required to pleasure a man in the bedchamber did not number amongst her accomplishments. Still, he reflected, she should not have to try very hard. Doubtless Dominic had expertise enough for both of them—and from the way his son had been watching his bride ever since the priest had pronounced their union, Hubert was confident the marriage would be consummated tonight, irrespective of any initial reservations Dominic might have harboured.

His gaze returned to Isobel. A pity William had not had time to complete her education, but then, had it not been for her headstrong behaviour, it was unlikely Hubert would ever have been able to bring about this marriage and gain for Dominic wealth and position beyond expectation. He sought out his son and nodded in the direction of the musicians.

"Are you not going to dance with your bride? Our guests will likely think it very odd if you do not."

Dominic had been thinking about the coldness with which Isobel had received his kiss in the chapel and contrasting it bitterly with the warmth she had subsequently shown to Alain and the twins. He shrugged.

"If it will please you, sir."

He claimed his wife from Lady Marguerite with a courtier's bow, noting with a flicker of annoyance that she once again appeared to shudder at his touch as he led her to the centre of the hall. She kept her head bent, seemingly intent on studying the elegant and costly tiles that graced Vaillant's magnificent floor, and Dominic's irritation finally got the better of him.

"You can look at me, you know," he gritted in lowered tones. "I will not bite you—at least not in public!"

Isobel flushed, missed a step, and concentrated even harder on the floor. In a sudden burst of insight it crossed Dominic's mind that there might be an altogether different reason for her reaction to him. Intrigued by the possibility, he decided to test his theory.

"Of course," he whispered, invitingly, "if you would rather not dance, then I am sure we could retire…"

Her head snapped up, and he found himself looking directly into her panic-stricken green eyes.

"I…I am content to dance, my lord."

Dominic allowed himself a smile. "As you wish, *ma* Bel."

When the carole finished, he was besieged by others claiming the privilege of dancing with his bride, and, finding no legitimate cause to refuse them, Dominic reluctantly relinquished her.

He watched her perform the various steps with a succession of partners, including her brothers, and was forced to admit that he could detect no dangerous undercurrents between his wife and any of the men with whom she danced. Dominic remembered Adam's insistence that his sister was an innocent and was suddenly assailed by the certainty that his friend had indeed been telling the truth—and that made his own reaction all the more disturbing. He had never been prey to irrational jealousy before, and he was surprised by the intensity of the emotion. When Isobel was near, Dominic felt as if his control was ebbing away, and it was not a sensation he liked. He might not be able to deny the powerful physical attraction he felt for his wife, but that did not meant he could not resent her for it. Desire, resentment, and frustration; they were a heady combination, and the thought of what she could do, should she ever discover the extent of her power, terrified him.

She was still dancing. This particular measure involved an exchange of partners, achieved by the women moving one place down the line with each completed *ronde*. Dominic noted with a stab of displeasure that Piers de Bracy had taken his place amongst the waiting men, but as the knight was a guest like any other, there was nothing to be done to prevent him from dancing with Isobel without causing offence. Dominic scowled.

De Bracy bowed courteously as Isobel was handed on to him by a rather portly older man. Her eyes widened in recognition, and she curtsied stiffly, disposed to treat him warily. Involuntarily her gaze dropped to the diagonal red scratch on his right hand and he followed its direction with a vulpine smile.

“Lady du Bois,” he acknowledged amiably. “You are completely recovered from your malady, I trust?”

Isobel inclined her head in silent assent and concentrated on putting a more comfortable distance between them as soon as the dictates of the dance permitted. Unperturbed, de Bracy responded by drawing her even closer on the next occasion.

“I should have thought that a little more wine

would have helped tonight, *petite*," he whispered mockingly.

Her puzzled expression seemed to amuse him. He made a show of laughing aloud, slanting a sly look at Dominic as he did so, and in that moment Isobel realised his action was deliberately calculated to make it appear as if she had been encouraging him. Anger fizzed through her.

Still smiling, de Bracy delivered her to the last man in the line, managing purposely to brush his knuckles across her breasts as he did so. It was too much. Isobel brought the heel of her foot down on his toes with as much force as she could muster. Since she was still wearing the doeskin slippers, the effect was not particularly satisfying, but she was gratified to hear him stifle an oath, all the same. Far from being deterred, however, he simply laughed the more.

"You really are a prize, *ma chere*—and one day we shall have a reckoning, you and I."

"When hell freezes over!" Isobel hissed at him.

The dance came to an end and she excused herself, anxious to seek out Dominic to ensure that he have the truth of her latest exchange with de Bracy. She spotted him apparently conversing amicably with Adam and was glad they seemed to have resolved their differences, for she had bitterly regretted being the cause of a rift between her adored brother and the man she knew he so admired. As she approached them, Adam reached out with one hand to pluck at the circlet of flowers adorning her hair. It had slipped a little during the dancing, and now he righted it with a smile and a deft flick of his wrist.

"What do you think, Dominic, would I make a

passable lady's maid—or do I need more practise?"

Isobel slapped his hand away.

"Let be, Adam," she said sharply. "I'm so tired of being poked and prodded today that I am like to floor the next person who touches me."

Adam looked at Dominic and exploded with laughter.

"That doesn't bode well for your wedding night, if you ask me, my lord."

Isobel's cheeks flooded with colour, and Dominic grinned back at Adam.

"I shall consider myself forewarned."

"Oh, Bel," Adam reproached teasingly. "That was ill done. I thought I'd taught you better than that. *Never* give the enemy advance notice of your strategy…ouch!"

A well-placed elbow made contact with the sensitive soft tissue between his ribs.

"*Jesu*, little sister—that hurt."

"*Oh, Adam*," she mimicked his tone. "A seasoned campaigner like you should know not to ignore the warning signs."

Her brother ceased rubbing his side and risked a rueful glance at his commanding officer. Dominic was shaking his head sadly.

"Was ever a man so foolish as I?" he asked of no one in particular. "I came here with just one de Lescaux snapping at my heels, and he was trouble enough. Now I find myself beset by a veritable pack of them."

"'Tis no one's fault but your own," Isobel shot back at him.

Conscious that they were being watched by several interested parties, Dominic leant towards his bride until he was close enough for her to feel the warmth of his breath against her ear.

"The majority of it, perhaps," he allowed, "but not, I think, the entirety."

It was a subtle reminder of the part she had played in her own downfall, and it was enough to silence her for the moment. A little of the colour ebbed from her face. Adam coughed discreetly.

"Talking of warning signs," he said dryly, "I think Aunt Rohese is trying to tell you that it is time for you to leave, sister mine." He could not fail to see the renewed panic in Isobel's eyes, and he felt a pang of sympathy for her. "Don't worry, Bel, everything will be all right. Just make sure you ignore any 'good advice' the old besom tries to give you."

"I'm not afraid of her," Isobel avowed stoutly. "Or of anyone else, for that matter," she added for good measure, looking deliberately at her husband as she spoke, just so he would be left in no doubt.

Dominic's lips twitched.

"I am delighted to hear it, *ma* Bel."

With his consent, she was led away through the raucous and increasingly bawdy company. Adam, remembering his own lessons with Father Padraig, silently wondered what, if anything, the elderly priest might have said to his sister about "the sins of the flesh." Somewhat less than he himself had been told, he imagined, and probably nothing that would be of much help to her this night. He watched her out of sight before turning to Dominic.

"I'm glad it will be you, Dominic," he said a trifle awkwardly. "I wasn't at first, but I am now. Whatever anyone might have led you to believe, I would swear on my life that my sister has no knowledge of what takes place between a man and a woman when they are alone together, even though she was always in the company of Alain and the twins, and probably continued to share their training right up until the time they left to enter your father's service." He grinned mischievously. "In fact, you may find that Isobel has some remarkable talents. When you next want an edge put on your poniard, I'd recommend you ask her to do it for you."

"A useful sort of wife for a man in my trade, then," Dominic observed.

"Oh, undoubtedly," Adam assured him, his face alight with laughter. He sobered again. "Dominic, she was only fourteen when Robert and Stephen left, and even at Lescaux there will always have been those about her who made certain she did not see or hear that which she should not. Besides, she was a child, with no interest in such matters. Believe me, her life has not been the sort to inspire romantic dreams. Whatever she might have said, I have no doubt that she *is* afraid of you, and of what is expected of her this night. She will need careful handling."

Dominic reached out and laid one hand on Adam's shoulder.

"Your sister is fortunate indeed to have so worthy a champion, my friend, but it is not necessary. If it is any consolation to you, I had already begun to conclude for myself that I had misjudged matters."

He let the hand fall, and turned it instead to the appropriation of a flagon of burgundy from a passing servant. Refilling his cup, he took an appreciative swallow and waited for Adam to do likewise. His brother-in-law dealt him a speculative look.

"So when did you begin to think that you might have 'misjudged matters,' my lord?"

Dominic considered the question. "When we danced together, I suppose. But had I been thinking clearly, I should have realised right there in the chapel, when that fool of a priest so generously granted me his permission to kiss my bride."

Adam raised his brows.

"Your sister's lack of response," Dominic obliged, "gave the lie to anything I might have believed."

Adam snorted and took another swallow. "You're a conceited oaf," he remarked without rancour. "Maybe she just doesn't fancy you—had you thought of that?"

"The possibility had crossed my mind," Dominic admitted, with a smile, "but then I began to wonder about the fact that she trembles whenever I am near…"

"Well, you can be rather intimidating," Adam allowed.

"And then when I suggested that if she did not want to dance we might, perhaps, retire…"

His companion gave an inelegant splutter, and Dominic thumped him on the back.

"Just don't get complacent," Adam warned when he had finished choking. "She doesn't only know how to hone a dagger properly—she can use one to good effect, too."

"Yes, I rather thought she might," Dominic admitted ruefully. Briefly he recounted the incident with de Bracy in the pleasaunce.

Adam frowned. "He followed her when she left the hall last night, too. Stephen told me he was there with her, and I doubt his intentions were honourable. He'll bear watching, Dominic."

"Oh, yes, him and de Clare both," Dominic agreed. "And there was I, thinking that marriage to your sweet sister was my means to a life of indolence and pleasure, not to mention the enticing prospect of living to a ripe old age."

"You'd be bored within a month," Adam assured him.

Dominic sighed, "Maybe, but it might have been nice to find out." He raised his wine cup. "To my wedding night, brother."

Chapter Twelve

Isobel's teeth were chattering as her Aunt Rohese, aided by Alais and a swarm of Lady Marguerite's other female guests, stripped her of her wedding finery in preparation for the arrival of her husband. She clamped her jaw firmly shut and tried to pretend it was the chill of the spring night invading the chamber that caused her to shiver so. In truth she was apprehensive enough already, without the addition of the inevitably boisterous male company that would shortly enter the bedchamber to witness her complete humiliation.

Alais was whispering in her ear, taking advantage of Aunt Rohese's preoccupation with fussing over the turning down of the sheets.

"Make sure there is enough blood," she hissed. "I made Will promise to shed his own if there was not enough of mine on the sheets in the morning."

"Blood?" Isobel uttered in astonishment.

Alais clapped a hand over her mouth. "Ssh. Do you want the old she-devil to hear?"

"Blood?" Isobel asked again, her voice this time an anxious whisper.

Alais rolled her eyes at the ceiling. "For goodness' sake, Isobel, you surely cannot expect me to believe you do not know what is expected when a girl beds with her first man. If there is no blood on the sheets, they will say you are impure."

Isobel opened her mouth to refute Alais' words but could not think of anything to say. Besides, her sister-in-law obviously was not expecting a reply.

"Anyway, if all they say of Dominic du Bois is true, there will probably be no need, for I am sure he will be more than man enough to do the deed, but you never know." Alais pursed her lips judiciously. "You have spent so much time careering around on that horse of yours…"

Isobel stared at her. "What has that to do with anything?"

Alais clucked her tongue. "You really haven't got a clue, have you? Never mind, just lie back and let him get on with it. It probably won't hurt all that much, especially if he is as good as they say. You might even enjoy it the second time."

"Who is 'they'?" Isobel wanted to know. "What do you mean, 'the second time'? Alais—wait…" But her sister-in-law was already disappearing in the direction of the door, and Isobel realised with a sinking heart that the moment she had been dreading could no longer be put off.

Dominic, already stripped beneath his bed robe, was borne into the room on the shoulders of several of his more-than-merry companions. Immediately his gaze sought and located the figure of his young wife in the centre of the room. The sheer level of noise and revelry had exceeded even his expectations, and, in the light of his conversation with Adam, he was anxious to reassure her, and to spare her as much of the indignity of the traditional bedding ceremony as he could. Taking in her terrified expression, he surmised that it might already be too late.

He found himself pushed none too gently towards her and urged by her father to disrobe her so that he might inspect her body for any blemishes. Frantically Dominic made eye contact with Adam, who responded with an almost imperceptible nod. Suddenly the five de Lescaux brothers stepped forward to form a protective circle around their sister and her husband, effectively shielding them from the eyes of all but their immediate relatives and the priest.

With an apologetic expression Dominic briefly dropped Isobel's robe from her shoulders and pronounced himself satisfied. He replaced and refastened the garment, unable to avoid brushing his knuckles across her breasts in the process. Isobel stifled a sharp intake of breath, and he stepped back, waiting for her to reciprocate, as custom demanded. At a sharp word from her father she reached upwards. The slender fingers that had only yesterday morning laced the neck of his gambeson were now trembling so badly that she was clearly incapable of the task. Ignoring William de Lescaux's growl of irritation, Dominic brought his hands up to cover hers, closing over them and undoing the ties for her. His robe dropped and he waited. Isobel barely glanced at his naked body, her cheeks burning in stark contrast to the pallor of the rest of her.

"I am content."

Somehow she managed the words that were expected from her, and it was over.

Adam bent forward, retrieved Dominic's robe, and assisted him to don it once more.

"Good job she did not want to look too closely," he murmured *sotto voce*. "You've got more scars on your miserable hide than a tiltyard dummy."

Dominic snorted appreciatively.

"Do me one more service tonight, my friend." He jerked his head at the chamber full of inebriated wedding guests. "Get this lot out of here."

Adam grinned. "Yes, my lord, of course, my lord!"

He began, with the assistance of his two elder brothers, to usher people back through the doorway. Lady Marguerite, straightening from the task of assisting Isobel into bed, paused beside Dominic, her eyes on the bare skin visible through his gaping bed robe.

"Very impressive," she said, dimpling at him. In response to his raised brows she tapped him lightly on the arm. "I meant your personal bodyguard, you wretch!"

"Oh, that." He looked away, smiling.

"Seriously, Dominic. It was well done, and an act of kindness that bodes well for your life together. I wish you joy of your marriage." She reached up and kissed his cheek.

With scant regard for custom or propriety, Robert and Stephen had seated themselves on either side of the bed and now proceeded to tease their beleaguered sister unmercifully whilst ignoring with equal success the outraged squawks issuing from their aunt, who had been unceremoniously herded into the corridor outside along with all the rest. Adam sighed gustily and motioned to Will and Henry, who each grabbed a twin by the scruff of the neck, hauled him to his feet, and marched him forcibly to the door.

"Ouch," Stephen complained vociferously. "Get off me, Will, you great brute! I haven't…"

At a look from Robert he subsided, but Adam was

instantly suspicious.

"You haven't what?" he demanded.

"Had time to do anything," Stephen admitted, somewhat grudgingly and with more than a hint of pique.

"The old witch kept this chamber so closely guarded all day, it was well nigh impossible," Robert contributed, alluding in this rather uncomplimentary fashion to his Aunt Rohese.

Will delivered his customary pompous reprimand about having respect for your elders and betters, and Stephen, waiting until his eldest brother's back was turned, stuck out his tongue.

"Not very mature," he excused, "but immensely satisfying."

"Well, Alais certainly seems to think so," Robert responded promptly, sending them both into fresh paroxysms of laughter.

"Out!" Adam ordered. "And if I find out that you have been up to your old tricks again, I promise I'll have you on slopping detail for the entire camp once we get back in the field."

The twins groaned in perfect unison.

"Old tricks?" Dominic asked with a hint of amusement, as he watched them go.

"Ask your wife," said Adam with a nod and an answering grin.

He fished in the leather purse attached to his belt and drew out a small, velvet-wrapped package which he dropped onto the bed beside Isobel.

"Happy birthday, sweeting. Did you think I'd forgotten?"

Then, with a brief kiss for his sister and a final

salute for Dominic, he was gone. The door closed behind him, and Dominic dropped the bar into place with an unmistakable expression of relief. He leaned against the timbers for a moment, and studied the girl in the bed. She was sitting upright again now, her back propped against the bolster.

"It is your birthday? No one told me."

Isobel shrugged her shoulders, causing the fine linen nightshift they had dressed her in to slip slightly. She hitched it up self-consciously.

"Why should they?"

Dominic decided this question was best ignored, since answering it might lead him to say some very ungenerous things about those he must now call family. He crossed to the bed and sat down on the opposite side from Isobel, continuing to regard her intently.

"For what it may be worth, I am sorry I did not know." He gestured at the closed door. "What did Adam mean, about them being up to their old tricks?"

A ghost of a smile lifted her lips. "It is because it is my birthday," she explained. "There was a time when they always tried to put something in my bed on my birthday. The first time I think it was a frog, another time a hedgehog, then a nest of mice—oh, and once they gifted me their prized collection of worms—all the usual things I suppose horrible little boys think will make girls run away screaming."

"But you didn't?"

Isobel shook her head, fingering the package Adam had left her, turning it over and over in her hands.

"You told Adam," Dominic guessed, "and he put a stop to it?"

Isobel glanced up at him. "I told Adam," she

agreed slowly, "but all he did was to suggest some things I might do to them in return."

Dominic snorted with amusement. "Yes, that sounds like Adam. Dare I ask what he told you to do?"

"Oh, I filled their half-boots with teasles, sewed up the ends of their hose, spread honey in their house shoes…"

Dominic spluttered. "*Jesu*, *ma* Bel, I must remember never to anger you."

He swung his legs up onto the bed and lay back with his arms folded behind his head, contemplating the hangings. He nodded in the direction of Adam's gift.

"Aren't you going to open it?"

She looked down at the package almost as if she had forgotten she was holding it. Absently she set it down on the night stand beside her and sat twisting the ring on her heart finger. The silence was almost deafening, and she wanted to scream. Finally, when she could bear it no longer, she reached out with a tentative hand. Dominic felt her touch on his arm and turned to look at her questioningly.

"My lord," she began hesitantly, "you will think me very ignorant, but…I do not know how to begin, you see. I…Is there something I should do?"

He made no response, and Isobel, fearing she had committed some grievous fault by broaching the matter, began to withdraw her hand, but Dominic suddenly caught hold of her fingers, the ball of his thumb moving gently back and forth over her knuckles.

"No, *ma* Bel." He smiled at her reassuringly. "There is nothing you should do—except, perhaps, go to sleep."

"Sleep?"

Had he not been so tired himself, he might have laughed. As it was, he sighed, using his free hand to massage his temples. "It has been a long day," he excused, "and we have far to travel on the morrow, if we are to cross into Wales."

She stiffened and turned her face away. "I understand," she said in a small voice. "Of course you are anxious to see what sort of bargain you have made."

"Oh, Christ!"

She flinched away from him, and involuntarily Dominic swore again, running a hand through his thick dark hair. Drawing on reserves of patience he had hitherto not known he possessed, he reached for her and drew her back to face him.

"I do not think you do understand, *ma* Bel, but if you are willing to listen, then I will try to explain."

Isobel tensed as he gathered up her unbound hair, sweeping it to fall over the shoulder furthest from him. Then he gently pulled her into the crook of his arm so his chin rested on the crown of her head. His fingers moved rhythmically, stroking lightly, and he felt her begin to relax a little.

"What do you know of your mother's dower lands, Isobel?"

The question clearly surprised her, but she responded readily enough, and in spite of his weariness Dominic was impressed. It was clear she had a quick mind and a fair grasp of the principles and economics of estate management—something his father had been at pains to ensure he also understood. He decided to test her further.

"And do you know aught of something called the Cambro-Norman alliance, or of a man called Richard de Clare?" he probed.

Isobel looked up at him through her lashes. On her part, it was a gesture completely without artifice, but it sent a jolt through Dominic all the same.

"Adam has made mention of both." She pulled a wry face. "Although you must know he is not the most diligent correspondent. Besides, Papa did not always let me…" She hesitated. "It was not always possible for me to read his letters," she amended diplomatically.

Dominic laughed and hugged her briefly. "My poor Isobel, I shall have to teach you the subtleties of spying." He looked down at her, merriment lurking in his eyes. "I have a suspicion you would prove an apt pupil—perhaps I should take you into my troop so that you may train alongside your brothers again?"

Isobel pulled away from him. "It pleases you to mock me, my lord." She sighed. "Thus far, I find there is little to distinguish a husband from another brother."

He swung his legs off the bed and moved to douse the night candle. A finger of pale moonlight stole through a gap in one ill-fitting shutter, touching the room with a faint glow. Keeping his robe on, Dominic slipped between the sheets and turned on his side so that he lay facing his wife.

"There are a great many differences between a husband and a brother, *ma* Bel," he assured her, "and I shall take time and pleasure to instruct you in each and every one of them. But I would give you a little time to accustom yourself to my company first."

She opened her mouth to speak, but he placed his index finger against her lips.

"Listen to me." He spoke swiftly, and in lowered tones. "Unless I am very much mistaken, we are both the unwitting victims of some devious political scheming here. Your dower lands lie close to the seat of Richard de Clare's earldom, and Robert Fitz-Harding made it his business to know that. Now, Fitz-Harding is King Henry's man, through and through—and he's just found a way to ensure the presence of a heavily armed troop in the very heart of de Clare's own demesne, under the command of a man who has every reason to be grateful to the king's man."

He judged it wiser for the nonce to leave out the additional complication of her shared borders with de Bracy's potential inheritance.

"And that, *ma* Bel, is why you and I find ourselves sharing this bed tonight. You must know that, for me, this marriage is an unbelievable opportunity—but I'd not force you to be my wife in anything but name before you are willing."

He knew that her eyes were wide, and he sighed.

"Given time, *ma* Bel, I think we could deal well enough together, but until you are ready I will not ask anything of you."

"I know my duty, my lord."

Dominic's mouth twisted wryly. "I am not sure that you do, sweet Isobel, and in any case, for myself, I prefer affection and respect over duty, every time."

"Affection and respect." Isobel repeated the words slowly. He could tell by the sound of her voice that she was troubled. "My Father will be very angry with me on the morrow if he thinks that I have not behaved as I should."

"Let me worry about that, *ma* Bel. It is, after all, her husband's displeasure with which a wife should concern herself, not her father's—and I am not angry with you. With others, perhaps, but not with you. Well, not at the moment, anyway," he qualified, smiling at her through the darkness, "although if I wake to find the insides of my shoes coated with honey, it may be another matter!"

Isobel moved cautiously back into his arms, which he had opened in invitation. Her body pressed against his as she settled, and she heard him stifle a groan. Instantly she froze.

"Is there something wrong, my lord?"

"No," he managed in a strangled voice, his breath warm against her neck. He could tell she was not convinced.

"Goodnight then, my lord."

"Goodnight, Isobel."

"Dominic…"

"Yes?" It was the first time she had called him by his given name since the priest had bound them together in Vaillant's chapel, and combined with the proximity of her warm, scented skin and his own recent abstinence, it was almost his undoing.

"Thank you."

He kissed the top of her head, gritted his teeth, and set himself to endure.

Chapter Thirteen

Isobel opened her eyes in the first grey light of a new day. She shifted slightly, trying to ease herself away from her husband without disturbing him. He stirred and muttered indistinctly but did not wake. Isobel edged a little further away, then drew her knees up under her chin and sat in silent contemplation. Now and then her gaze strayed back to the man who slept beside her. It was still hard to believe she was married at all, let alone to Dominic du Bois, a mercenary soldier with a ruthless reputation for selling his not inconsiderable skills to the highest bidder.

Yet he had been surprisingly gentle with her, she realised. She bit her lip anxiously, wondering what would happen when the linens were changed and there was no bloodstained sheet to proclaim her purity, as Alais had said there should be. What would her father say? He would surely never believe that her husband had not consummated their marriage because he craved affection and respect from his wife. She started as warm fingers trailed lightly over one exposed shoulder.

"Good morning, sweetheart." His use of the endearment clearly surprised her. Dominic smiled quizzically. "That's a very pensive look for a wife to be wearing the morning after her wedding night."

Isobel flushed. "I was wondering…I mean, I was thinking about the sheet…" Her voice dropped to a whisper. "What will people say?"

It took Dominic a moment or two to realise what she was talking about, for he had always been at pains to ensure that the women who shared his bed were experienced enough to provide only what he sought—a pleasurable interlude and a necessary physical release. He studied Isobel's worried face and once again felt an overwhelming urge to reassure and protect her. He placed his forefinger on her bitten lips and gently teased them apart.

"I would not have you worry, *ma* Bel, for it is a thing easily remedied." He swung his legs out from under the covers, and Isobel leapt backwards.

Dominic frowned. "I meant what I said, Isobel—you need not fear me. I have never been a man who gained satisfaction by the use of force."

As soon as the words were uttered he realised how incongruous they must sound, coming from the mouth of someone who earned his living by inflicting defeat on others. He grinned mischievously. "Well, not in the bedchamber, anyway."

Reaching for his belt, he withdrew his eating knife. "How are you at binding wounds, my lady wife?"

She continued to regard him with an expression of deep mistrust, and Dominic's patience deserted him.

"For Christ's sake, I'm not going to use it on you!"

He made a competent nick on the smooth, muscled surface of his lower left arm where a thin line of blood welled in immediate response. Dominic threw back the top sheet and liberally smeared the middle section of the bottom one. "There," he pronounced. "Honour satisfied. Now, be a good girl and find me something to stanch this with. There should be some clean cloths in my coffer."

Still not entirely sure why this was so important, and not having the courage to ask, Isobel tore her eyes away from the bloodied linen and struggled with the hasps on Dominic's travelling chest. Used to the twins and the cheerful abandon with which they strewed their belongings around, she was surprised to find the contents of Dominic's coffer were neat and orderly, and she said as much to him as she drew out the bandaging strips.

He shrugged dismissively. "Old habits. You learn to travel light and keep things to hand when you lead an existence such as mine."

Isobel sought the flagon of spiced wine that had been left for them last night. She sniffed it cautiously and, judging it to be undiluted, poured a little onto a fresh pad and applied it without warning to Dominic's arm. He gave a hiss of pain as the astringent liquid made contact with the new wound.

"I'm sorry." She looked up quickly and found herself staring straight into her husband's eyes. They were, she realised, a deep, hypnotic, summer-sky blue, fringed with lashes as thick and dark as his hair. She could see her own image reflected in his pupils. She swallowed convulsively and wadded the damp linen into a ball. "Someone once told me that washing with a little wine will cleanse a wound and encourage it to heal cleanly," she offered tentatively.

"*Someone* was right," Dominic confirmed tersely, "but they obviously neglected to add that it also stings like the very devil."

He turned his back and dropped his bed robe. Isobel gasped, and he guessed that she had either closed her eyes or at least averted them. He grinned to himself, remembering how she had hardly dared look at him when they had been stripped for each other at the bedding. He shrugged into a fresh shirt, relishing the prospect of teaching her to know and pleasure his body in the coming months and helping her to discover the secrets of her own in return.

Out of deference to her sensibilities, he kept his back to her until he was sure she had scrambled into her undershift, and when he at last turned round it was to see her sitting on the edge of the bed, with Adam's gift open in her lap. Curiosity got the better of him, and he leant forwards as she drew the velvet wrappings away. Inside was a gold cross of definite Irish workmanship, set with small chips of Baltic amber.

Dominic knew it to be a costly piece, for he recalled Adam haggling for it. It had been purchased from an itinerant merchant in Dublin, not long before they returned to England, and at the time he had surmised it to be either a generous farewell gift for his lieutenant's current mistress or a tempting inducement to the next likely candidate. Now, of course, he knew better. Adam must have been drawn to the amber because it would complement his sister's colouring. There was also a thin rolled-leather thong, ready to be attached to a loop at the head of the cross so it could be worn around the neck.

Seeing that Isobel's fingers shook as she attempted to pass the thong through the loop, Dominic reached over and took it from her, intending only to complete the task. As he did so, however, he realised she was wearing what he had come to think of as her "cautious" expression, and he immediately guessed the direction of her thoughts.

"He loves you very much, Isobel," he said softly. "Even when he could not be there for you, you have never been far from his thoughts—but I was wrong to think what I did, and I am sorry for it."

He lifted her hair out of the way and placed the cross around her neck, his fingers brushing against the bare flesh as he deftly tied the ends of the cord in a firm knot. Isobel's skin quivered at his touch, and Dominic stepped back somewhat hastily, still surprised by the swiftness of his own response. Her eyes were bright with unshed tears.

"*Jesu*, Isobel, do not look at me like that. I..."

Whatever he might have been going to say was lost in the arrival of Alais de Lescaux and Rohese Pascale. Dominic turned away after unbarring the door, and busied himself re-packing the contents of his travelling chest.

"What was it like, then?" Alais whispered, nudging Isobel slyly, as the bloodied sheet was exclaimed over and summarily removed to be displayed downstairs. Making sure that her husband was nowhere nearby, Alais allowed her eyes to dwell hungrily on the man who was now her brother-by-marriage. "Are the rumours true?"

"How would I know, seeing as I have never heard them?" Isobel parried.

She wished that Alais would leave her alone, lest she say anything in her ignorance that would give the lie to the stained linen that had so triumphantly been borne off to the hall.

"Oh, come on, Isobel," Alais cajoled. "You can tell me. After all, we are both married women now. They say he is twice the man that others are—if you take my meaning!" She giggled.

Isobel blushed scarlet, and Alais pouted with disappointment. She patted her sister-in-law's shoulder consolingly, shooting a reproachful look at Dominic. "Never mind, Izzy, it will probably be better for you next time."

He was standing so close he could not fail to have heard, and Isobel almost choked on a mouthful of watered wine at the expression on his face.

"Forgive me, Lady Alais," he interrupted smoothly, "but we have some distance to travel before nightfall and needs must be on our way. Perhaps you can prevail upon your husband to let you visit us soon? I would not deprive my wife of the company of her female relatives."

Alais preened visibly. "We would be honoured, my lord," she fluttered coyly. "But I am sure that first we must allow you and your new bride some time alone."

She kissed Isobel on both cheeks and extended her hand to Dominic, who obliged by raising it to his lips before turning back to his wife, who was regarding her sister-in-law's retreating back with a distinct lack of enthusiasm.

"Don't worry, 'Izzy,' " he murmured in her ear, smiling as her mouth twisted in a sour grimace. "I'm sure we can find a suitable excuse when the time comes."

"My father"—Isobel sighed deeply—"thinks I should strive to be more like her."

Dominic reached out and tugged the end of her braid.

"*Jesu*, *ma* Bel, if you ever become like her, then I

swear I will find a means to put you aside."

"I'll bear that in mind, my lord," she said sweetly.

He responded by catching her to him in a surprisingly swift move and planting a kiss on her cheek.

"Don't get any ideas, *ma chere*," he murmured in her ear. "What I have, I hold." He released her and flicked the flat of his hand across her behind. Isobel glared at him and stalked away, her nose in the air.

Chapter Fourteen

Their farewells made to their respective families, Dominic, Adam, and the twins stood in Vaillant's bailey, amidst the preparations for their departure. Isobel's mare whickered a greeting and, laughing delightedly, she palmed the expectant horse a crust of bread. One of Dominic's troopers, a seasoned campaigner by the name of Sim Walters, to whom the task of holding the restive animal had fallen, now shook his head gloomily.

"Not a lady's mount, this, my lord," he opined.

"Oh, she's bound to be a little fresh," Isobel excused. "After all, she has not been ridden for two full days."

Dominic glanced enquiringly at Adam.

"Don't look at me," his lieutenant responded. "I'm not getting on it!"

Dominic noted, however, that Adam did not look particularly worried, and the twins were openly grinning at their sister as she took the reins from his pessimistic sergeant. With the familiarity of long practice, she bent to check the girth. The mare lifted a threatening hind leg and was rewarded with a competent knee in the ribs, together with a reprimand for her manners. Without waiting for assistance, Isobel set her foot in the stirrup and swung into the saddle. Ignoring the open-mouthed astonishment of both her husband and his man-at-arms, she settled her divided skirts around her.

"If you will excuse me for a moment, my lord..."

It was something of a rhetorical question, Dominic realised, for neither horse nor rider had any intention of waiting for his say-so. Roisin sprang forward as soon as she felt Isobel's weight in the saddle.

"Like I said, sir, not a lady's mount." Sim stood his ground and sucked his remaining teeth in disapproval.

"Will she be all right?" Dominic asked Adam uncertainly, for he was inclined to agree with his sergeant.

"I expect so. She probably only needs a good gallop to sort her out."

Dominic favoured him with a pained expression.

"Who, your sister, or the horse?"

Adam spluttered, unable to contain his mirth.

"*Jesu*, Dominic, you've only been married to her for one day. How are you going to cope with a lifetime?"

"God knows," he muttered, gaining the saddle of his destrier, which Robert had been holding for him. "Should I go after her?" he wondered aloud.

Adam glanced up from checking the buckles on his saddle roll and shrugged. "If you think you can catch her."

Dominic threw him a look that promised a reckoning. He jerked his head at the assorted men and baggage littering Vaillant's courtyard.

"Get this lot sorted and move out. We need to make Bristol by this evening."

"Shall I come with you, my lord?" Robert hovered at his stirrup.

"No, on this occasion you may stay here. I'll deal with your sister."

The twins followed Adam's lead in saluting as Dominic rode out beneath Vaillant's gatehouse.

"Pity he didn't want you to accompany him," said Stephen with relish. "I'd like to know what he's planning to do when he catches up with her—*if* he catches up with her."

Adam smothered another laugh. He could imagine only too well what Dominic would do when he caught up with Isobel, and it served to remind him that it had been some considerable time since he'd been able to indulge himself in a similar manner.

****

Isobel heard the sound of another horse coming up fast behind her. Twisting round in the saddle, she saw a single mounted man in pursuit and surmised that since she did not recognise the horse it was not one of her brothers. She spared a moment to admire her husband's unquestionable horsemanship before Roisin gave another of the exuberant bucks which she generally employed to illustrate her displeasure at being held on too tight a rein. Isobel, who had actually been keeping the mare in check up until then, allowed her to have her head. The horse was fit and unlikely to take any harm from a flat-out gallop, so Isobel set herself to the task of watching the terrain as best she could and steering her mount away from uneven ground.

The mare's stride lengthened, and Isobel crouched low over her neck, laughing joyously. She had chosen a tree in the distance as her marker, and as it drew closer she began gently to draw rein. Roisin, her temper as ever assuaged by a short burst of speed, responded willingly by easing into a controlled canter, then back to a sedate trot. Isobel turned a wide circle in a walk, eventually stopping by the tree, just as she had planned. She slipped down from her saddle and let the leather girth out a notch.

With a critical eye she watched the approaching destrier. Much bigger and heavier than Roisin, it was still capable of covering the ground at an impressive rate, and as Dominic drew closer Isobel's heart began to jump a little in her chest, for she could see that his face was tight with fury. He dismounted, eased his own horse's cinch, and unloosed a stinging rebuke.

"Don't ever do that again! Do you hear me?"

"I hear you," she said mildly. "I should imagine half the county can."

Roisin's head snaked round, and she snapped at Dominic's stallion, which had dared to sniff at her rump. The big horse backed off, looking affronted, and Isobel giggled. Dominic, still half out of his wits from anxiety for her safety, seized her shoulders and jerked her towards him. He looked down at her flushed face, laughing eyes and parted lips, and could not help himself. He lowered his mouth to hers. Her gasp of surprise gave him the advantage, and he instinctively deepened the kiss, thrusting forward with his tongue.

Isobel's arms crept up round his neck, and her fingers bunched in the fabric of his tunic. Her whole body seemed to soften while his grew tense and hard. The sensations were new and exciting. She wanted to know more, but already Dominic was drawing back from her. She took a deep breath to steady herself, gratified to note that her husband seemed no less disturbed by what had occurred between them.

"See what happens when you provoke me?" he said huskily. "Let that be a lesson to you."

"I did not provoke you," Isobel shot back at him. "Is it my fault that you came chasing after me?"

"Someone had to, and none of your brothers were volunteering for the task," he retorted.

"Of course not. *They* have more sense."

Dominic grunted and turned away to hitch Roisin's girth up again. Predictably, the mare bared her teeth at him, but he ignored her.

"Come. It is time we left. There is somewhere I want to go before we rejoin the others on the road to Bristol."

As he seemed to be expecting it, Isobel allowed him to assist her into her saddle.

"Where are we going?" she asked curiously.

"To the convent of St. Therese."

He knew he had surprised her, but his mother had expressed a desire to meet her daughter-in-law, and Dominic could not be sure when they might pass this way again.

Sister Emily welcomed him as courteously as ever, but her eyes bulged with curiosity, and Dominic realised his mother must have said nothing to her fellow sisters about his marriage. From Sister Emily's expression, it was all too obvious what she was thinking. He decided to disabuse her straight away of the notion that Isobel was some court butterfly he had brought to St. Therese to conceal her shame. He introduced her as his lady wife and watched with amusement as astonishment replaced the disapproval on the little nun's face.

Dominic led Isobel through to the receiving

chamber where he had last seen his mother not two days since, and gestured her to be seated on one of the cushioned benches.

"Why have we come here?" There was a hint of apprehension in her voice, and he was unable to resist teasing her.

"Because your behaviour has convinced me that you are an unruly wife, and I want no more of you," he intoned sternly. At her stricken look, he relented. "I have brought you here to meet my mother, you goose—she is a sister in the order here."

"Your mother?" Isobel was clearly taken aback.

His lips twitched. "What's the matter, *ma* Bel? Don't tell me you've been listening to guardroom gossip?"

Her brow furrowed.

"I believe the rumour goes that I am not of woman born but sprang fully formed from the jaws of He—"

"Dominic!" The voice was full of reproof.

"My apologies, *Maman*. I had not realised you were here."

"And you feel that is adequate excuse?" Marie du Bois' shapely brows rose in mild query.

Dominic found the grace to look ashamed. "Evidently not," he acknowledged with a wry twist of his mouth.

Marie inclined her head significantly and extended her hand for her son to kiss. He dutifully raised it to his lips, at the same time drawing Isobel forward.

"We are on our way to Wales, and as I am not certain when we will next return to England, I judged it expedient to call on you again, so that you might at least be acquainted with one another."

“I am pleased to meet you, *ma dame*.” Isobel curtsied.

Marie du Bois studied the face of the girl her son had married. That she was possessed of rare beauty could not be denied, but Marie also sensed underlying determination in the set of that fine-boned jaw, and secretly she was delighted. The tendrils of red-gold hair escaping from the edge of Isobel’s wimple, and those remarkable green eyes, merely confirmed that here indeed was a match for her beloved Dominic. Her own eyes sparkled with warmth and appreciation.

“And I am pleased to meet you, my child.” Artlessly she turned to Dominic. “Dominic, my dear, it is so fortunate that you have returned—the answer to my prayers, I know it.” Ignoring the blatant scepticism on her son’s face, Marie continued, “Reverend Mother’s horse is quite lame, and no one seems to know why. As you are so much more experienced in these matters than any of us, perhaps you would take a look at it?”

Not for one moment deceived by this obvious ploy to banish him from the room, Dominic did not see any way to refuse his mother’s request, so with a nod of assent and an eloquent look he went.

Marie winked at Isobel in a most un-nunlike manner.

“That’s better,” she said, settling on the bench and motioning her new daughter-in-law to sit beside her. “He can be downright intimidating at times—not to mention incredibly tiresome.”

A tentative smile lifted the corners of Isobel’s mouth. There had been few female role models in her life and never, she was sure, one quite like Dominic’s mother.

"I confess he scared me at first," she admitted shyly, "although you may be sure I did my best not to let him know it."

"Quite right, too." Marie nodded approvingly. "And now that you are wed?" she probed gently. Isobel coloured and studied her hands, which were neatly folded in her lap.

"He has shown me great kindness," she acknowledged. Marie reached out and touched her lightly.

"Then I believe I was not wrong when I told him that I felt there was hope for him in this marriage."

Isobel was startled. "You knew about it already?"

Marie patted her hand. "Of course, my dear. Dominic came to see me on the eve of your betrothal. He told me something of the circumstances of your meeting."

Isobel blushed and looked down again. "Oh."

"Yes, 'oh' indeed!" Marie's forefinger raised her chin, and Isobel saw that her eyes were alight with mischief. "I believe you will lead my son a merry dance, Isobel, which will be all to the good. It would never do for Dominic to become bored."

She rose gracefully and busied herself pouring two cups of watered wine from a jug on the nearby trestle.

"I fear you must make some allowances for him, however," she cautioned, returning to press one of the cups on Isobel. "After all, being a husband is as new to Dominic as being a wife is to you. My son is used to giving orders and to having them obeyed. He may appear somewhat heavy-handed and autocratic in his dealings with you to begin with."

Isobel was silent, remembering Dominic's reaction to her headlong gallop on the mare.

Marie laughed delightedly. "I see that I am right. Do not worry so, daughter—I am confident you will soon have him eating out of your hand."

At this Isobel looked so doubtful that Marie could not resist the urge to fold her in a brief but unmistakably maternal embrace. For Isobel the experience was a novelty and one she wished she could have savoured for longer, but approaching footsteps signalled her husband's return, and Marie du Bois set her gently away.

"Dominic," she said guilelessly, turning to her son, "how did you find Reverend Mother's horse?"

"By crossing the yard and following the path to the stables," he retorted sarcastically. "It has the gravel, *Maman*—a fact of which your horse master seemed well aware and was, surprisingly enough, quite knowledgeable about treating."

"Yes, well, it never hurts to have a second opinion in such matters," his mother told him firmly.

Dominic opened his mouth as if he would say something more to her, then obviously changed his mind and spoke instead to Isobel.

"It is getting late, my lady, and we must be on our way."

She rose and curtsied to him. "Yes, my lord," she responded, very properly.

Dominic looked at her suspiciously, then back at the serene face of his mother, sensing he was the victim of some feminine conspiracy but unable to detect it for himself. With a mixture of amusement and irritation, he bade his mother farewell and set out once more for

Bristol, from whence he had arranged to take ship and sail round the coast to either Milford or Pembroke, that being the quickest way to reach Isobel's manor.

Chapter Fifteen

He caught up with Adam at their pre-agreed meeting place, a Bristol hostelry known affectionately as the Hole in the Wall. Robert and Stephen cast openly curious glances at their sister, but Adam merely saluted, making no comment as to his commander's tardiness. He greeted Dominic with the news that Piers de Bracy had passed them on the road, apparently in some haste. It seemed that Sir Roger Allyngton's ailing body had at last given up its struggle, and de Bracy was riding hard to comfort his betrothed in her grief.

"Belike he'll add to it," Dominic commented sourly. "If the girl has any sense, she'll lace his wine with henbane and do us all a favour."

"You'd recommend such a course to a new bride, then, my lord?" Isobel remarked innocently.

Adam spluttered, and Dominic, still feeling somewhat nettled about the empathy between his wife and his mother, rounded on her indignantly.

"No, I would not, you impertinent baggage!"

"Have a heart, Bel," Robert protested. "If my lord gets suspicious and requires his food to be tasted, it'll be me who gets the job."

Isobel pretended to give the matter serious consideration. "Hmm, it's tempting. What was that proverb Father Padraig was so fond of? The one about killing two birds with one stone?"

Her brother swung his arm at her threateningly, and she ducked, at the same time manoeuvring Roisin to barge the quarters of Robert's dun. Dominic, his mood unaccountably lightened by their childish squabbling, shook his head at Adam.

"You de Lescauxs are all as bad as each other. Mind, I hope your siblings are better sailors than you."

Adam could not disagree, remembering with a shudder his acute discomfort on the crossings to and from Ireland. "Still," he remarked optimistically, "this channel is not like to be as rough as the Irish Sea, and in any event, we'll not be travelling further today, since it would seem de Bracy has beaten us to both vessel and tide on this occasion."

Dominic glanced at his wife. Although she was still engaged with the twins and clearly intent on giving as good as she got, her face was pale, and faint blue shadows shaded the fine skin beneath her eyes. "It'll do no harm to take a night's rest," he decided.

Unfortunately this remark was overheard by several of his men, already taking their ease in the inn's spacious courtyard, and prompted a barrage of ribald jests, which Dominic parried good-naturedly, but Adam detected a certain tension about his brother-in-law and was puzzled. His concern grew when Dominic courteously bade Isobel goodnight and she retired alone to the private sleeping loft Adam had been at some pains to secure for them.

"Is Bel unwell again?" he probed, suspecting he already knew the answer.

Dominic withdrew his gaze from the direction of the stairs and shrugged.

"I don't think so. Why do you ask?"

"Oh, come on, Dominic, you're a newly married man."

"She's tired," he excused, "and we have at least another full day's travelling ahead of us. I thought it best to let her sleep tonight."

His companion said nothing, but it was a silence that spoke volumes. Dominic thrust one hand through his hair in frustration.

"Listen, Adam, you're my second in command, my brother-in-law, *and* my closest friend, but my marriage to your sister is most assuredly *my* affair, so if you, or any other member of your family, think to interfere between Isobel and myself..."

Adam had not served four years with the man beside him without learning the wisdom of tactical retreat. He threw up his hands in a gesture of submission.

"*Pax*," he said, amicably. "I get the message—and I'll try to keep my over-long nose out of your business from now on. In fact, I'll even try to ensure that the rest of the de Lescauxs do likewise, although you'll have a hard time trying to conceal anything from my Aunt Rohese, or Alais, for that matter. They are like terriers with a rat, especially where Isobel is concerned."

"Adam..." Dominic growled menacingly.

"I know, I know." Adam spread his palms apologetically. "It's just that when you've been accustomed all your life to looking out for someone, it becomes a hard habit to break overnight. I just need time to get used to the fact that the privilege is no longer mine."

His customary irrepressible grin twitched at the corners of his mouth, and he saw Dominic began to relax a little. With an inward sigh of relief, Adam twisted slightly and waved to attract the attention of one of the prettier girls engaged in serving before turning back to Dominic.

"Since we appear to be stuck with one another for the evening, you can tell me everything you know about Piers de Bracy's newly acquired fortune—but I warn you, I'm likely to need plenty of our host's finest in order to wash *that* tender morsel down."

The girl approached with evident enthusiasm, but when Adam took the proffered jug of ale with no more than a nod of thanks and a cheerful wink she pouted and flounced away, clearly disappointed that he did not intend to further their acquaintance. Dominic could not help but quirk one brow in sardonic amusement. Adam gave a self-deprecating shrug in response.

"You'll lose your reputation," Dominic prophesied, with a shake of his head

Adam looked unconcerned. "Not on the strength of one missed opportunity."

He hooked another bench towards him with his foot and proceeded to prop the heels of his boots comfortably upon its scarred and pitted surface. The redoubtable Bristol alewife frowned her disapproval, though whether it was for his apparent lack of interest in one of her best whores or for his cavalier treatment of the furniture it was difficult to tell. At any rate it did not seem to bother the young man, who merely raised his tankard in silent approbation of her undisputed brewing skill.

She huffed and turned away, doubtless muttering darkly under her breath about men in general and mercenary soldiers in particular, although as her harassed husband was at pains to point out to her later, in the comfort of their own well-appointed bedchamber, her profits would show a healthy increase as a result of the troop's overnight sojourn.

"So, where were we? Ah, yes, de Bracy." Adam looked enquiringly at Dominic.

"I am not sure there is much more I can add to what I told you upon our arrival at Vaillant," Dominic mused, idly tracing a pattern in the dregs of spilled ale on the table.

"You told me you suspected the holdings he would gain lay close to Isobel's own—how did you come to know that?"

"Let's just say that *someone* made sure I knew just enough to pique my interest and set me to find out more."

Adam was not slow to comprehend. "Fitz-Harding!" The name emerged as a bitter expletive.

"The very same," Dominic agreed. "It would seem he carried out his reconnaissance with admirable diligence, and, though I doubt it's much consolation to any of us, he clearly intended all along to send me venturing into de Clare's heartland, one way or another. As it turned out, he did not have to try very hard to bring his plans to fruition."

"I bet he was practically crowing with delight when he saw a way to engineer a marriage between you and Isobel," Adam gritted.

"Yes," Dominic nodded thoughtfully. "I'm not sure how he would have sought to secure my services otherwise."

"Perhaps he originally intended to enlist de Bracy to spy on de Clare, instead?"

Dominic shook his head broodingly. "I doubt it. If so, why take the trouble to ensure that I should know about de Bracy's 'good fortune'?" He took an appreciative swallow of ale, then sighed. "Fitz-Harding is playing a deep game, Adam—and it's my belief he does not trust de Bracy any more than he trusts Strongbow himself."

Adam was silent for a moment, seeming to consider this possibility. "But it was Fitz-Harding who recommended Strongbow to McMurrough in the first place," he said slowly. "Why would he do that if he did not trust him?"

Dominic snorted. "That's easy. De Clare owed him money, and Fitz-Harding reckoned that a few coffers of plundered Irish gold would be an ideal way to settle the debt. The fly in the unguent was that they actually needed the king's permission for their little war, and Henry was less than keen to give it, since he also has a deep mistrust of de Clare."

"And are you going to enlighten me as to why the king doesn't trust de Clare either?" Adam asked expectantly.

Dominic frowned. "I'm not entirely sure," he admitted. "But I do know that Henry has a long memory, so it could be something to do with the fact that de Clare's father switched loyalties during the conflict."

This was clearly news to Adam, who had settled into a comfortable slouch. He sat up again.

"Oh, yes," Dominic responded to his questioning look. "At the outset, Gilbert de Clare supported King Stephen and received the earldom of Pembroke, amongst other lands and titles, for his pains, but then

Stephen made the mistake of imprisoning Gilbert's young nephew and namesake, Hertford, as a hostage for the good behaviour of Ranulf of Chester—who just happened to be the boy's other uncle."

"*Jesu*! And you thought *my* family were trouble?"

"Oh, they are," his commander avowed, grinning at him, "especially your sister."

Adam swung a lazy fist, and Dominic ducked, laughing.

"Behave, boy, else I decide not to finish this little bedtime story I'm telling you. Now, when Ranulf of Chester defected to the empress' cause, Stephen retaliated by stripping Hertford of his family's castles and lands. Naturally this enraged Gilbert de Clare to such an extent that he changed sides too—that was the point at which Stephen revoked his right to Pembroke. Of course, Gilbert wasn't too bothered at the time, because he thought the tide was turning, and he was confident that when Mathilda triumphed he would get everything back—and probably more besides. Unfortunately for him, it did not quite work out the way he planned; Maud got defeated, Stephen was re-crowned, and Gilbert died, leaving it to his son to petition Henry for the return of what he considered his rightful inheritance."

"And the king has always refused to recognise de Clare's claim," Adam concluded thoughtfully. "But why?"

Dominic shrugged. "Maybe he's just wary of men who can change their loyalties as easily as they change their linen. For myself, I am more inclined to believe it is because Henry knows that to recognise any claim based on tenure granted during the anarchy would create a dangerous precedent."

Adam took a long swallow of ale and reached to replenish his cup before framing his next question. "If Henry mistrusts de Clare so much, how was he ever persuaded to grant his blessing for the Irish campaign?"

"Fitz-Harding, of course," Dominic responded promptly. "He used his influence to convince Henry to let de Clare raise an army and take ship for Ireland. And now that the situation looks to be going sour as last summer's vintage, he's desperate to find a way to redeem himself. Arranging to send me and my men to keep an eye on de Clare and forcing me to act as a buffer between him and de Bracy is obviously Fitz-Harding's way of attempting to reassure the king that he still has everything under control—and it hasn't cost him a penny," he added bitterly. "You have to admire the man, Adam, even if he is an unprincipled son of a…"

Dominic's words alluding to Fitz-Harding's parentage were lost to posterity, since at that moment a dispute over a game of dice erupted between some local lads and several of his younger recruits. Both he and Adam were forced to wade into the fray to separate the protagonists, amidst vociferous complaint from mine host's wife, and the remainder of the evening was spent ensuring that a fragile peace prevailed until the local boys left and Dominic's men were persuaded to roll themselves in their cloaks and bed down for the night.

Chapter Sixteen

Isobel sat on her travelling chest at the edge of the wooden jetty, watching the play of sunlight on water as her husband of two days supervised the loading of thirty men, horses, military equipment, and sundry other baggage onto the vessels that were to take them across from Bristol to Pembroke. Never having seen anything quite like it before, she was fascinated by the sights and sounds of the Welsh-Back, so-named on account of the frequent trade crossings made between the two countries.

"I could stay here forever," she told Adam as he motioned her to stand up so he could check the ropes securing her chest and see to its loading. To her surprise, his only comment was a noncommittal grunt.

Dominic approached, extending his arm towards her.

"Are you ready, Wife?"

Isobel jerked her head in Adam's direction. "What's the matter with him?" she asked suspiciously. "Did he drink too much last night?"

Dominic smothered a snort of laughter and gestured at the numerous docked ships which rose and fell in the gentle swell that tugged at their moorings. "Adam is feeling a little uncomfortable at the prospect of our voyage. I'm afraid he suffered rather badly on the crossings to and from Ireland, and it has given him a distinct distaste for seafaring."

"Green as grass and puking over the side all the way, according to Sim," Robert added gleefully as he passed them with a pile of harness destined for the waiting ship. "He wanted to know if we were likely to be the same."

"And are you?" Dominic enquired curiously.

It was Stephen who answered. "Shouldn't think so," he opined cheerfully. "Most of us de Lescauxs have stomachs lined with lead—not much that makes us heave."

"Apart from poppy syrup," Robert reminded him darkly.

"And that look Alais uses on Will when she wants something," Stephen conceded magnanimously.

Robert pulled a hideous face, put two fingers down his throat and mimed retching with commendable credibility. Dominic ran a hand through his hair in exasperation.

"*Jesu*, what am I going to do with them?" he asked Isobel, ruefully.

"Well, I'd keep them away from Adam, for a start," she advised, accepting his proffered arm as he ushered her up the gangplank. "At least until we're back on dry land—it wouldn't be fair otherwise."

Dominic rolled his eyes skywards. "A temporary cessation of hostilities between the de Lescauxs—I believe I have witnessed a miracle!" A thought struck him. "Were they including you in the 'stomachs lined with lead' bit?"

"I expect so," his wife replied, not seeming in the least offended, and Dominic surmised it was probably no more than she was used to.

As it turned out, the twins' optimism proved well-founded, and Adam, who had managed to avoid the indignity of actual vomiting only through a combination of sheer strength of will and a judicious decision to break his fast on nothing more than dry bread and water, could not help but feel a little aggrieved at the injustice of it. Still feeling slightly nauseous, he turned his back on the water and joined Dominic in studying the fortifications of the de Clare stronghold. The turf and timber defences built by Arnulf de Montgomery in the days of William Rufus had yet to be completely replaced by the prevailing preference for stone, although here and there was evidence that the process was underway.

Once the building works were completed, the castle would be a formidable fortress. It was strategically positioned on the highest point at the head of the river estuary and commanded control of approach by land or sea. Adam began to understand why Henry was so reluctant to make official acknowledgement of de Clare's claim, and from the grim expression on Dominic's face he knew he was not alone in his opinion. Dominic's voice was curt as he gave the order to move out, and the troop began the final stage of its journey.

As they drew near their destination, Dominic acknowledged that whatever William de Lescaux had or had not done for his daughter, no one could accuse him of neglecting her inheritance. As with most castles, the site had clearly been selected for its strategic value, but, unlike Pembroke, Pyr already boasted its construction entirely in stone. Impressive turrets and crenellations topped imposing curtain walls linked by powerful corner towers, and the whole structure was visible from some distance off. Beneath its walls lay an equally well-constructed fish pond, and beyond that an orchard, bounded by a grove of coppiced hazel. The overwhelming impression was one of power and wealth—a startling combination of beauty and function.

The castle was approached by a narrow valley carved by two streams which flowed down towards the sea. On the crown of the opposite ridge William de Lescaux had commissioned a church. It faced the castle challengingly across the divide, its lime-washed tower given a mellow golden cast by the early evening sun. God and man in juxtaposition, Dominic acknowledged wryly, still scarcely able to credit the unlikely chain of events that had led to him becoming its custodian.

Adam, too, was captivated. Like Isobel, he had been aware of the basic economic facts concerning the demesne, and he knew it was a profitable holding, producing considerable revenues from its wheat harvests and from fishing, but nothing could have prepared him for the reality. It was, quite simply, a prize.

They passed over the drawbridge, Dominic's professional eye noting the well-greased chains, and beneath a fine gatehouse topped by strong battlements and interspersed with numerous arrow slits. Craning his head at the roof, Adam was gratified to see that his father had ordered the incorporation of the appropriately named "murder-holes" through which either hot liquids or solid missiles could be hurled down at an enemy trapped between the two portcullises. On the western and southern walls of the inner ward were the usual lean-to timber structures connected with stabling and blacksmithing. There was also a huge barn and what looked to be a complex hall-range. The place was a hive of well organised domestic activity, from which William de Lescaux's ageing and increasingly frail steward emerged with all the haste of which he was capable to greet the new lord and his wife.

Sion Prys did his duty by his new lord, but it was on the face of the Lady Isobel that his faded brown eyes lingered. Belatedly conscious that he was staring, he bowed low over her hand.

"Forgive me, my lady, but you are so very like your mother, God rest her."

Isobel's eyes widened. "You knew my mother?"

"I had that honour, lady."

"Are there many people here who remember her?" she demanded breathlessly.

The old man shook his head with a sad smile. "Not many, Lady Isobel, but there are still a few of us." His eyes strayed behind her and, with a deferential bow to Dominic, he continued, "If you will forgive my boldness, sir, there is no mistaking my lady's brothers, either, for each of them are clearly their father's sons."

Robert and Stephen appraised each other's faces and wrinkled their noses in such identical expressions of disgust that all those who had heard the steward's remark could not help but laugh.

"Welcome, my lord and lady." Sion bowed again as he ushered them towards the main hall.

Chapter Seventeen

Isobel leaned as far out of the window as it was possible to go and craned her neck towards the sea. The day was warm, and the distinctive scent of may-blossom drifted towards her on the breeze. She sighed with frustration and looked down at the grubby circle of linen stretched over her embroidery frame. Her intention to work a design along the edge of a piece of fabric destined to become a new wimple had seemed a good one, but, try as she might, her sewing skills remained at best lamentable. Whenever she bewailed such shortcomings to her husband, he simply laughed, tugged her braid as was his habit, and pointed out that there were women aplenty who could sew, but not many who could hone a dagger blade so well as she, and he knew where his preference lay.

Considering what he had once suspected of her, Isobel reflected sourly that she might now be forgiven for thinking there was truth in the rumour surrounding Dominic and Adam, and that his *preference* definitely lay with her brother. They were rarely out of each other's company, either practising their swordplay or bending their heads over some plan or other for improvement of the castle's defences. Today they were engaged in a lively discussion with the blacksmith concerning the practicalities of demolishing the existing forge and replacing it with a larger, more substantial structure against the west wall. Robert and Stephen were remarkably busy, too, Dominic having decided that the best way to keep them out of mischief was to keep them fully occupied and under the more or less constantly watchful eye of Sim Walters, with whom they seemed to have struck an instant rapport.

Isobel was, quite simply, bored. The day-to-day routine of Pyr was so well-established that it ran without interference from her, and there seemed nothing else for her to do. With a sigh she dropped the offending scrap of fabric into her workbasket and quitted the solar. Outside, in the sunshine, she paused and sniffed the air. The urge to be truly free, as she had been in her childhood, was too strong to ignore, and she skipped across the inner ward with a lack of decorum that would have outraged her Aunt Rohese.

Sion spied her heading for the postern gate, which opened out onto the seaward side of the castle. He shook his head, smiling at the memory of her lady mother behaving in much the same manner. It had been on just such a day as this that Lady Anwen had first met the young Lord William de Lescaux, when a lame courser had caused him to become separated from his hunting party. Lord William had wandered for hours, hopelessly lost in the Welsh countryside, until Lady Anwen had come upon him. A stormy and illicit courtship followed, but there had never been any question in the lady's mind when her Norman lordling had come to claim her, in defiance of both his family and her own. She had gone without a backward glance, taking with her nothing more than the clothes she had worn. Her father had been nigh on incandescent with rage, and privately Sion thought it was nothing short of a miracle that Rhys ap Pyr had never carried out his threat to disinherit his only child.

A strong suspicion that the lady's daughter might prove just as wilful, coupled with the rumours Sion had lately heard concerning the new Lord of Penllan, sent him hurrying to find Lord Dominic. The sentry on duty at the postern was commendably reluctant to let the young Lady du Bois pass through the gate unaccompanied and indeed did his best to persuade her to wait until a suitable escort could be found, but short of detaining her by force, there was little he could do in the face of her direct order that he stand aside. He did so most unwillingly, and Isobel guessed with a spurt of annoyance that he would not be slow to alert someone to her departure. With a discerning eye she surveyed the lie of the land, deciding with some satisfaction that the sand hills would lend themselves admirably to a game of hide-and-seek. If nothing else, it might serve to alleviate her boredom.

She was thus in no particular haste as she wandered down the pebbled road leading towards the beach, where she found the miller's daughters playing bare-legged on the edge of the stream, their skirts kilted up and tucked into their plaited leather girdles. On impulse she pulled off her shoes and hose and joined them, paddling in the shallows, admiring their various treasures, and taking joy in their simple pleasure. Narrowing her eyes against the dazzling sunlight, Isobel glanced back towards the castle and immediately spotted the two figures winding their way down the narrow track from the postern. With a smile for the little girls, she gestured at the soldiers, putting her finger to her lips and shaking her head. They nodded solemnly in mute understanding as she swept up her belongings and ran.

By the time Dominic caught up with the men who had been summarily despatched by the captain of the watch in pursuit of his wife, he found them lying prone on their stomachs, almost hidden from view amidst one of the tall clumps of rough grass cresting the sand dunes. Like most of his soldiers, Matt Williams and Giles le Blanc were vigorous young men in their prime, not many years older than Isobel's twin brothers, and as soon as they had realised the lady knew they were following her, they had settled down to play her game of cat-and-mouse with evident enjoyment.

"You can tell she's Sir Adam's sister," Matt greeted in low tones, saluting as Dominic dropped down beside him. "She's good—even managed to give us the slip for a minute or two when she stripped this off." He flourished Isobel's blue overdress. "It made her so much more difficult to spot against the sand. She almost had us for a while, until we found it and realised what she'd done."

Dominic muttered something colourful under his breath and took the garment from Matt's hand.

"Thank you, Williams. I am indebted to you."

"Would you like us to stay, my lord—as reinforcements?" Le Blanc sounded almost hopeful.

Dominic cuffed him affectionately. "Are you suggesting I can't take her by myself?" he scoffed. "Watch and learn, stripling!"

As he eased himself down the dunes towards the beach, Dominic was smiling. He had been married to Isobel for over a month now, and in that time there had been ample opportunity for him to observe her behaviour. The doubts that had once plagued him had been well and truly vanquished, and he was now able to accept with a touch of pride the admiration of men like Matt and Giles for his beautiful and, admittedly, unusual wife. It probably helped that three of her brothers were in his service and that despite her being married to their lord they continued to treat her more or less as they had always done—with teasing indulgence and brotherly affection. The remainder of his men seemed to take their cue from that, and although it was clear many of them admired her, Dominic knew Isobel did nothing to encourage them. Indeed, she was largely oblivious of their regard and, unlike her brothers, seemed to have neither the inclination nor the skill to indulge in flirtation.

Isobel gained the far end of the beach and knew she was clearly visible to the two men charged with following her. Once she had established that their orders must be simply to keep her in sight, she had set out to make the game worth the candle, but now she had tired of it. She crouched over a tidal pool and idly dabbled her fingers in the clear water, sending a tiny crab scurrying for cover.

Dominic found his wife's shoes on top of a flat rock at the base of the dunes, her discarded hose stuffed inside them. Of her wimple there was no sign. He shook his head, grinning, as he placed the neatly folded overdress next to the other items. Shading his eyes against the glare of the afternoon sun on the water, he scanned the shoreline. Isobel was at the furthest end of the beach, apparently intent on something she had found in one of the many pools that formed in the rocks at low tide. He saw her reach out and poke experimentally with a piece of driftwood at whatever it was that had caught her attention.

Seeing as he had to negotiate a bank of loose shingle, Dominic considered that he managed his approach with commendable stealth, relying on Isobel's preoccupation and the gentle rhythmic sound of the waves to cover any sound he made. He moved carefully, keeping his shadow from falling across her so as not to alert her to his presence until he was in touching distance.

"So, madam, I have found you!"

Isobel gave a yelp of surprise and, but for the speed of his reflexes, would have pitched forward into the water.

"You devious bastard!" she spluttered.

The words were uttered without conscious thought, and immediately Isobel clapped one hand over her mouth in horrified consternation as she realised exactly what she had just said. Dominic's hold on her tightened, but, far from being offended, he appeared to be struggling not to laugh.

"An allegation I can't deny," he acknowledged, "on either count."

Still off balance, Isobel swung at him. He ducked adroitly. "Now, now, sweeting," he admonished, "be very careful, or I might just be tempted to let go."

He turned in the direction of the dunes and thrust his free hand into the air, thumb pointing skywards in an unmistakable gesture of triumph. Isobel saw her two watchdogs wave in response before swinging round and heading back towards the castle.

"They were very good," she acknowledged grudgingly, her eyes on the retreating figures.

"Hmm." Her husband frowned down at her. "I suppose it would not hurt to tell you that they returned the compliment. Come, my errant wife, let us return you to your bower—and next time you wish to rend the chains of domesticity asunder, at least have the decency to let me know. I might want to come with you!"

"Ah, but where would be the fun in that?" she riposted. "This way, I keep you on your toes."

"Literally," Dominic admitted, thinking about the way he had been forced to cross the shifting bank of shingle.

He steered her away from the water and back up the beach. Isobel sat down next to the flat rock where she had left her shoes and brushed ineffectually at the loose sand on the soles of her feet.

"I suppose I should thank you for not being angry with me," she offered.

"Who says I'm not?" Dominic teased, watching as she struggled to put on her hose only to abandon the exercise a moment later. She found one shoe, slipped it onto her bare foot with a faint grimace, and cast about for the other.

"Isobel..."

The missing shoe dangled invitingly from the end of Dominic's index finger. He held it out towards her, but as she leant forward to take it he stepped back again, keeping it just beyond her reach.

"What's it worth?" he asked, grinning wickedly.

"You avoiding a humiliating and ignominious defeat?" Isobel offered, sizing him up with determination.

Dominic pretended to consider her response.

"Hmm, spoken with more bravado than conviction,

I think…"

Isobel lunged, intending to use the same technique as she had used to floor de Bracy in the pleasaunce, but Dominic was ready for her. Hooking his ankle round her calf he took her down with him, and they landed together in the soft sand. He rolled swiftly, trapping her beneath him. She was furious, and the fact that Dominic was practically helpless with laughter did nothing to improve her temper.

"Let me up, you miserable, misbegotten son of a…" Isobel flailed wildly with her fists.

"Now, sweetheart," Dominic reprimanded with mock severity, "is that any way for a lady to speak to her husband?"

Wedging one leg between her thighs, he used the weight of his left arm across her stomach to keep her pinned beneath him. With his other hand he caught hold of her wrists and brought them both up above her head. The action drew the fine fabric of her undershift taut across her breasts, and Dominic eyed the result appreciatively.

"Are you ready to concede yet, madam?" he asked pleasantly. "We could negotiate terms—you never know, I might be prepared to be generous…"

Isobel glared up at him defiantly.

"You may take your terms and stuff them up your…"

She gave a muffled gasp as his mouth closed over hers, and Dominic was instantly and painfully aware that what had begun in all innocence as a game between them had suddenly become something entirely different and infinitely more dangerous. Knowing full well that he should be the one to call a halt, but unable to resist the temptation, he bit down gently on her lower lip, and as she opened her set teeth to protest against the intimacy he thrust forward with his tongue. There was a moment of shocked hesitation before slowly, tentatively, he felt her begin to return his kiss.

Jesu, she was sweet! Sweeter than anything he could ever remember tasting. His body responded instinctively, clamouring for a release long denied. Beneath him Isobel writhed, still attempting to free herself, and Dominic's discomfort increased tenfold. Shuddering with the effort, he levered himself onto his elbows and rolled away. For a moment he lay still, then as Isobel sat up he jerked backwards, fearing that if she touched him again he would not have the control to stop. He risked a glance at her face and wished he had not when he saw the hurt in her eyes.

"What is it?" she asked in a small voice. "Did I do something wrong?"

"Christ, no!"

He swallowed hard and shook his head vehemently in an effort to reassure her. He wanted to tell her there was nothing wrong—that it was all too right. He wanted, above everything, to take her back into his arms and make her his wife in every sense of the word, right here and now. The difference was that he *knew* where this was leading, and he was very conscious that a sandy beach, where they might be chanced upon at any moment, was not the best place to initiate his virgin bride into the intimacies of marriage. From somewhere he summoned a smile for her, although it was somewhat strained.

"I took advantage of you, *ma* Bel—and of the moment. It was not very chivalrous of me, and I apologise." Dominic stood up and extended his arm. "I suppose I must now think of some way to atone for my sins," he continued as he pulled her to her feet. A devilish gleam entered his eyes. "I have to ride into Pembroke tomorrow for provisions. Perhaps I can bring you back some new embroidery silks?"

Isobel's lips tightened ominously. She drew back her arm, and Dominic, realising her intent, set off at a run. The shoe hit him squarely between his shoulder blades, and he mentally added an accurate aim to her list of unusual accomplishments.

Chapter Eighteen

When Dominic told Isobel he needed to visit Pembroke for provisions, he was not lying—but he was also in search of something else. The small town was alive with all manner of stall holders offering their wares, as might be expected on market day, and there were also a number of merchantmen docked at the quay. It was amongst these that Dominic hoped to find that which he was seeking.

Having left his wife in the care of her twin brothers and with sufficient coin to purchase a range of domestic necessities, Dominic excused himself on the pretext of needing to sort out transport for a load of timber he had bought in connection with the new smithy project. In reality, this business was speedily transacted, and he quickly proceeded to a small waterfront tavern where he had directed Adam to meet him.

The door was open, for the day was warm and trade brisk. Customers spilled out onto the street, and it took Dominic several minutes to work his way through the press of men to reach the interior. He stood on the threshold, allowing his eyes time to adjust from the bright spring sunlight outside to the darkness within. Crowded, noisy, and stinking of unwashed humanity mixed with the lingering scent of garlic from last night's pottage, it was just the sort of place he had become accustomed to frequenting.

Adam was seated on a blackened oak settle sunk in one of the inglenooks on either side of the empty hearth, deep in conversation with the captain of a Scottish merchantman with whom Dominic regularly traded for information. He was frowning, and Dominic felt the familiar lurch of his gut that bespoke trouble. As if sensing his presence, Adam looked up and shifted along the settle to make room for him.

"Well?" Dominic asked urgently, sliding down beside him.

"MacMurrough is dead."

"What?"

"Aye, it's true," Archie MacPherson confirmed dryly, "and yon fool de Clare has assumed the kingship of Leinster, in the name of his wife."

Dominic swore, following up the colourful epithet with some concise if decidedly uncomplimentary remarks alluding to de Clare's parentage.

"Oh, aye," Archie agreed amiably, "he is that—and now he's gone and upset the Archbishop of Dublin with his nonsense, if you please. So much so that His Grace has roused the Irish chieftains and raised an army against him. Last I heard, de Clare was besieged in Dublin, with Roderick O'Connor and Domnall O'Brien camped outside the walls, baying for his blood."

"And like to get it," Adam commented sourly. "What with Henry's writ against aid coming from England or Normandy, and the Irish preventing him from getting supplies any other way, he must be *in extremis*."

"He'll have to offer terms." Dominic nodded.

"Oh, he's tried that already," Archie supplied gleefully. "He offered to hold Leinster as O'Connor's vassal, but O'Connor's having none of it. He's demanding total surrender—the return of Dublin, Wexford, and Waterford, *and* a complete withdrawal from Irish soil."

"Henry will never stand for that," Dominic warned. "Whatever de Clare's immediate fate, this will ultimately mean war."

MacPherson pocketed the proffered purse of coin with a genial nod.

"A pleasure doing business with you, gentlemen, as always. I fancy I'll be back this way again in three weeks or so, if you've a mind for any further purchases." He winked significantly at them. "Now, you being a newly married man, Sir Dominic, there must be something I could tempt you with for your lady wife?"

Dominic grinned. "Well, now that you mention it, I believe she does have need of some embroidery silks."

****

Piers de Bracy watched with narrowed eyes as the de Lescaux twins escorted their sister around the various booths and stalls of Pembroke's market. Like most people, he was fascinated by their identical faces, although he gave no credence to the foolish gossips who intimated they shared more than looks and were endowed with some supernatural power.

His interest in their sister was of a much more basic persuasion. He cast a disparaging glance at the diminutive figure of his own wife, following a respectful three paces behind him on the arm of his squire. Her hood was drawn up over her pale hair, and her slate-grey eyes were modestly cast down, the lashes starkly black against the almost translucent pallor of her skin. Beside the laughing, vivacious incandescence of Isobel du Bois, she was akin to a common tallow dip placed beside an expensive beeswax candle. He caught hold of her wrist and dragged her forward with such abruptness she almost stumbled.

"Come, madam, you must exchange pleasantries with our neighbours. It would not do for you to gain a reputation for discourtesy."

She made no response, but that was not unusual. Piers had discovered his wife barely spoke these days except to answer yes or no to a direct question, and he found it did not bother him unduly.

"Lady du Bois!"

He put himself directly in Isobel's path, so she had no choice but to stop. She was aware of Robert and Stephen on either side of her positively radiating hostility, and she saw their right hands close simultaneously over the hilts of the poniards sheathed at their hips.

"You seem surprised to see me, my lady, but surely it is not so unusual for neighbours to meet on occasions such as this?" De Bracy gestured expansively at the market.

"We are neighbours?" Isobel's shock was real, but when she turned to share it with her brothers she realised that they, unlike her, were clearly not in ignorance of this fact.

"Your land shares a border with his," Robert confirmed tautly, his eyes never leaving de Bracy's face, whilst Stephen watched Louis Montierre with similar concentration.

"How…interesting," Isobel floundered.

Wondering how to extricate the twins from this

situation without bloodshed, she was still desperately casting about for something else to say when, to her great relief, she saw Dominic and Adam working their way through the crowds. In an attempt to buy time, she swallowed the bitter taste in her mouth and forced herself to be polite.

"My husband has mentioned that you, too, are recently married, Sir Piers. May I offer you my congratulations?"

"Yes, indeed, de Bracy. In this my wife speaks for both of us."

Isobel sent up a silent prayer of thanks as Dominic arrived at her side. He eyed de Bracy impassively. "Is your lady not with you today?"

Piers turned slightly and indicated behind him as he said, "Of course. Aleyne, I would have you meet Sir Dominic du Bois, lately become Lord of Pyr, and his wife, the Lady Isobel. These other gentlemen are Lady du Bois' brothers."

He spoke as if to a simpleton, or perhaps a child, and Dominic's first thought on seeing Aleyne de Bracy was that if Isobel had seemed overly young for marriage, then Sir Roger Allyngton's daughter was indeed still a child.

She was small, not reaching even to his shoulder, and now she had moved closer Dominic could see that the body beneath her cloak was thin and coltish. Smiling courteously, he took her fingers and raised them to his lips in formal greeting, noting that despite the heat of the day her hands were ice cold. His stomach churned at the thought of this vulnerable girl at the mercy of the kind of man he knew de Bracy to be. Somehow he doubted Piers had extended to his wife the same courtesy offered to Isobel in refraining from her bed until she expressed herself willing, and his suspicion became a certainty when the girl raised her head and looked at him. He heard Adam's sharp intake of breath, saw the revulsion in his eyes, and knew he was not alone in his misgivings.

For the first time ever Adam de Lescaux found himself actually *wanting* to kill a man, but the rush of burning rage was quickly followed by a sense of pity, and of such helplessness that he felt suddenly sick, as if someone had punched him in the gut. The sensation was so intense Adam feared he would be unable to control it, and on the pretext of needing to make a purchase from the harness maker's booth before the man packed up his stall, he bowed and excused himself.

De Bracy watched him go with a mocking smile before returning his attention to Dominic.

"You will have heard the news, I suppose?"

Dominic nodded curtly, judging there was no advantage to be gained from dissembling.

The knight's gaze roamed over Isobel with insulting familiarity.

"It seems we shall barely have time to beget our heirs before we must be off to war, du Bois."

Embarrassed colour flared under Isobel's skin, and Dominic's face tightened. He dipped his head in the barest acknowledgement of civility and steered his wife away, motioning as he did so for Robert and Stephen to fall in behind him.

Chapter Nineteen

Adam closed the door and crossed the solar to where Dominic sat, one booted foot resting casually on a footstool, the other leg stretched towards a brazier lit against an unexpectedly chilly late-spring evening. Isobel sat in the window embrasure so as to catch the last of the fading light as she worked on her household accounts. The air of tension between the couple was tangible.

Dominic responded to Adam's customary evening report with merely an affable nod, indicating that he should help himself to a drink. Adam glanced across at his sister, but she seemed engrossed in what she was doing and did not look up. He swallowed hard, half inclined to think he would rather face the entire army currently besieging de Clare than tackle the present situation. With a sigh he propped himself against the wall, and, keeping his voice deliberately low, addressed himself to his brother-by-marriage.

"Dominic, what is wrong between you and Isobel?"

Dominic withdrew his gaze from contemplation of the burning logs and favoured him with an urbane smile.

"What makes you think there is anything wrong between us?"

"The fact that I have known her all her life, and

you for the past four years," Adam answered scathingly.

Innate honesty prevented Dominic from uttering the rebuke he would have delivered had the words been spoken by anyone else. He shrugged.

"We quarrelled over the meeting with de Bracy this afternoon. She felt I should have told her about Penllan's borders marching with ours."

Adam snorted disparagingly. "So you should, but that is not what I meant, and you know it. Are you aware there are rumours about your marriage, Dominic—rumours that could undermine your position here? Speculation abounds as to its validity, despite the evidence you so obligingly provided the morning after your wedding."

Dominic's tone remained neutral. "Your sister is young, and our marriage was made in haste. I told her I would give her time to become accustomed to me before I made any demands on her."

Adam exhaled slowly. "So it is true, then—you have not consummated the marriage. For God's sake, Dominic, many girls are wedded and bedded before they are Bel's age."

There was an uncomfortable silence as the memory of Aleyne de Bracy's haunted eyes rose between them.

"You are within your rights," Adam reminded him flatly, knowing the words carried no conviction.

"By law, yes," Dominic acknowledged. His eyes strayed to the figure of his wife silhouetted in the window. The rays of the setting sun created a nimbus of gold around her, making her look like one of the painted icons in the church across the valley. "But I find I would have more from her than her duty—am I so wrong to want that?"

Adam shook his head impatiently. "No, of course not. But I think perhaps a misplaced sense of honour has you blinkered like a carter's nag. Make her your wife in deed as well as name," he urged. "I think you will find the experience rewarding enough."

Dominic gave him a repressive look. "I made your sister a promise, and I will not break it."

His tone caused Isobel to raise her head and look in their direction. Adam smiled back at her in what he hoped was a reassuring manner.

"You know what lies ahead," he reasoned grimly. "Would you have Fitz-Harding or de Clare make her a widow before you have made her a wife?"

Dominic swore under his breath. "*Jesu*, Adam, you know where to stick the knife, I'll give you that."

It was Adam's turn to shrug. He pushed himself away from the wall and wandered over to his sister.

"I am for bed," he announced, stretching his long frame. He bent and whispered something in Isobel's ear, and her face flamed. Then he laughed and tweaked her braid affectionately, in much the same manner as Dominic often did. He kissed her cheek, saluted her husband, and was gone.

"Your brother missed his vocation," Dominic opined sourly as the door banged shut. "He'd have made a fine fool."

She made no response. He sighed and tried again.

"I should have told you about de Bracy before," he offered ruefully, pushing a wayward lock of hair out of his eyes. He had been considering asking his wife to barber it for him, but such had been the violence of their quarrel that afternoon he had fancied she would be more inclined to use her shears to slit his throat. "At the time, I thought you had enough on your trencher, but I would have told you eventually."

"When?" Isobel demanded angrily, getting up from the window seat and whirling to face him in a flurry of skirts. "When did you plan to tell me? When de Bracy turned up at our gates with a siege engine? This is *my* home—my inheritance. Its well-being, and that of its people, are as much mine to consider as they are yours, and you had no right to keep such information from me."

It was Dominic's turn to remain silent, for he recognised that she had a point and therefore did not try to defend himself. From the way she was now pacing about the confines of the room, past experience suggested Isobel was looking for something to throw at him. Considering the possible options, he devoutly hoped she would select one of the damask cushions in preference to any of the pottery cups or the fire irons. She picked up a cup, and he ducked instinctively, throwing up a hand to protect his face. When nothing happened, he risked a cautious upward glance and saw that his wife had come to stand directly in front of him.

"Do you want wine?" she asked sweetly.

He took the proffered cup and scowled at her over the rim.

"You and Adam seemed to have plenty to say to one another this evening. Are you going to share any of it with me, or do I have to find out for myself, as usual?" she challenged, throwing herself back down on the window seat.

Dominic hastily gathered his wits, mentally sifting through the evening's whispered conversation with her brother and knowing there was no way he could tell her its true content. She was clearly waiting for him to answer, and he settled for giving her an edited version of what they had learned in Pembroke.

"It may be in the nature of cold comfort to you, but it's likely de Bracy will be too busy elsewhere to worry about making trouble at home, at least for the time being," he concluded.

Isobel eyed him narrowly. "If there is a war between Pembroke and the king, you will go back to Ireland, won't you?"

He shrugged uneasily and avoided looking at her. "It's what I do."

She stood up, shaking her head. "You will go because you have to—because you owe service to the king now. You'll go because he bought you—with me."

His head came up at that. "I'd have gone regardless of you," he corrected. "Have you forgotten what I am, Isobel? What your brother is? We are professional soldiers. It is our livelihood—if not in Ireland for King Henry, then in France or Outremer or anywhere else that men make war on other men."

She had turned away again and was staring out of the window. Dominic stood up. He walked over to her and set his hands on her shoulders, turning her round to face him.

"Don't fret, *ma* Bel," he told her, sweeping the side of his index finger down the curve of her cheek. "I'll make provision for you before I leave."

"Provision!" Isobel dashed his hand away as she hurled the word back at him. "And just what provision do you plan to make for me, Dominic du Bois? Am I to go back to my father? Or perhaps you intend to send me to dwell with my esteemed sister-in-law, so that we may keep one another company? Mayhap we could take bets on who will be the first to bury her husband? Or would you have me enter a nunnery, like your mother?"

She punctuated her accusations with a series of half-hearted blows to his chest until Dominic caught her wrists and held her slightly away from him, his blue eyes bright with an emotion he was reluctant to define. He bent his head and touched his lips to hers softly. It was a butterfly caress, meant only to comfort, but having learnt from their two previous encounters, Isobel surprised him by opening to him almost at once, inviting him to deepen the kiss.

Aware she was intensely vulnerable in this moment, Dominic reined himself back, fully intending to draw away, but he had not allowed for the fact that Isobel's arms crept up round his neck, and now she curled her fingernails into the fine stuff of his tunic, holding him fast against her.

"Please, Dominic," she whispered. "Please."

He was not even sure she knew what she was asking for; but he did, and in his mind Adam's words about making her a wife before others could make her a widow mingled with de Bracy's remark about begetting heirs, their combined urgency making it even more difficult to resist her impassioned plea. Freeing one of her hands, he guided it between them, down the length of his body.

"Can you feel what you do to me?" he whispered.

Her widened eyes and heightened breathing gave him answer.

"*Jesu* God, Isobel," he murmured against her mouth. "Do not be swayed by anything that Adam—or anyone else—has said to you. You must be very sure this is what you want, for once the deed is done there is no undoing it."

"I am your wife," she said simply, her hand returning to his chest, where she could feel the rapid beat of his heart. "You asked for affection and respect—you have earned them both in good measure." She looked up at him, through her lashes, just as she had done on their wedding night, but this time Dominic knew the action was entirely calculated. "You also promised you would teach me the difference between a husband and a brother, my lord—and I would hold you to that promise, for I am so very weary of brothers."

He could not help laughing, and some of the tension ebbed from him.

"I seem to remember I told you there were many differences, witch," he corrected, allowing her hand to return to his shoulder, "and that I would delight in teaching you *all* of them."

Dominic drew away to head across the solar in the direction of the adjoining bed chamber. When barely inside the doorway, he paused to divest himself of his tunic, and his voice came muffled through its folds.

"Besides, you already know one, for I sincerely trust none of your brothers has ever kissed you the way we have just kissed."

"No, my lord," Isobel acknowledged demurely, close behind him.

Crossing to the canopied bed they had shared without intimacy every night since their arrival at Pyr, Dominic sat down and kicked off his boots. He patted the coverlet beside him and waited until Isobel had removed her overdress before encircling her slender waist with his arms and pulling her into his lap.

"And now you may tell me, madam wife, whether or not you have enjoyed your lessons thus far."

She wrinkled her nose at him. "It is hard to tell, my lord, for they have been somewhat infrequent. My father always says that in order to master a skill, one needs to practise it often."

"Your father," Dominic growled, nipping her ear, "has a great deal to answer for. However, in this matter I am persuaded he may be right. Shall we put his theory to the test?"

He sought her mouth, this time exploring it thoroughly, his lips warm and firm against hers. He teased her, breaking away when she opened for him and trailing kisses along her jaw, upwards to the sensitive skin behind her ear. Isobel twisted in his arms, and he felt himself harden as the movement ground her lower body against his pelvis. There was no time to dwell upon this pleasant sensation, however, as she had curled her fingers into his hair and was directing his mouth back to hers. This time Dominic acquiesced to her demand and took the kiss to a breathless conclusion.

He drew back to concentrate on regulating his breathing and steadying the erratic pulsing of his heart, fully aware that his control, already perilously stretched by a prolonged period of abstinence, had limits. Although he had never before bedded a virgin, Dominic was sufficiently worldly to know that this first time there must inevitably be pain for Isobel before there could be pleasure, and he badly wanted to give her enough pleasure to counterbalance that pain.

"You are an apt pupil, *ma* Bel," he told her, a trifle unsteadily. Placing one arm under her knees, he swung his own legs upwards and took her with him, so that they were both now lying on the bed. He turned on his side and propped himself on one elbow to gaze down at her. She returned his regard, emerald eyes wide with expectation.

"Lesson number two?" he queried mischievously.

"I am ready, my lord."

"Not yet, sweet Isobel," he told her, enjoying her slightly uncomprehending frown and the power of his own superior knowledge.

He motioned for her to turn so he could reach the lacings at the back of her chemise, and his fingers proceeded expertly to accomplish their task. When her mouth pursed in a censorious pout at his obvious skill, Dominic kissed her again, laughing.

"What did you expect, my lady wife—that I would be a novice at the game?"

"My sister-in-law was more than happy to disabuse me of that notion on our wedding night, my lord," she came back at him, somewhat waspishly.

His hands stilled. "I am twenty-seven years old, Isobel, and it would be accounted strange indeed if there had not been women in my life before now, but I swear on my honour that there have been none since the day I promised myself to you, and I have no intention of breaking that vow, whatever you may think or others may tell you."

She could feel his breath, warm against the skin at the nape of her neck, like a caress. Isobel gave an impatient moan and pushed her body against the length of his. Carefully Dominic eased the unlaced shift down over her shoulders, exposing her smooth flesh inch by inch to his covetous exploration. He pushed the garment down to her waist and returned his attention to her uncovered breasts. Isobel gasped and shuddered at the sensations wrought by his mouth and hands on her body.

"Slowly, *ma* Bel," he cautioned, as much for his sake as her own. His fingers trailed fire across her stomach and then dropped lower, questing. He felt her stiffen against him uncertainly, and immediately he drew back, smiling reassurance.

"It is permitted for me to touch you so, sweeting," he encouraged, "and if you will let me, I promise I can give you pleasure." His voice was husky, a persuasive throb that echoed the growing rhythm of her blood and caused warmth to pool at the juncture of her thighs as he coaxed her shift down still further, easing it from under her hips until he could strip it away altogether. Then he dispensed with her hose and her soft leather shoes. She lay dazed and naked beneath his hot gaze, and the summer-sky colour of his eyes darkened to a deep midnight blue with the intensity of passion.

Dominic doffed his linen shirt so that he too was naked but for his woollen braies. He lay down beside her again and took one of her hands in his own, gently opening the fingers until he could place her palm to his. Then he dipped his head and drew his lips across the tip of each finger in turn, sucking gently. He felt her shiver of response and pressed her trembling fingers to the warm muscle of his chest, inviting her to explore his body in the same way he had been discovering hers and silently vowing she would never know what it cost him to permit those hesitant hands to proceed at their own pace. They roamed upwards and over his shoulders to travel across the hard planes of his back, then back round over the ridges of his rib cage and across the flatness of his abdomen. She felt his swift intake of breath as she traced the faint line of dark hair that arrowed downwards from his stomach.

"*Jesu*, woman, enough!" he uttered thickly. Isobel snatched her hand away as if it had been burned. Dominic was breathing hard now, and there was a faint sheen of perspiration on his forehead and upper lip. He rolled away and stood up with his back to her. He loosened the drawstring of his braies and dropped them to the rush-strewn floor. He had not been able to exert as much control over his body as he had planned and was already much harder than he had intended to be at this stage. He swore inwardly, his heart heavy. There was no way he could take Isobel's maidenhead without causing her considerable hurt, yet he was too desperate now in his own need not to complete what they had begun.

"Close your eyes, ma Bel."

He knew she would be puzzled, perhaps even a little frightened, by his request, but it was a gratifying indication of her trust in him that she did as he asked. He returned to the bed and covered her body with his own, kissing her down-swept lids. "Now, open them, and look at me," he commanded forcefully. "Do not take your eyes off my face."

Easing one knee between her legs, he nudged them apart and then used his hand to guide himself. Bewildered, Isobel felt him then, hot and hard, at the moist entrance to her body, and in that moment her natural fear of this ultimate invasion reasserted itself. She began to panic and thresh beneath him. Hating himself, Dominic thrust forward. Her cry tore through him with the force of a crossbow bolt, and he strained every muscle to hold her still, afraid of increasing the pain.

"*Jesu*, Bel, I'm sorry, I'm so sorry." He repeated the words over and over like a litany, all the time softly stroking the hair back from her forehead. "Truly, I am sorry, sweetheart, but there was no other way."

At his penetration she had squeezed her eyes tight shut again in denial. Now she glared up at him and beat at him furiously, her fists impacting against the taut muscles of his back.

"Sorry?" she shouted as she bucked furiously beneath him. "Sorry? You deceitful, lousy, conniving, bastard mercenary! You don't know the meaning of the word. But you will. Oh, yes, you will, I promise you!"

Dominic swore, for her tirade of insults was punctuated by the heaving rotations of her hips as she struggled to dislodge him. In reality, all she achieved was to drive him deeper, sending ripples of beckoning sensation coursing through him. He concentrated on preserving his precarious control and fancied he would have succeeded had it not been for his wife. Quite suddenly her frantic pushing settled into a new and rhythmic motion and the stream of invective directed at him faded until it was lost altogether in her increasingly rapid breathing. For a split second Dominic remained motionless, unable to believe what was happening, but then his body began to respond instinctively to the exquisite play of her internal muscles on his sensitised flesh. Soon Isobel's urgency was matched by his own. He drove relentlessly into her, meeting thrust with thrust until he feared he could bear it no longer. The last remnants of self-control dissolved in a blinding rush as he felt Isobel spasm repeatedly against his shaft. An exultant cry of relief was torn from his throat as Dominic let go and spilled himself inside her.

With the return to conscious thought came the knowledge that Isobel was once again shifting impatiently beneath him. Dominic cautiously opened one eye.

"Well? Don't just lie there like a felled tree," she demanded indignantly, giving him a pointed jab in the ribs. "Get off me."

He winced slightly in protest and levered himself away. Collapsing back onto the down-filled mattress, Dominic turned his head so he could look at her at his side. The expression on her face was reassuring.

"If that is your idea of making me sorry," he told her with a lazy grin, "then I take leave to tell you that I shall be happy to apologise to you on a very regular basis."

Isobel sat up, pulling the sheet with her, and scowled at him. " *'Close your eyes,* ma *Bel,'* " she mimicked, swinging the long rope of her braid back over one bare shoulder. "That was a dirty trick."

Dominic spread his palms upwards and shrugged in token remorse. "What else would you expect from a '*deceitful, lousy, conniving, bastard mercenary*'?—I believe those were your exact words."

"I said nothing that you did not deserve." She heaved the bolster out from underneath them and threw it at him, following it up with a further attack on his ribs.

For answer Dominic caressed the smooth skin of her upper thigh in a subtle circular motion. "It won't hurt like that the next time, trust me," he cajoled.

"*Trust you*? I would not trust you further than I could throw you, you miserable wretch. Anyway, what makes you think there's going to be a 'next time'?" she challenged.

Dominic struck quickly then, pulling her over and positioning her so that she was straddling him.

"Count on it, *ma* Bel," he told her, smiling into her startled eyes. "Count on it!"

His fingers worked deftly to loosen her braid to let her red-gold hair cascade around them both like a waterfall. Admiring her lithe and supple form, Dominic could not deny that whatever misgivings he might have about his wife's upbringing, William de Lescaux's training had endowed her with a magnificent body. He drew her down so he could kiss her again, using his not inconsiderable expertise to coax a response despite her lingering annoyance with him. Although he would have pronounced himself well satisfied just moments ago, Dominic was gratified to feel his manhood thickening again, and it was something that his wife, sitting as she was, could not fail to notice.

"Alais told me they said you were twice the man others were," she remarked provocatively. "Of course, at the time I had no idea what she meant."

Dominic snorted. "Shameless wench!"

"Who, me or Alais?"

"Does it matter?" he whispered huskily, tumbling her beneath him.

Chapter Twenty

Dominic watched his wife indulgently as she proceeded to trounce one of her twin brothers at merels whilst the other looked on, giving what he judged, by the exasperated expressions on the faces of the players, to be less than helpful advice.

Archie MacPherson, lately docked at Pembroke, had ridden the three miles to Pyr to dine by invitation of its lord, and was now taking his ease in the solar with the family, it being much more private than the great hall.

"She's a bonnie lass," he acknowledged, running an appraising eye over Isobel and grinning as she reached out to competently box the ears of the interfering twin. "And useful, by the look of her, too!" He fumbled in the soft leather bag that lay at his feet, withdrew an oiled canvas wrapper, and placed it on the table. "I brought the embroidery silks you asked for, my lord."

Dominic opened it up and eyed the rainbow colours dubiously. "Dare I give them to her?" he wondered aloud, grimacing at his brother-in-law. "Knowing your sister, she'll probably fashion them into an elegant garrotte and use it to strangle me in preference to sewing with them."

"Take no notice of him, Archie," Adam advised, drawing up a stool to sit with them. "I guarantee my sister is as sweet and dutiful a wife as you may care to wish for."

Remembering what his "sweet and dutiful" wife had called him when he took her maidenhead, Dominic could not help but smile. He waited until Adam had settled and poured himself a measure of wine, and then the three men raised their cups in a silent toast.

"So," said Dominic, leaning forward slightly across the table. "What news is there from Ireland?"

"Oh, I've a fine tale for you this time, my lord." The Scotsman took another mouthful of wine, swallowed deeply, and rubbed his hands together with a definite air of relish. "You will recall that when we last met I told you Strongbow was stuck in Dublin, trying to negotiate with O'Connor?"

Dominic nodded.

"Well, it would seem that whilst he was busy trying to find a way out of the city, young Domnall Cavanagh was doing his damnedest to get in—he'd been sent by Fitz-Stephen to tell Strongbow that Wexford was besieged and to demand assistance, if you please."

Adam choked on a mouthful of wine. "Good old Fitz-Stephen," he spluttered, "applying his keen and penetrating mind to the problem as usual. God knows why McMurrough ever bothered ransoming him from the Welsh in the first place—I'd as soon have left him there."

"Granted he's something of a liability in the field," Dominic admitted, "but he's got powerful family connections, you know. Fitz-Gerald, Fitz-Henry, and Raymond le Gros are all tied to him by blood, and I rather suspect their support for McMurrough was somehow dependent upon him using his influence with his Celtic cousins to negotiate Fitz-Stephen's release. Still," he mused, "I'd give a great deal to know exactly what McMurrough offered Rhys ap Gruffydd in return."

"Do ye two clapper-tongued buggers want tae hear what happened, or not?" MacPherson growled in a disgruntled tone.

Dominic slanted him an apologetic look. "Sorry, Archie. Pray continue."

The Scot made a disparaging sound. "Well, now, Strongbow decides that if Cavanagh can get *in*, then he can get *out*, so he takes six hundred men and bursts through the gates bold as you please…" He paused to savour the effect of his words.

Adam's soft expletive confirmed to Dominic that, not unusually, their thoughts shared a similar bent. Survival in their world depended upon an unerring instinct for self-preservation, and both were well aware of the fine line that separated tactical genius from rank stupidity, its boundary being defined only in terms of success or failure.

"Did it work?" he asked, wondering whether he really wanted to know the answer.

"Oh, aye." The Scotsman was smiling, still enjoying their reaction.

"*Jesu*!" Adam shook his head in disbelief.

"Took the wind right out of O'Connor's sails." MacPherson chuckled. "The story I heard is that he was bathing in the Liffey when Strongbow attacked, and by all accounts he evaded capture only by the skin of his teeth. Now that's what ye call being caught with yer breekes down, wouldn't ye say?"

Dominic and Adam grinned appreciatively.

"So where is de Clare now?" Dominic questioned.

"Sitting back in Dublin castle, crowing like a dunghill cock," Archie responded promptly. "It's said he's looted enough corn meal and salt pork from O'Connor's camp to provision the city for a whole year."

"He still needs to do something about Henry's trade embargo," Adam pointed out. "He's bound to have sustained some losses when he stormed out of Dublin like that, and the king's writ put a stop to him recruiting men, as well as obtaining supplies."

"Aye, ye mebbe right at that," MacPherson conceded. "I've a notion that'll be what's on his mind now. There's talk he's sent another emissary to the king, and the word is that this time it's Hervey de Montmorency who's acting as his errand boy."

Adam snorted. "I doubt it will do him any good."

"Hmm, I'm inclined to agree with you there," Dominic admitted. "Good old Uncle Hervey will be received courteously enough, I'm sure, but then I think he'll find himself returning to Ireland on the next available tide with nothing to show for his trouble save a less than polite request for de Clare to get his arrogant arse back to England in person."

"And you think he'll come?" Adam sounded doubtful.

Dominic shrugged. "God knows. But if I were him, I'd be considering my position very carefully. If he doesn't return of his own free will, then I think Henry may very well decide it's time to go over there and drag him back. Either way, I would say Pembroke is lost to him for good, wouldn't you?"

"Better to lose an earldom than your head," Adam observed pragmatically.

Dominic's expression was grim. "If he does decide to return, whatever the circumstances, the chances are he'll come here first."

"And where does that leave us?" Adam asked, having a horrible suspicion he already knew the answer.

Dominic's mouth twisted sardonically. "Oh, I think you'll find that Fitz-Harding's expecting us to provide the welcoming committee."

There was an exclamation of pure disgust from one of the merels players.

"I don't believe it," Stephen complained. "You've won again! How is it that you always win?"

"Because she's smarter than you," Robert told him, with brotherly candour.

His wife was smiling in a manner Dominic was rapidly coming to recognise.

"I don't recall the last time *you* beat me at merels, Robert," she invited, gesturing towards the board.

He groaned and ran his hands through his hair while Archie MacPherson studied the tableau with interest.

"You take yours, I'll take mine?" Adam offered magnanimously, alluding to their respective squires.

"Oh, no." Dominic shook his head emphatically. "That way, *I* still get stuck with two of them. You can have your brothers. I'll deal with my wife."

Adam grinned. Whatever Dominic was planning to do with his wife, he doubted they would be requiring the merels board.

"Done," he said cheerfully. "Care to join me, Archie? I have a feeling I'm going to need reinforcements here."

With a dexterity born from years of practise, he interposed himself between Isobel and the twins, using the presence of their guest to divert his sister by reminding her of her duties as chatelaine.

"You owe me," he told Dominic, as he propelled his brothers forcibly towards the door.

"Yes, I rather think I do," Dominic acknowledged with a gleam in his eye. He lowered his voice so that Isobel, now engaged in animated conversation with MacPherson, would not hear. "Not least for whatever it was you said to your sister that night in the solar."

Adam smothered a snort of laughter. "Never accuse a de Lescaux of cowardice," he advised, "it's as good as a gage in the teeth, any day!"

Chapter Twenty-One

"For the love of God, Richard, stop this," Hervey de Montmorency urged. "Have you forgotten what happened to the last man who thought he could challenge Henry's rule? Christ, if being archbishop wasn't enough to save Becket, what chance do you think you have?"

With a bellow of impotent rage, Richard de Clare smashed his fist into a finely wrought prie-dieu for no other reason than that it had the misfortune to be within range. Montmorency winced, recognising the piece as one of several which had been included in Aoife MacMurrough's dowry. It was of impossibly delicate workmanship—a costly item that reacted to such harsh treatment by splintering into hopeless disrepair. Cursing and cradling his bruised knuckles but apparently otherwise unrepentant, de Clare stalked to the open window and glared out contemptuously at the town of Dublin, his upper lip curling back to display still surprisingly sound teeth for a man of his years.

"I forget nothing," he snarled. "It is Henry of Anjou who conveniently *forgets.* For all his promises, that misbegotten spawn of a she-devil never had any intention of recognising my claim."

"As I recall it," Hervey reminded him patiently, "Henry did not make any promises to you at all. You seized upon a chance remark and interpreted it to suit yourself—as is ever your way, Richard."

"So I am to go running back to England like a tame dog, to lick his boots and beg for a few more meaningless words of favour?"

"I would," Hervey told him with brutal frankness. He sat down, feeling suddenly immeasurably weary. "The fact of the matter is that you have exceeded your licence and now you are being called to account. If you have any sense at all, you will expedite your return to England and at least pretend a degree of humility. That way, there is still a chance you may be able to salvage something from this affair. However much it may hurt to swallow your pride, Richard, I would think it a far more attractive proposition than facing permanent exile—and infinitely preferable to sharing Becket's fate."

"And I suppose Fitz-Harding agrees with you?"

"Fitz-Harding's only interest lies in protecting his investment," his uncle replied with barely concealed irritation, "and he's astute enough to know he'll get precious little return from your rotting corpse."

De Clare kicked moodily with the toe of one boot at a patch of distempered plaster where wall met floor.

"What does Henry want of me?" he demanded petulantly, his handsome features twisted with frustration. "What must I do to hear him say the words that will give me back what's mine by right of blood? I have done everything in my power to gain his approval. I have secured Leinster, routed the Irish army, sent O'Connor back to Connaught with his tail between his legs, and reclaimed Dublin, Waterford, and Wexford in his name. Have I not served him well?"

"You have served yourself better," Hervey felt

compelled to point out. "Henry's agreement was to you aiding McMurrough in regaining what O'Connor took from him by force. He did not expect you to marry the man's daughter and set yourself up as a king in your own right."

"Was it my fault McMurrough went and died?" his nephew countered angrily.

Hervey cast his eyes at the painted ceiling and prayed that God would grant him patience.

"Richard, go back to England and make your peace with the king while you still can," he counselled.

De Clare was silent for a moment, chewing thoughtfully on his thumbnail. "Is Fitz-Godebert still close by Haverford?"

Hervey shrugged. "As far as I know. Why?"

"Because I am going to send him a message. I wish him to know that I am returning to England to make my report to the king, and that I shall require a small armed escort for my safety, for which purpose I should like to engage his services. He can meet us at Pembroke."

Hervey nodded slowly. Richard Fitz-Godebert was a Flemish mercenary who commanded a small but efficient troop of men on a holding not far from the Welsh town of Haverford. It was no secret that Fitz-Godebert had seen service with MacMurrough in the early days of his battle to regain Leinster from O'Connor but had returned to Wales in disgust when MacMurrough had seen fit to treat with the enemy after his defeat at Carlow.

"Probably a wise move," he acknowledged, rubbing his chin as he contemplated his nephew's plan. "There's no saying what Henry's intentions are towards you at the moment."

De Clare snapped his fingers to summon of one of the ubiquitous page boys who waited patiently for just such a call. There was a glimmer of a smile on his face. "Oh, rest assured, dear uncle, if I am going to step into the lion's den, I mean to make certain I have plenty of meat about me."

****

Fitz-Godebert was both entertaining and being entertained when he received the news that a messenger had arrived from the Earl of Pembroke.

"Earl of Pembroke, my arse," he spat derisively as he sat up, abruptly tipping his pouting companion out of his lap. "I'll be Earl of Pembroke before he is." He hoisted an expensive silver-gilt flagon to his lips, took a deep draught, and swallowed, wiping his mouth on his shirt sleeve. "Well, what does the arrogant little git want from me?"

"Your services, my lord," the reluctant herald edged further forward into the room. He was scarce out of boyhood and, to the ill-disguised amusement of Fitz-Godebert's guest, clearly embarrassed by the presence of the two scantily clad whores. "He is returning to England to make his report to the king, and he requests that you meet him at Pembroke. He wishes to engage you to travel with him, my lord, as his escort."

"He's got you marked out as crow fodder, Richard," his guest taunted maliciously.

Fitz-Godebert grinned laconically. "You're just jealous because he's asked for me and not you."

Piers de Bracy snorted, plainly more interested in the enticing cleavage being offered for his inspection. "I doubt Strongbow even remembers my name," he said, his voice muffled by the woman's ample breasts.

"Then perhaps we should remind him, Piers—especially as it looks as if he is coming home. I should imagine he would be quite grateful to know he could count upon your support."

De Bracy pushed the whore away. In the light from the rush dips, the gleam of avarice was clearly visible in his eyes. "How grateful?"

Fitz-Godebert smiled invitingly. "Let's see, shall we?"

****

Adam lounged against the wall of the gatehouse with his back to the sun-warmed stones, watching the approach of his squire with critical appraisal. In the last month or so his brothers had each gained a good inch in height, and even he felt bound to admit that they now boasted an impressive physique. He smiled to himself, recalling Dominic's caustic observation that if the twins were to persist in their habit of stripping off their shirts and heading to the well house after sword practice, his wife had best repair to her still room and lay in supplies of restorative tonic for the benefit of the more susceptible kitchen maids.

He waited with barely concealed impatience as Stephen dismounted and took the reins over the gelding's head.

"Well?" he demanded.

Stephen shrugged, continuing in the direction of the stables. "He seems sound enough."

Adam scowled and fell into step beside him.

"Very amusing. That's not what I meant, and you know it."

Stephen grinned infuriatingly.

"Pembroke's buzzing," he confirmed. "The rumour

is that de Clare's on his way back and has asked Fitz-Godebert to attend him."

Adam let out a low whistle.

"It gets better," Stephen promised, leading the horse into a vacant stall and dropping the bar into place behind him. He removed the bridle and replaced it with a rope halter, tying it short to prevent the horse from nipping his backside as he turned to unfasten the girth. Lifting the heavy saddle away, he set it carefully down on the partition between the stalls and bent to snatch a handful of dry bedding from the floor, sidestepping neatly as the gelding lashed out at him.

"Your bloody nag's got no manners," he remarked, deftly twisting the straw into a wisp and using it with firm strokes on the glossy bay hide.

"Try letting someone geld you and see how it improves your manners," Adam advised dryly. "Anyway, you're my squire. It's your job to teach him some."

Stephen winced and shuddered. "Lost cause," he concluded.

He dropped the wisp, dusted off his hands, and released the horse's head, ducking nimbly under the bar to avoid its snaking neck and snapping yellow teeth.

"Hah, missed me again, you miserable old bugger," he taunted, with unmistakable satisfaction. Flopping onto a pile of sweet meadow hay, he proceeded to settle himself, folding his arms behind his head and crossing his long legs at the ankles.

"Comfortable?" Adam asked sarcastically.

For answer Stephen smiled and patted his impromptu mattress, indicating that Adam should sit down beside him.

"De Bracy's been seen in Fitz-Godebert's company a good deal of late," he revealed, turning his head slightly to look at his brother. "By all accounts, the two of them are so close they're practically sharing the same hauberk."

Adam frowned. "Are you certain?"

Stephen nodded. "Pretty much—although you seem disinclined to believe me?"

"I am," Adam acknowledged grudgingly. "I've campaigned alongside Fitz-Godebert often enough to feel that I know him well, and I'd not have thought there'd be much common ground between him and the likes of Piers de Bracy. Where did you get your information?"

A faint tide of colour washed over Stephen's angular cheekbones.

"I heard it in a tavern," he confessed, "but not by way of ordinary gossip."

His tone was decidedly defensive, and he looked as guilty as sin. Adam hid a smile.

"There's nothing wrong with a little tavern gossip," he allowed. "I'll even admit to having indulged in it myself from time to time…"

"Generous of you," Stephen sniffed. Adam ignored the interruption.

"Am I to understand, however, that on this particular occasion your source was a woman?"

"A rather disgruntled whore," Stephen admitted reluctantly, slanting him a wary glance.

Adam concentrated hard on affecting a suitably stern countenance and managed to deliver the reprimand that his youngest brother was so clearly expecting.

"They're a dangerous breed, boy," he intoned sonorously. The result was extremely gratifying. Stephen's jaw dropped.

"*Jesu*, Adam," he exclaimed in tones of horrified fascination. "You're starting to sound like Papa!"

It was the expression of utter dismay which accompanied this dire pronouncement that finally proved Adam's undoing, and he was unable to prevent himself from exploding with laughter.

"So what happened?" he asked at length, wiping his eyes. "Did someone forget to pay her?"

"Fitz-Godebert, apparently," Stephen responded with a rueful grin. "She and her friend were engaged in pleasuring him and his guest when a messenger arrived from de Clare—and it would seem they rather lost interest at that point."

"I trust *you* remembered to pay her?"

His brother pulled a face. "I paid her for the information, nothing more." He gave a delicate shudder. "I found I had no fancy to go where the likes of de Bracy or Fitz-Godebert—and God knows how many others—had already gone before me."

Adam sighed and shook his head.

"Whoever heard of a discriminating mercenary?" he teased remorsefully. "I wouldn't tell anyone about this if I were you, Stephen. It could ruin your fledgling reputation."

He stood up, giving his erstwhile squire an affectionate poke in the ribs with the toe of his boot and ignoring the predictable yelp of outrage his action provoked.

"Come on, shift yourself, you lazy brat. I need to report to Dominic before supper. And you"—he sniffed pointedly and screwed up his face with exaggerated distaste—"need to wash off the stink of the stables before presenting yourself in the hall." Eyes alight with mischief, he asked, "Shall I get Isobel to have a tub prepared for you, or just warn her that you're planning to sluice off in the well house as usual?"

Stephen's answer was a swiftly extended foot, carefully contrived to send his lord and master sprawling onto the stable midden, and it was a creditable effort. Adam, well aware he had avoided the indignity more by luck than anything else, gave a bloodcurdling yell and lunged after his squire. The ensuing tussle carried them across the bailey to an accompanying medley of hoots, catcalls, encouragement, and advice from their fellow men-at-arms.

Chapter Twenty-Two

Drawn by the commotion, Dominic halted at the top of the steps leading to the great hall and surveyed the scene with a mixture of exasperation and amusement as he acknowledged Sim Walters' cheerful salute.

"Good evening, my lord."

"It was," the Lord of Pyr responded dryly. "Dare I ask who is winning?"

Sim grinned broadly. "Difficult to tell at the moment, my lord, but I'd say the smart money is on your lady wife."

He gestured in the direction of the kitchens, and Dominic groaned as he saw Isobel advancing upon her brothers, armed with a brimming pail of water and clear intent.

Drawing level with the combatants, she launched the contents of the bucket at them, thereby earning herself a rousing cheer from the onlookers. They broke apart immediately, spluttering and protesting loudly. Adam shook himself like a dog and grimaced, whilst a dripping Stephen glared balefully at his sister.

"What did you have to go and do that for, Bel?" he asked in an aggrieved tone. "I almost had him then."

Adam snorted derisively. "In your dreams, little brother," he scoffed.

Isobel folded her arms and regarded both

protagonists with an expression of extreme disfavour.

"You," she said, jabbing a finger at her youngest brother, "are most certainly lacking in respect for your lord. As for *you*…" She rounded on Adam, who was looking distinctly smug. "You should be old enough to know better! I'll teach you to brawl in *my* bailey, Adam de Lescaux…"

Dominic decided it was time to intervene. He hastened down the stone stairway and placed his hands firmly on his wife's shoulders, pulling her off balance and back against him.

"I think you already have, sweeting," he murmured, closing his arms about her waist and giving his brothers-in-law what he hoped was a suitably quelling look. "Go and get yourselves cleaned up," he ordered as sternly as he could.

He steered Isobel back towards the hall, trying to ignore the fact that Robert had quickly fallen into step beside his twin, with whom he now appeared to be in earnest conversation. He had little doubt the subject under discussion was Stephen's performance against their older brother, and that the twins would be doing their utmost to engineer a return match at the earliest possible opportunity. Dominic sighed, and fleetingly wondered whether he should warn Adam, before discarding the notion on the basis that all the de Lescauxs—including his wife—were each as bad as the rest.

"If I were given the task of besieging Lescaux," he said darkly, "I think I should just camp outside its walls and take my ease whilst I waited for you to slaughter one another—it would surely be only a matter of time."

Cheeks flushed and eyes sparkling, Isobel leaned

provocatively into his embrace.

"Ah, but in adversity, my lord, we are as one," she answered pertly. "It is only in peacetime that we de Lescauxs make war upon each other."

Dominic drew her closer. "At this moment, *ma* Bel," he whispered, "making war is the last thing on my mind."

Unable to resist the temptation, he spun her round and kissed her full on the mouth, much to the delight of the assembled audience. The bawdy shouts of encouragement were enough to remind him that he had not yet gained the privacy of the solar, and he drew back, regretfully conceding that he must temper his desire for now, but the expression on his face told Isobel that he considered their personal skirmish far from over. The fact that she returned his look with interest almost made him forget again where they were.

****

Adam, tawny hair still damp from his impromptu bath, accepted Dominic's invitation to sit down and settled himself on a cross-legged stool in front of the fireplace. In doing so, he glanced towards his sister, and his jaw dropped, for she appeared to be thoroughly immersed in the exclusively feminine and undeniably domestic preserve of spinning. Fascinated, Adam found himself following the hypnotic drop and twirl of the weighted spindle—until a discreet cough jolted him from his reverie. He realised Dominic was grinning at him.

"An engaging sight, is it not?"

"I hardly dare ask by what means you have wrought such a miracle."

"Oh, it was easy enough." Dominic was disposed

to enlighten him. "I simply wagered with her that she would not be able to do it."

"Poor Bel," Adam reproached sorrowfully. "She really doesn't stand a chance against an unprincipled wretch like you."

Dominic snorted. "Don't waste your sympathy," he advised. "I have an unpleasant notion that your little sister is already at least one step ahead of me and this will likely cost me dear."

Adam's brows arched speculatively as he considered the expression on his brother-in-law's face.

"I don't suppose you'd care to tell me the nature of this wager?" he essayed hopefully.

Dominic's smile broadened. "Not particularly."

He poured himself a measure of wine and sat down.

"So, what has young Stephen been up to that you needs must beat him about the bailey in so public a fashion?"

Adam grunted. "Little runt tried to pitch me into a pile of horse shit."

Dominic attempted to look suitably grave and disapproving. "One of the disadvantages of having your own brother for your squire, I would say. Mind you, I feel compelled to point out that if you were to call me a 'little runt' I might take exception too."

"I didn't call him that to his face," Adam defended indignantly.

"Probably just as well, in the circumstances." Dominic paused to drink some of the wine in his cup. "Runt or otherwise, your *squire* was gone a while this afternoon."

Adam gave him a wry look.

"I should have known you would mark his absence—there's not much that gets past you, is there? I sent him to Pembroke to see what he could find out."

Dominic leant closer. "And?"

Adam slanted another glance in Isobel's direction to reassure himself she was still otherwise occupied before regaling his brother-in-law with an edited version of Stephen's tale. Dominic propped one elbow on the table and cradled his chin thoughtfully between thumb and index finger. His other hand splayed idly across the smooth, polished wooden surface.

"How reliable do you think Stephen's source was?"

Adam's lips twitched. "Reliable enough."

Dominic's eyes narrowed suspiciously.

"You really don't want to know," Adam assured him. Dominic afforded him a pained look, and Adam almost choked.

"*Jesu*, there's no need to look at me like that. Stephen's no innocent, believe me. And he understands the rules of engagement. I checked."

"God help me if Isobel ever finds out what you've been up to," Dominic muttered feelingly. "No doubt I'll be accused of corrupting another of her precious brothers."

"All the more reason for me to spare you the details," Adam argued reasonably. "That way you can plead ignorance in all honesty. Does Bel really think you corrupted me?" He seemed to find the prospect extremely diverting.

"Of a certainty."

Dominic's response initiated a fresh bout of mirth from Adam, causing Isobel to look up from her task. She frowned repressively at him before returning her attention to what she was doing.

Adam sobered. “So what are we to do now?” he asked.

Dominic shrugged. “What Fitz-Harding intended. Send an immediate despatch to the king and continue to monitor the situation. We need to see if we can intercept de Clare’s link with Fitz-Godebert—find out when he is expected to land and make sure we are in Pembroke at the same time.” He smiled wolfishly. “Coincidentally, of course.”

Adam nodded. “I’ll see to it.” He pushed himself to his feet as the dinner horn sounded. “At least de Clare seems to have realised that the game is up,” he offered cautiously.

“That rather depends on why he’s coming back,” Dominic countered. “If he really is planning to make his peace with the king, then he’d do well to make all haste. My information is that Henry is hell-bent on sailing for Ireland to deal with the matter in person.”

The thread snapped, and Isobel swore. With a well-aimed kick, she consigned her spindle to a corner of the solar, much to the amusement of the room’s two male occupants. She glared at them, as if daring them to say anything.

“Looks like you might win your wager yet,” Adam quipped.

Dominic favoured Isobel with a distinctly lascivious smile.

“I’m counting on it.”

She sniffed disdainfully and stalked towards the door.

“You’ll not be laughing when you’ve no clothes on your back,” she promised, alluding to her lack of skill with the spindle.

Adam grinned slyly at Dominic, deliberately choosing to misinterpret his sister's words.

"Ah, so it was that kind of wager, was it?" He shook his head in mock reproof. "Really, Dominic, I'm surprised at you."

Dominic twitched his shoulders and spread his palms apologetically.

"Men!" Isobel pronounced scathingly.

The sound of their laughter followed her all the way to the hall.

Chapter Twenty-Three

Dominic shrugged out of his robe and sat down on the edge of the bed in which his wife already lay, waiting for him. It was a warm night, and with the exception of the top sheet she had dispensed with the covers. He gave the thin linen a cursory glance and made to draw it back, but Isobel prevented him. Surprised, he let his hand fall.

"What is it, *ma* Bel? You are surely not still angry with me about that business before supper?"

Isobel jerked her head dismissively.

"There are spinsters and cloth merchants aplenty to furnish your needs, without my paltry contribution, and well you know it. What concerns me, my lord, is what you are trying to hide—you and my brother both. You are forever whispering in corners these days."

She sat up, the movement sending waves of red-gold hair cascading over her shoulders and dislodging the sheet. Noting the direction of Dominic's gaze, she hitched impatiently at the fabric. He reached out and idly caressed one bared shoulder, his tanned fingers lingering on the smooth, creamy skin. Isobel gritted her teeth.

"Don't seek to cozen me," she warned.

"Could I?" Dominic asked, already knowing the answer.

She ducked her head and bit his hand. He cursed

under his breath, and his temper, heightened by a substantial helping of lust, flared suddenly. Dominic struggled against the urge to take her there and then, in the heat of his anger. He knew he could do it—was confident he could lose them both in the intensity of physical sensation and force her to acknowledge his mastery, but of late he had found himself wanting something more.

The affection and respect he had once declared was all he required no longer seemed to be enough, and he wanted to feel that when Isobel lay beneath him he possessed not just her body but her entire being—heart and soul. The realisation that he was willing—even eager—to give himself similarly in return, struck him with all the force of a well-placed jousting lance, and he fell back against the bolster, struggling with this newfound and unlooked-for complication. Was this what the troubadours meant when they sang of "love"? Was it possible he was in *love* with his wife?

"Dominic?"

He heard the anxiety in her voice and, for a moment, was almost tempted to tell her the true course of his thoughts. She would probably think he had run mad. Dominic sighed and angled his head slightly, the better to look at her.

"Strongbow is on his way home," he said, hoping she would accept this news as the reason for his preoccupation.

He watched Isobel's fingers work the edge of the sheet into a series of pleats and silently congratulated himself on having successfully avoided the real issue.

"Does this mean there will be trouble?" she asked eventually.

He responded with a harsh bark of laughter.

"God knows! It rather depends on how Henry reacts to the news—and whether he is prepared to wait any longer for de Clare to come to him. I fancy it may already be too late. I think it likely he is even now making for Pembroke with every intention of sailing for Ireland on the first available ship."

"Is that what your father thinks?"

He regarded her with evident surprise, and it was Isobel's turn to laugh.

"Do not look so astonished, my lord," she chided gently. "I have eyes. I guessed it must be one of the Vaillant men who rode in yesterday, from the way Robert and Stephen greeted him. Since he was not from Lescaux, the most likely explanation was that he belonged to your father's household."

Dominic shook his head. "You are too clever by half, *ma* Bel."

If he had thought to distract her with the compliment, he failed miserably. Isobel worried her lower lip between her teeth, unaware that the gesture served to remind Dominic of just how much he wanted to kiss her.

"What will you be expected to do now?"

He smiled engagingly as he reached for her.

"My duty, sweetheart, what else?"

She deliberately evaded his grasp once again, and Dominic groaned in frustration. He sat up.

"I will try to find out why de Clare is here, and whether he poses any threat to the king," he admitted. "Are you satisfied now, madam?"

She ignored him, intent on pursuing her own line of questioning.

"And if he does—what then?"

Dominic shrugged his shoulders.

"Then the threat will have to be removed," he told her uncompromisingly.

"You will kill him?"

He avoided looking at her. "I took an oath, Isobel. My loyalty is to the crown." Dominic ran his hands through his hair. "*Jesu*, I am getting too old for all this."

"Indeed," Isobel murmured. "It is a sore trial for me to be wedded to such a greybeard, but then it seems I, too, must do my duty."

He recoiled as if she had dealt him a physical blow, and Isobel, who had spoken the words by way of a jest to lighten the mood between them, was alarmed at the expression on his face.

"I do but tease, my lord," she offered hastily.

Swift as summer lightning, one arm snaked out and strong fingers closed around her wrist. Dominic jerked her towards him.

"Do you, *ma* Bel, I wonder? Will *this* ever be any more than a duty for you?"

His lips closed over hers in a kiss of breathtaking intensity. When he released her, his eyes were dark with the very emotion he refused to name, but Isobel, for all her lack of years and experience, was quick to recognise it for what it was. She raised her free hand and trailed her fingers down his face, tracing the line of his jaw from cheekbone to chin, feeling the roughness of his beard stubble graze her fingertips.

"It has never been just duty, Dominic," she said softly.

He shook his head in denial.

"You are very young, sweet Isobel. How can you

be so sure, when you have nothing with which to compare?"

"Trust me," she breathed, her lips moving persuasively against his. "Call it women's knowledge, if you will."

She felt his lips curve upwards in the beginning of an answering smile. Dominic raised his head slightly, regarding her quizzically. "Women's knowledge," he mused, his solemn tone belied by the glint in his eye. He lifted her chin on his thumb. "Like knowing how to spin, perhaps? I don't know, ma Bel, if I should trust this knowledge of yours…"

He yelped as, for the second time that evening, Isobel sank her teeth into his unsuspecting flesh.

"Vixen! I will teach you manners yet."

He rolled her beneath him, but instead of the passionate assault on her body that Isobel had hoped for, he began to tickle her. She cried out, her voice muffled against his chest as she writhed in his grip until she was breathless with laughter.

"Oh, please, Dominic, stop, I beg you…"

He knew he should not, but he badly wanted to hear her say it.

"And what is it that you beg for so prettily, sweeting?"

Isobel had no hesitation.

"You, my lord," she said simply. "I want you to love me."

Dominic's heart soared.

"Until the last breath leaves my body, *ma* Bel," he promised, surrendering them both to a pleasure that surpassed all others.

****

Matt Williams lounged against a pile of wooden crates stacked ready for loading. He appeared to survey the dockside comings and goings with the air of a casual observer, but in reality he was watching carefully for the agreed signal from his companion, Giles le Blanc, who was seated on an upturned barrel some fifty yards further along the quay, seemingly engaged in coiling a length of rope. With an almost imperceptible inclination of his head, Giles indicated a fresh-faced youth, clad in expensive Flemish weave, who had just alighted from the merchantman tied up at the jetty. Without haste, Matt drew himself upright and followed.

The task of apprehending de Clare's envoy had fallen to Robert and Stephen de Lescaux, and it was one they had embraced with enthusiasm, but Adam had deemed it expedient to ask the more experienced Matt and Giles to shadow his brothers, just in case anything went awry with their plan. Neither man had objected, since Dominic's latest recruits were universally regarded by their fellow soldiers as convivial company, as well as being something of an intriguing novelty. That aside, the opportunity to visit a thriving local town was never to be missed. Matt smiled to himself. Having been made privy to the twins' intentions, he thought it unlikely that he and Giles would need to dirty their hands on this occasion.

Sauntering down the quay, he nodded genially in Stephen's direction, mentally applauding the ease with which the young man detached himself from the pretty fishwife with whom he had elected to pass the time. Matt dropped back slightly, and Stephen fell discreetly into step behind their quarry. Some ten paces further on, his twin brother stepped suddenly from the shadows of one of the many narrow alleys that linked the quayside with the town. The moment had been timed to perfection. De Clare's messenger halted abruptly, some sixth sense warning him this was no accident. He pivoted quickly on his heel, intending to run, only to find that his adversary had somehow beaten him to it and was already behind him. His head swung round, and his expression changed to one of incredulity.

The twins exchanged a smile, for the reaction of their victim was precisely as they had intended it should be, and before the unfortunate youth had managed to work out exactly what was happening to him, he had been manoeuvred into the alley, where Robert and Stephen set about extracting the information Dominic sought.

Across the street, Matt waited impatiently for them to reappear. When they did so, he was not disappointed. The twins emerged separately, melting into the crowd like mist dispersing in sunshine. Well satisfied, Matt headed back to the hostelry where they had left their mounts.

Both the twins and Giles were there before him, and he greeted them with a grin.

"Well?" he asked expectantly.

"Two weeks from today," Giles confirmed. "Market day again. Presumably he thinks it will be good cover."

Matt nodded, and Giles finished attaching the length of neatly coiled rope to his saddle. He turned to look closely at the twins, studying their faces intently. Dressed identically as they had been for the purposes of their mission today, it truly was impossible to tell them apart—even down to the smug grins on their faces.

"Do you think it was wise to let him go?" he demanded of neither in particular.

"Safer than killing him," one of them answered, through a mouthful of hot mutton pie purchased from one of the many cook shops serving the town. "Fitz-Godebert will be expecting a message from de Clare. If it doesn't arrive, he'll get suspicious."

Giles grunted. "But will the boy talk?"

"Doubtful," commented the other, filching a morsel of pastry out from under his sibling's nose and earning himself a threatening glare. "He was too bloody scared—kept babbling on about devils and witchcraft. Now, if you were him, would you be falling over yourself to carry a tale like that to Richard Fitz-Godebert?"

Giles laughed appreciatively. The Flemish mercenary was renowned for his lack of superstition, and likewise his inability to tolerate any man who was foolish enough to harbour such beliefs. Clearly the twins had discovered this for themselves, and they had put the information to good use. He gave each of them a good-natured shove in the small of the back.

"Come on, then, you pair of hell-spawned brats. I reckon you've time to buy your 'nursemaids' a drink before we head back to Pyr." He winked at Matt. "God knows, we've earned it!"

Chapter Twenty-Four

Beneath the heat of the July sun, Aleyne de Bracy was beginning to feel distinctly unwell. For some weeks now she had been plagued by sickness on rising, and a lowering sense of fatigue that persisted throughout the day. Understandably, she had not mentioned this discomfort to her husband, for she knew it would be of no interest to him. Indeed, when she had dared to demur at the prospect of accompanying him today, he had simply resorted to his customary manner of persuasion, cuffing her round the face and reminding her that she had taken a vow of obedience before the priest who had wed them. Wisely, Aleyne had refrained from pointing out to him that then, as now, she had been given little choice in the matter.

Her husband's friendship with Richard Fitz-Godebert was something to which she had hitherto given little consideration, save to thank God for the fact it had frequently kept him from home and out of her company. Now, riding between the two men, with her stomach churning at every forward motion of the horse, she found herself wondering at it.

Contrary to Piers' assumptions, Aleyne was no simpleton. She was young, being even now only six months past her fourteenth birthday, and she was undoubtedly lacking in worldly experience, but her mind was keen enough, and she had sufficient wit to realise that the Flemish mercenary commanded respect with the same casual ease that Piers bedded women. She cast a covert glance in his direction and was disconcerted to find him watching her. He smiled, inclining his head towards her in acknowledgement of her regard, and Aleyne looked away hurriedly, fearful of drawing her husband's attention.

Fitz-Godebert studied de Bracy's young wife with unease. She was present at his suggestion, to lend credence to the impression that today's outing was no more than a routine shopping expedition. He did not for one moment consider that it would have occurred to her husband to tell her the real purpose of their trip, but from her wan face he doubted anyone would actually be stupid enough to believe she was enjoying herself.

De Clare's instructions were that he was to be met with an armed escort, but Fitz-Godebert, who had long ago made the decision to play by no man's rules but his own, had chosen not to turn his men out in such an obvious show of force. To his practised eye, Strongbow's young messenger had been even more uncomfortable than usual at their last meeting, and the mercenary was certain the boy had been hiding something. He judged it more than likely that at least one other also knew exactly when Richard de Clare was due to set foot on Welsh soil, and so he had ordered a dozen of his best men to make their way independently into town and lose themselves amongst the everyday comings and goings in the vicinity of the quay.

As they drew to a halt before one of the town's less notable hostelries, Fitz-Godebert set his hands about Aleyne de Bracy's slight waist and lifted her from her horse. It was clear to him that she was close to fainting, but neither her husband nor his mannerless lout of a squire seemed disposed to offer her such assistance. Even though his touch was impersonal, he felt her shrink from it and deduced she was accustomed to rough handling. A flicker of pity stirred in him. Surprised by the unwelcome emotion, he turned away from her, focussing his gaze on the busy waterway. Several ships were navigating their way up the narrow channel on the incoming tide, and it was impossible to tell from this distance which one might carry Richard de Clare. There was nothing to do but wait, and since a goodly number of his men were already in position, he suggested to de Bracy that they might seek refreshment for themselves whilst they waited for the ships to dock. It was, of course, entirely unsuitable for Aleyne to accompany them within, and a surly Louis Montierre was thus ordered to see to their horses and attend her outside.

The stench from the untidy, sprawling midden that served the inn grew steadily stronger as the sun climbed higher, and Aleyne's delicate stomach heaved in protest. Blindly she reached out for something against which to steady herself, her fingers closing in desperation around Louis Montierre's leather-clad shoulder. He quickly dislodged them, thrusting her away with such force that she half fell onto a pile of discarded sacking.

"If you are about to disgrace yourself, *lady,* I'd as lief you did not do it over me!"

Aleyne doubled over, retching miserably, while her husband's squire watched with barely concealed amusement.

"Shall I inform my lord of your indisposition?" he

asked, grinning with malicious anticipation. He would not have thought it possible for the girl to lose any more colour than she already had, but to his gratification her pallor increased. She shook her head weakly.

"No, please do not, Louis," she gasped, using his given name in the vain hope of appealing to his long-dormant better nature. "I shall be recovered shortly, I am sure—but if you could perhaps find me some water?"

Montierre needed no second bidding. With a curt obeisance he was gone, disappearing swiftly in the direction taken by Fitz-Godebert and her husband. Aleyne thought it unlikely he would hurry back. She closed her eyes and concentrated, willing the nausea to subside.

"Lady de Bracy?"

Her lids fluttered open, and she blinked at the man leaning over her. They had met only once before—and briefly at that—but a face like his was not easily forgotten. When last he had looked upon her, it had been with an expression of unmistakeable disgust; now, however, Adam de Lescaux's striking hazel eyes held nothing but concern.

"It is Lady de Bracy, is it not?" he persisted. "What do you here alone, my lady? Are you lost?"

Aleyne opened her mouth, intending to reassure him that she was not, only to be assailed by another bout of vomiting. Unlike her husband's squire, he did not back away but instead crouched beside her, supporting her gently until the spasm passed. Detaching a leather costrel from his belt, Adam opened it and offered it to her.

"I would advise small sips," he cautioned with a

wry smile, "even though it is only water."

Not without difficulty, Aleyne swallowed. About to return the flask to him, she suddenly tensed, her eyes widening with fear. Adam did not need to be told why. Slowly he unfolded from his crouch and got to his feet.

"De Bracy," he acknowledged with the merest hint of civility, the fingers of his right hand straying automatically to cover the pommel of the sword at his hip.

"Well, well, well, if it isn't the noble Adam de Lescaux," Piers sneered. "And what brings you to town on this fine morning?" He flicked a glance at his wife. "Aside, of course, from the desire to practise your own peculiar notions of chivalry."

"The same as you, I imagine," Adam responded evenly, heeding the inner voice that told him there was nothing to be gained from trading insults with the likes of de Bracy. He shrugged his shoulders carelessly and schooled his features to impassivity. "It is market day, is it not?"

De Bracy snorted and turned his attention to his wife.

"You are ill, madam?"

"It is nothing, my lord, truly."

Her voice was soft, barely above a whisper, but still Adam could detect the inflection of near panic. Unconsciously his fingers tightened on the sword's serviceable leather grip. De Bracy must have seen the movement, for he smiled. He caught hold of Aleyne's wrist and jerked her roughly to her feet.

"Sweetheart, you should have told me!"

The words appeared solicitous, but she knew he mocked her. The bile rose in her throat again, and she made a small choking sound. Piers released her abruptly and gave her a small push in the direction of his squire.

"Look to my lady's comfort."

Montierre inclined his head with every semblance of dutiful obedience, but the fingers he placed beneath Aleyne's elbow pinched cruelly, and she was unable to stifle a small whimper of pain. Adam forced himself to remain still, well aware that he was being deliberately goaded. A mocking smile dared him to interfere, and for one wild moment he almost considered it.

In pleasurable anticipation, de Bracy observed the muscles in Adam de Lescaux's throat cord with the effort of restraint. His disappointment, when it became obvious the younger man was not going to lose control, was almost tangible.

"Lady de Bracy," Adam bowed stiffly, "I hope you will soon be recovered."

"I should give it about another seven months, my friend," a guttural voice murmured in his ear, "provided, of course, that bearing the babe does not kill her."

Fitz-Godebert affected an air of amused detachment as comprehension dawned and Adam struggled to conceal his shock. The Fleming threw back his head and laughed.

"Christ's bones, de Lescaux, after four years in the company of Dominic du Bois, I'd have thought you beyond caring." He scanned the crowd expectantly. "I take it he is somewhere hereabouts?"

Adam did not trouble to deny it.

"Hmm—I thought as much."

Ignoring de Bracy's outraged expression, Fitz-

Godebert placed his arm about Adam's shoulders in a gesture that bespoke old acquaintance, reflecting that had Dominic not beaten him to it, this man might even now be serving in his own company. Deliberately he drew him slightly away so they might converse without being overheard.

"I hear that your lord is also recently wed—and to your sister, no less. Quite a coincidence, is it not, that her dower estates should lie in this part of the world?"

"You are no more a believer in coincidence than I am, Richard," Adam retorted tersely. "You know exactly why we are here."

Fitz-Godebert nodded. "Then I do but return the compliment. Tell me, what did you do to de Clare's messenger?"

Adam's bland expression neither confirmed nor refuted any involvement, and Fitz-Godebert grinned.

"Ah, well, it is of little consequence. Listen to me, Adam. I've no quarrel with you or Dominic—although God knows it is easier to make enemies than friends in our business. Whichever side we may find ourselves fighting for in the immediate future, you should know that de Bracy waxes most eloquent on the subject of your sister, especially when he is in his cups. Tell Dominic from me to watch his back—and hers."

"Honour amongst mercenaries?" Adam asked sardonically.

"Tell anyone else, and you're a dead man," Fitz-Godebert promised.

Adam inclined his head in the briefest acknowledgement and was gone, leaving Fitz-Godebert to dwell with increasing disfavour upon the petulant countenance of his present comrade-in-arms.

"How is it that you are on such friendly terms with du Bois' lapdog?" de Bracy demanded aggressively.

"Jealousy does not become you, Piers," the Fleming counselled him, rather in the manner of a tolerant parent reprimanding a tiresome child. "And you would do well to remember that more flies are caught with honey than with vinegar," he added cryptically.

Chapter Twenty-Five

Dominic lounged watchfully against the outer wall of Richard de Clare's principal keep whilst his wife negotiated what she considered to be a fair price for six inches of beautiful—and potentially lethal—pattern-welded steel. His twin brothers-in-law had remained at home on this occasion, since it was likely de Clare's emissary would be amongst those accompanying his master on the voyage home, and Dominic was keen that they should not run the risk of being recognised. Naturally, they had been disappointed, but they had also been entirely sensible of and gratifyingly in agreement with his reasoning. Catching sight of Adam wending his way along the crowded main street, he raised one arm by way of greeting.

"Is that wise?" Isobel's brother asked, with a nod and a smile in her direction as he arrived at her husband's side.

"Probably not," Dominic admitted ruefully, "but you know I like to live dangerously, and that pretty toy she uses for eating would be no use to her against anything tougher than a stuffed capon."

Adam frowned, recalling his encounter with Fitz-Godebert.

"Are you worried for my safety?" Dominic teased.

"Christ, no." Adam shook his head. "Leastways not from her," he qualified.

Dominic's amused look turned to one of mild enquiry, and Adam sighed.

"I've just seen Fitz-Godebert down on the quayside," he offered by way of explanation, "in the company of de Bracy and his unfortunate lady."

"Did he see you?"

"Oh, yes. More than that. He acknowledged me openly."

Dominic nodded thoughtfully. "What did he say?"

"Enough to confirm he's still in de Clare's pay at present, and to let me know he's aware you are here on behalf of the crown. He asked me what we'd done to Pembroke's messenger."

Dominic laughed. "I trust you didn't tell him?"

"No," Adam agreed. "But he told me something—two things, really. First and foremost, he seemed anxious to assure me that he personally has no quarrel with either of us."

"I suppose that's comforting to know," Dominic conceded cautiously, "and the second thing?"

Adam glanced uncomfortably at Isobel. "The second thing was a warning to you. He said to tell you that de Bracy displays an unhealthy interest in your wife, and that you should watch your back—and hers."

Dominic's mouth tightened. He had first encountered Richard Fitz-Godebert in his early days on the tourney circuit, and, since then, had fought alongside him on many occasions. The Fleming was astute, experienced, and not easily unnerved. If he had seen fit to issue such a caution, it would not be without reason. His eyes rested broodingly on the slender figure of his wife.

"Dominic?" Adam touched him lightly on the arm.

With difficulty he tore his gaze from Isobel and focussed once again on her brother.

"I remember you telling me on my wedding night that your sister knew how to keep and use a blade?"

Adam grinned. "You must be doing something right, or you'd have found out for yourself by now."

Dominic very properly ignored him.

"In the circumstances, perhaps it's just as well she's had such an unusual education. Did you manage to find Archie?"

Adam shook his head. "No, but he was here yesterday. He sailed for France on the morning tide, with a cargo of hunting dogs, would you believe? He left a message for you, though—with the landlord of *Y Ci Du*—rather appropriate, don't you think?"

Dominic stared at him blankly.

"The Black Dog," Adam translated obligingly. "Honestly, Dominic, don't tell me you haven't managed to learn any Welsh at all yet."

Dominic grunted. "I have not your flair for languages, it would seem."

"If you think I am quick, you should hear the twins," Adam told him. "It's a pity they're so tall and fair—otherwise we might have been able to pass them off as Cymru born and bred within another couple of months. Now, that would have made them really useful."

"Oh, I think your little brothers have more than proved their worth already," Dominic responded dryly. "What was the message?"

"It is as your father predicted. Henry has tired of waiting for de Clare to come to him, and now he's coming here."

"Hell and damnation!" Dominic swore softly. "Do we know when he is expected?"

Adam shrugged. "As to that, I cannot be sure—but thanks to your telling him when de Clare was expected to arrive, I would say that of a certainty he plans to be here before Strongbow has a chance to consolidate his position, so tomorrow, maybe, or the day after."

Dominic's gaze narrowed. "Do you think Fitz-Godebert knows about this yet?"

"No." Adam was definite. "He is not stupid. I fancy he would not risk his men in open confrontation against the kind of force Henry could raise, whatever de Clare might have promised him."

Dominic nodded, seemingly satisfied. "Then I need to see him, and without his friend Piers in attendance. It's just possible that Fitz-Godebert might be able to talk some sense into de Clare before it's too late."

"What makes you think he would be willing to try?" Adam was curious.

"Because," said Dominic, with a wry twist of his lips, "I shall promise him that, whether he succeeds or not, he may be sure Fitz-Harding—and the king—shall hear of his diligence."

Adam shielded his eyes from the glare of the sun whilst he judged its position. "They will have docked by now. Are we going to make our presence known?"

Dominic shrugged. "I see no reason not to, especially since Fitz-Godebert is already half expecting us—I'd hate to disappoint him." He sauntered over to Isobel, who was in the throes of concluding her business with the knife-seller, and enquired as to the amount she had agreed to pay. When she named the figure, he could not help but be impressed.

"Your lady drives a hard bargain, my lord," the beleaguered merchant informed him in an aggrieved tone.

Dominic flashed him a commiserating look as he tendered the required sum.

"Tell me something I don't know!" He placed a proprietary hand on his wife's arm and guided her back to where Adam waited for them.

"Is Captain MacPherson here?" Isobel asked hopefully. The Scotsman had fascinated her with his interesting and apparently inexhaustible store of anecdotes when he had been persuaded to stay the night at Pyr.

"Why, haven't you made enough assaults on your husband's purse for one day?" her brother teased. "Surely you cannot have used *all* those silks already, Bel—what can you have been doing with them?"

Isobel smiled sweetly at him. "Would you care to see my latest purchase, Adam?"

She brandished the package invitingly and he flipped it deftly out of her hands, ignoring her indignant protest.

"I think I'd prefer to admire this from a distance," he told her, with a conspiratorial wink at Dominic. "I did try to tell your doting husband that he was making a grave mistake, but he would have none of it."

Dominic snorted as Adam presented the neatly wrapped parcel to him with a flourish and a grin. Isobel retaliated by poking out her tongue at him, whereupon he promptly returned the gesture, with interest. Dominic rolled his eyes and shook his head.

"*Jesu*, you two are every bit as childish as Robert and Stephen."

Chapter Twenty-Six

It was just a little after midday when Richard de Clare's feet, clad in a particularly fine pair of gilded leather boots, stepped off the ship that had brought him home. He paused to savour the moment, relishing the warm July sunshine and sniffing the air like an old hound on the trail of a familiar scent.

Betraying no hint of his growing lack of enthusiasm for the task, Fitz-Godebert moved forward to greet his paymaster with a suitably deferential bow, but his mood of disquiet intensified when de Clare made only cursory acknowledgement of the salutation, his gaze sweeping dismissively over the mercenary and coming to rest on his three companions.

"Where is my escort?" he demanded.

For an instant Fitz-Godebert actually considered telling the self-proclaimed Earl of Pembroke to go to hell, before the discipline of years re-exerted itself and instead he tendered his prepared explanation.

"My lord, as I could not be entirely certain what other arrangements might have been made in respect of your return, I judged it best not to draw such attention to your presence. As you can see, I am presently in the company of Sir Piers and his good lady, but my men are nearby, and do but await my command."

"Very commendable," Hervey de Montmorency was heard to approve from somewhere behind his nephew's left shoulder.

De Clare ignored the interruption.

"You have reason to believe that my arrival may be anticipated?" His piercing eyes settled unerringly on the liveried youth bringing up the rear of his small entourage.

Fitz-Godebert saw the boy's face pale to the unhealthy hue of raw pastry and was once again assailed by the same sense of pity that Aleyne de Bracy had aroused in him. Seriously wondering whether he was beginning to lose his edge, he nevertheless sought to draw Strongbow's attention away from the lad.

"My lord may have heard—Dominic du Bois has recently been granted land in this vicinity?"

"Du Bois?" De Clare tested the name, then shrugged. "Should I know him?"

"He served you in Ireland, my lord," Fitz-Godebert enlightened. "His profession was, until lately, the same as my own."

"A common soldier?"

De Montmorency winced inwardly and risked a glance at the Fleming's face, but if the mercenary had taken offence he gave no sign of it.

"Not so very *common*, my lord," Fitz-Godebert advised. "Dominic du Bois is the natural son of Hubert le Vaillant."

De Clare assimilated this detail, the corners of his mouth twisting scornfully. "Really? And what, I wonder, can Vaillant's by-blow have done to merit such largesse?"

"I understand he married, my lord," Fitz-Godebert responded smoothly. "It is, I believe, a most effective means of preferment—for bastards and nobles alike."

De Montmorency choked, earning himself a repressive frown from his nephew.

"And to whom did he manage to ally himself quite so advantageously?"

"To the daughter of William de Lescaux, my lord."

"De Lescaux?" Strongbow was clearly surprised. "I did not even know he had a daughter. You are certain of this?"

"The girl's existence was something of a revelation to us all, my lord." De Bracy chose to enter the conversation, taking advantage of the moment to bring himself to de Clare's notice.

The earl snorted contemptuously. "Is she some ill-favoured simpleton, that her father should seek to keep the world in ignorance of her?"

De Bracy opened his mouth to reply, but Fitz-Godebert forestalled him.

"Why not judge for yourself, my lord?" he invited, indicating in the direction of the steep pebbled slope that served as the principal thoroughfare between the quayside and Pembroke's main street.

Observing the startled expression on de Clare's face, Fitz-Godebert knew an almost irresistible urge to smile. Whilst Dominic's name had meant nothing to the arrogant earl, it was clear he had immediately recognised the man himself.

"His companion is Adam de Lescaux," he supplied helpfully, enjoying Pembroke's discomfiture and seeing no reason why he should not add to it. "He is Lord William's third son and du Bois' second in command."

De Clare's lips thinned.

"I'd hardly describe *that* as ill-favoured," Hervey de Montmorency commented dryly, his eyes on the figure of the young woman who walked demurely between the two men. "Although whether or not she is a simpleton remains to be seen."

"Oh, there is naught wrong with her mind, either," de Bracy assured him with a salacious grin.

Strongbow regarded him with renewed interest. "You are well acquainted with Lady du Bois, Sir Piers? Perhaps, then, you can enlighten me as to why her father and her estimable brothers would have agreed to such an obvious *mesalliance.*"

The knight coloured angrily. "Le Vaillant would have it that the match was an arrangement of long standing, my lord, but I have good reason to believe it was arranged hastily, and that William de Lescaux agreed only to avoid the shame of his daughter's dishonour."

At this, de Clare threw back his head and laughed. "So Dominic du Bois is the author of his own fortunes?" he mused. "Mayhap the difference between us is not so great after all. As it would seem that congratulations are in order, I think I shall presume upon our previous acquaintance."

He stepped forward with an air of such regal assurance that his companions were left staring open-mouthed after him. Fitz-Godebert was the first to recover his scattered wits.

"*Jesu*, it's no wonder King Henry is worried for his crown," he muttered under his breath, as he hastened in pursuit.

Hervey de Montmorency, following close behind, said nothing, but his face was troubled.

Dominic bowed before the undeniably commanding figure of the Earl of Pembroke, managing with commendable aplomb to conceal his surprise as his wife sank into an elegant curtsey at his side, the like of which he had not known she numbered amongst her accomplishments.

De Clare bent his head a mere fraction in response before extending his hand to Isobel and assisting her to rise.

"Dominic du Bois, is it not?" He spoke with careless confidence, his eyes raking Isobel's figure with a boldness that verged on insolence. "I was informed that you had recently married—it would seem you are indeed to be congratulated on your good fortune."

Dominic reclaimed his wife's hand from de Clare's and carried the fingers caressingly to his own lips, exerting a slight warning pressure before releasing them.

"As you can see, my lord, I am entirely sensible of my *good fortune* and intend to do all in my power to safeguard it."

The words were double-edged. Subtle advice, if Strongbow cared to heed it.

"A man does what he must," de Clare responded obliquely, choosing to continue the deliberate ambiguity of the conversation.

"Indeed, my lord," Dominic inclined his head in agreement.

De Clare nodded affably and strolled back to his waiting companions. He watched with narrowed eyes until Dominic and his party had passed out of sight, then turned to Fitz-Godebert.

"I want *him* put out of the reckoning," he said, uncompromisingly.

"Permanently, my lord, or just temporarily?" The

Fleming had drawn his dagger during de Clare's exchange with Dominic and was now examining the blade minutely, as if assessing its suitability for the task.

"That's your affair," the earl responded with supreme indifference, choosing to ignore his uncle's hastily smothered gasp of protest.

De Bracy stepped forward eagerly. "Permit me to take care of du Bois, my lord? A little distraction on his own borders should be enough to keep him from meddling in matters that are no concern of his."

De Clare regarded him impassively. De Bracy had made no attempt to hide his interest in the admittedly tempting Lady du Bois, and it took little imagination to envisage what form his planned "distraction" would take. His lips compressed again as his gaze fell on the hunched figure of de Bracy's own wife. The girl seemed to retreat even further into the shadow of her hooded cloak beneath his stare. It was hardly surprising that her husband needed to look elsewhere for his satisfaction. Still, it was the man's own fault for taking a child bride and bedding her before she was ready. He smiled to himself. De Bracy was a fool and therefore expendable.

"As you wish," he nodded curtly.

Fitz-Godebert summoned a sour grin in response to de Bracy's look of triumph, whilst reflecting that the troubled waters in which he had initially thought to dabble for his own profit were rapidly becoming far too deep and murky for comfort. Uncle Hervey had been busy telling anyone who would listen that his nephew's sole reason for returning to England was to effect reconciliation with his liege lord. But if that was indeed the case, why would de Clare be so keen to have Dominic du Bois removed from the field? If he really intended to make his peace with the king, then Dominic, obviously the recipient of royal favour at present, should surely be cultivated rather than cut down? Whether de Montmorency was privy to his nephew's plans or not, Fitz-Godebert was willing to bet the renegade earl was not yet ready to abandon his ambitions entirely; and that made his own position precarious.

Unless he was very much mistaken, the majority of de Clare's support remained firmly on the other side of the glittering expanse of water separating Ireland from Wales. Even had it been camped nearby and ready to mobilise at a moment's notice, it was Fitz-Godebert's professional opinion that Strongbow's chances of waging a successful campaign against the combined might of the Angevin empire were negligible. His instinct for self-preservation, honed to a high degree by more than a decade at the top of his profession, was screaming at him to do what he must and distance himself from the disaster that would inevitably follow outright rebellion.

There was also the matter of his admittedly ill-conceived association with de Bracy. The man's obsession with Dominic's wife unsettled Fitz-Godebert greatly. By his own peculiar code he had always taken pains to avoid using women and children as bargaining counters, and he possessed an inherent contempt for anyone who fell short of his own exacting standards.

Fitz-Godebert decided it was time to seek a meeting with Dominic du Bois, and to see about getting himself back on the winning side.

Chapter Twenty-Seven

"Well?" Adam queried impatiently, as he fumbled a crust of bread from his pouch and proffered it to the inquisitive muzzle thrusting expectantly against him. "What do you think?"

"God's teeth, how am I supposed to know?" Dominic exploded, tugging at his hair with frustration. "He's about as transparent as a horn beaker! You heard him for yourself: 'A man does what he must.' It could mean anything. Pembroke may just be a convenient stopover on his way to prostrating himself before the king in abject apology, but he could just as easily have come here in the hope of persuading the Welsh to join the Irish in a full-scale revolt. It's impossible to tell."

He gnawed his thumbnail distractedly.

"Adam, I want you to escort Bel home. Take Matt Williams with you. Then come back here with the rest of the troop, including Robert and Stephen. Leave those currently on light duties to protect Pyr—and tell Sim that he is to take command of the garrison."

He glanced at his wife as if anticipating some protest from her, but she said nothing. It occurred to him that she was unnaturally pale, and he was assailed by an uncomfortable feeling that her pallor had some special significance, for he seemed to recall having seen her look similarly once before. He racked his memory trying to recapture the occasion and, in the same moment it came to him, he knew Adam too, had guessed what was wrong.

"Oh, *Jesu*, Bel, not now," her brother groaned.

"I'm all right," she flared at him. "You needn't worry that I'll slow you down."

Adam looked searchingly at her, wondering uneasily whether his sister could be suffering from the same malady as Aleyne de Bracy and realising, with an uncomfortable jolt, that it was entirely possible. He opened his mouth as if to say something, then thought better of it. "I'll find Matt," he offered helplessly.

"Well, get a move on," Isobel snapped back irritably. "The sooner, the better."

Watching him go, she clenched her hand, pressing the knuckles against her mouth. She dropped her head quickly, but not before Dominic saw the telltale glint of tears. With an oath, he gathered her to him.

"Bel, don't, please. It will serve no purpose."

"Do you think I do not know that?" she retorted. "I vowed that when the time came I would not be like this, but now I find I cannot help it." She broke free of his hold and looked up at him. "Will you promise me something, Dominic?"

He looked uncomfortable. "If it be within my power."

"Don't take any unnecessary risks."

He could not help laughing. "There speaks a true mercenary's wife." He smoothed a stray tear from the curve of her cheek with the ball of his thumb. " 'Don't take any *unnecessary* risks.' Yes, I believe I can promise you that, sweetheart, and gladly, but you in return must do something for me."

He reached to his belt and withdrew the carefully

wrapped package. As he unwound its protective bindings, sunlight flashed blindingly on the wickedly sharp silver-blue blade. Isobel took it from him and felt the carved bone handle warm almost immediately to her touch. It was oddly reassuring.

"*No unnecessary risks*," he repeated her own words, looking at her sternly. "It is a bargain between us—agreed?"

"Agreed," she murmured softly.

Taking her old knife from its wool-lined leather sheath at her girdle, she settled the new one in its place, rewrapped the spare blade, and thrust it down her boot.

Dominic smiled and shook his head ruefully. "Bel, you are a jewel beyond price, and I most assuredly do not deserve you."

For answer, she stood on tiptoe and touched her lips to his. His arms came round her again, and he pressed her close.

"Take care, my lord," she murmured.

"And you, *ma* Bel."

Abruptly she disengaged from his embrace. Accepting Matt's assistance to mount, she sent her mare forward into a canter without warning and was quickly gone. With a startled oath, the young man swiftly gained his own saddle and hastened after her.

"Be back before curfew." Dominic spoke tersely to his brother-in-law. "I'll be at the Rose."

He named the waterfront tavern where Archie had first told them of MacMurrough's death and de Clare's claim to the kingship of Leinster. Adam nodded and, with a final salute, spurred his horse in the direction of the main gate.

"Christ's bones, du Bois, don't tell me no one ever

counselled you against the folly of wearing your heart on your sleeve for all to see?"

Dominic spun round sharply to find Richard Fitz-Godebert's grinning face level with his own. "Mind, I'll grant you she's a pretty piece—I might even have been tempted myself."

With lightning speed Dominic's arm snaked out, and to his astonishment the Fleming found himself pinned back against the stableyard wall. The savagery of the response surprised him, and he automatically raised open palms in a universally recognised gesture of submission.

"*Pax*, Dominic. As I told your brother-by-marriage earlier, I've no quarrel with you—and I'd as lief keep it so. We need to talk."

Dominic loosed his hold. "I was about to come looking for you," he admitted tersely.

"So I've saved you the effort," Fitz-Godebert said equably, straightening the heavily braided neck of his tunic with a reproachful look at the man responsible for its disarray. "*Jesu*, man, you look as though you need a drink—I know I do—and since I don't suppose either of us would care to have this conversation overheard, 'tis best we take it somewhere else."

Forging a determined path through the crowds, Fitz-Godebert set off in the direction of a row of slate-roofed cottages that bordered the far side of the market square. He stopped outside one whose smooth walls were tinted a delicate shade of pink—a local specialty which Dominic knew was achieved by the not-so-delicate means of adding a quantity of fresh pig's-blood to the lime wash. Stooping to peer through the unshuttered window, Fitz-Godebert gave a grunt of satisfaction.

"All the comforts of home," he pronounced, pushing open the door. "Although from what I hear, your expectations these days may be somewhat higher than mine."

Dominic arched his brows questioningly, and Fitz-Godebert responded with an eloquent grin.

"It belongs to a friend of mine," he explained, "and as you can see, she's out."

One hand on his sword hilt, Dominic ducked warily under the lintel. If this was a trap, then in all likelihood his enemies would strike now, whilst he was still adjusting to the sudden darkness after the bright sunlight outside. He held his breath, waiting.

Fitz-Godbert favoured him with a longsuffering look, then glanced once back up and down the thoroughfare before quietly closing the door. Gesturing at the two rough-hewn chairs drawn up beside an equally crudely fashioned table, he indicated Dominic should sit down. From a stone cist by the open hearth he retrieved an earthenware flagon and two pottery beakers. The wine was cool, smooth, and surprisingly good.

"Won't your 'friend' object to you making so free with her hospitality in her absence?" Dominic asked wryly.

Fitz-Godebert shrugged. "I pay her enough for her understanding." He raised his cup in salute. "Besides, this is mine anyway—believe me, it would be wasted on her." He took a deep drink and swallowed, savouring the taste. "So are we going to sit here exchanging pleasantries, or are you going to tell me what you're up to?"

Involuntarily Dominic smiled. "I'll show you mine, if you'll show me yours?'"

"Something like that," Fitz-Godebert grinned back in return.

Dominic leaned forward suddenly. "I want to know what stakes de Clare is playing for."

The Fleming sighed mournfully and shook his head. "And there I was hoping you would be able to tell me." His eyes gleamed. "Damn it, du Bois, does that mean I've enticed you here and plied you with my best Anjou all to no purpose?"

He raised his cup to his lips again and took another draught, swilling it appreciatively round his mouth.

"All I've been asked for so far is to provide him with a small armed escort, ostensibly for his own personal safety. As I understand it, I am to accompany him to wherever Henry requires him to present his miserable carcass, and then I am to kick my heels in some antechamber whilst he pleads his cause. Mind you, if it all goes horribly wrong, then I'd lay odds he's counting on me to risk my neck and get him out of there with his intact."

"Well, at least you'll be spared the additional hazards of a lengthy journey," Dominic advised him consolingly. "According to my information, Henry has grown tired of waiting. He's on his way to Pembroke now, although I doubt he'll be in the mood to listen to any of the minstrel's lays de Clare may be planning to sing for him."

Fitz-Godebert swore colourfully. "When do you expect him?"

"Today or tomorrow."

"What kind of force is he travelling with?"

“I don’t know—and that’s the truth,” Dominic added hastily, in response to the Fleming’s sceptical expression. A solitary woodlouse trundled industriously across the table between them. “Do you think de Clare’s amenable to reason?”

Fitz-Godebert spluttered into his drink, and Dominic raked his fingers through his hair in frustration.

“Look, Richard, there’s no profit in this for either of us at the moment. You must know that de Clare is still heavily in debt to Fitz-Harding, and you don’t need some conjuror with a crystal ball to tell you that if Henry decides to arraign him for treason, you won’t get so much as a penny for your trouble. If, on the other hand, *you* were able to convince de Clare to be suitably contrite by the time the king gets here, then I guarantee Fitz-Harding will get to hear who was responsible for such a miraculous feat.”

The Fleming groaned. “It would be a bloody miracle, at that! Why is it, whenever I find myself working with you, du Bois, *I* always end up with the shit part of the bargain?”

Dominic flashed him a smile and clapped him on the shoulder bracingly.

“Cheer up, Richard. This one’s a winner for you either way. Even if de Clare manages to resist your blandishments, I promise to make sure Fitz-Harding knows you tried.”

“You are going to owe me,” Fitz-Godebert threatened, “in this life and the next.”

“You’ve a better chance of getting your dues from me than from Richard de Clare,” Dominic assured him. “Thank you for the warning, by the way.”

"Warning?" Fitz-Godbert's brow creased. "Oh, Christ! Listen, Dominic, after your interesting little interlude on the quayside with de Clare, he ordered me to see to it that you were 'taken out of the reckoning,' as he so quaintly put it, and whilst I was still busy trying to thinking of a way to answer him, de Bracy stepped in and offered to do the job for me. He suggested that a distraction on your own borders would be enough to keep your nose out of other people's business. He means to snatch your wife, Dominic, and when it comes to what he intends to do with her, I doubt you'll be needing conjurors and crystals any more than I will."

Dominic swore and thumped the table with his fist. "*Jesu*, Richard, why didn't you tell me this before? I've just sent her back to Pyr, with only Adam and one other man to escort her." He shot to his feet and Fitz-Godebert, correctly anticipating his intention, thrust himself hurriedly between Dominic and the door.

"Wait!" The single word was barked like an order, and it was the tone more than the command itself that halted Dominic in his tracks.

"For Christ's sake, use your head," Fitz-Godebert urged. "If you don't, you'll end up walking straight into whatever trap he sets to catch her, and then he'll have both of you. Just imagine what that would do for the little turd's self-esteem."

"I don't give a damn about his self-esteem." Dominic forced the words through lips white with fury. "What the hell were you thinking of, harnessing yourself to a gutter-sweeping like him?"

Fitz-Godebert pulled a face. "An unfortunate lapse of judgement on my part, which, believe me, I have been regretting ever since I sobered up enough to realise the full implications of my folly." He shook his head. "I'm getting old, Dominic—starting to make mistakes. Maybe it's time I thought about retiring."

"Not before we've settled this."

Fitz-Godebert sighed and nodded in resignation. "Agreed. So what would you have me do?"

Chapter Twenty-Eight

Although his acquaintance with Isobel du Bois was one of comparatively short duration, Matt Williams was confident the lady well understood the dangers of out-riding her escort. Accordingly he had followed at a tactful distance, thinking to allow her time to regain her composure. Aware that someone now approached from behind at speed, Matt's head whipped round as he transferred both reins into one hand in a practised movement and placed the fingers of the other in readiness on the pommel of his sword. As horse and rider drew close enough to be recognised, he saw that he need do no more than raise his arm in greeting. Having done so, he returned his attention to Lady Isobel. She had drawn rein and was now apparently waiting for him to catch up with her, but as Matt closed the distance between them, he realised with a growing sense of unease that his lord's wife was peering intently towards an untidy tangle of brush bordering the strip of woodland that edged the road ahead.

"My lady?"

Isobel flashed him an apologetic smile. "I am worse than Roisin," she excused. "Belike I am jumping at shadows."

Matt followed the direction of her gaze, scrutinizing the thick foliage carefully. Had such sentiments been expressed by any woman other than the one currently at his side, he might readily have agreed; but such was his respect for Lady Isobel that he was disposed to be cautious. He waited expectantly.

"I cannot be sure…" Isobel admitted hesitantly, "but for a moment I thought I saw…"

"Sunlight catching on the edge of a blade," Adam advised grimly as he rode up to join them.

He attempted to manoeuvre his own mount protectively closer to his sister's, only to have the ungrateful Roisin respond with a snake of her long neck and a vicious snap of teeth. Adam swore, just managing to wrench himself out of the way in time.

"Christ *Jesu*! Get that *thing* under control, Bel."

Isobel scowled at him and ran a soothing hand down the mare's neck, allowing Matt to ease himself as close to the fractious Roisin as he deemed prudent. One by one, mounted men began to emerge from the trees.

"Outlaws?" Matt suggested hopefully.

"God knows," Adam muttered, glaring back at his sister. "But I think it's safe to assume that if they were about any honest business they'd be using the road openly, like the rest of us."

"So what do we do?" Matt probed. "Make for home and try to outrun them, or turn and ride hard back to Pembroke?"

To his surprise, it was Isobel who provided the answer.

"You and Adam will go back, and I will go on—alone."

Both her escorts gaped at her in utter stupefaction.

"Those are de Bracy's men," she said quietly, as if that would settle the matter.

Adam reached across and grabbed hold of her arm.

"And just how, pray, can you know that?" he demanded angrily.

Isobel sighed. "I don't, not for certain, but his squire is most definitely with them."

Her fingers tightened unconsciously on the reins, causing Roisin to sidle sideways and barge the shoulder of Matt's gelding. The bigger horse backed off on its hocks with a surprised snort, and Isobel immediately relaxed her grip, automatically tendering an apology. She uttered a soldier's oath that, despite the gravity of their situation, had Matt's lips twitching.

"This will be de Clare's doing!"

"You just said they were de Bracy's men," Adam reminded her irritably.

Isobel shot him an impatient look.

"For heaven's sake, Adam, de Clare's no fool, even if you are. It's obvious he recognised you and Dominic this afternoon. He knows you've been sent here to safeguard the king's interests, so now he's seeking a way to control the damage you can do, and he thinks to use me as his bargaining piece. As to these being Piers de Bracy's men, I have no doubt their master is only too eager to do de Clare's bidding, especially if he thinks it will further his own ambitions into the bargain. You must return to Pembroke at once. Warn Dominic, tell him…"

Adam exploded. "*Jesu*, Bel, what do you imagine Dominic is going to do to me—and Matt, here—if we return without you? Never mind our admitting we actually *allowed* you to be taken. I'll tell you, shall I?" Adam continued, ignoring the fact that his sister had opened her mouth to respond. "He'll find the nearest serviceable crossbeam and string us both up, that's what he'll do, and you may rest assured that my being his brother-by-marriage will not deter him for an instant!"

Isobel shook her head. "Adam," she urged, "you are not thinking clearly. If I am right, I am their main objective, and I'm willing to wager that whoever is responsible for this will have given orders that I am not to be harmed. You and Matt, on the other hand, will have no such protection. We are outnumbered, and they will have no compunction about killing you. Their orders will be to take me. If I run, they will have no option but to pursue me. They will not waste time and men in chasing after you. Do you not see? It is your only chance."

From the agonised expression on Adam's face, Isobel could see that he knew the sense of her argument, and she gathered her reins in readiness, but even as she did so, her brother leant forward again, grabbing hold of Roisin's bridle. His eyes were bright with emotion, every fibre of his being screaming denial against what he was about to let her do. He maintained his grip, ignoring the mare's squeal of protest. Against the dark, well-oiled leather, his clenched fingers were white with tension.

"What the bloody hell am I meant to tell Dominic?" he wondered aloud. "Assuming, of course, that he grants me the opportunity of saying anything at all, once I confess to having lost you."

Isobel considered the question for a moment, then her lips curved upwards in the beginnings of a smile.

"Tell him I decided that this was *a necessary risk*."

"You think that will make a difference?" Adam derided.

Isobel shrugged. “Very well, you may tell him also that I said he is to remember that he is the king’s man—bought and paid for—and he is to do whatever he must.”

“Christ, he’ll kill me for sure!”

“Well, better him than de Bracy’s rabble,” Isobel responded prosaically. “Anyway, it will not come to that. He will understand, I promise you.”

There was a hint of anxiety in her voice now, for Louis Montierre and his companions had begun to advance. Soon they would be surrounded, and then there would be no escape for Adam or Matt.

“We are outnumbered, Adam,” she reminded him. “If you remain here, it is almost certain you will die, both you and Matthew, and I would not have that on my conscience.”

His gaze rested on her pale face for a moment, the agony of indecision clear to see; then abruptly he let go of the mare’s bridle.

“You are to stay alive, Bel, do you hear me?” Adam’s voice was fierce. “No matter what they…” He broke off, battling the memory of Aleyne de Bracy’s haunted eyes. “No matter what *he* does to you, you are to stay alive. Do you understand me?”

The look she gave him was almost pitying.

“I am not a child, Adam. I have seen the way Piers de Bracy looks at me. I know what he wants to *do* to me.”

She did not add that her preference would likely be to die by her own hand rather than give him the satisfaction. Adam swallowed hard to dispel the bile that threatened to choke him.

“Are you ready?”

For answer, Isobel gathered her reins again, winding the already fractious Roisin until she was taut as the rope on a primed mangonel, and then she set her heels to the mare's side and sprang away. She heard a shout of surprise and then the sound of rapid pursuit, but she did not dare look back. She gritted her teeth and tried to convince herself that the tears streaming from her eyes were caused merely by riding into the wind.

Chapter Twenty-Nine

Adam saw the blow coming, but although he ducked instinctively he did nothing else to defend himself—in truth, he did not want to. To his surprise, however, his brother-in-law's fist did not connect with his jaw, having been halted in midair by the vicelike grip of another. The sinews and tendons on Fitz-Godebert's wrist bulged with the effort of holding Dominic back, and he cursed fluently in his own tongue.

"Christ's bones, du Bois, have you taken leave of your senses?"

Dominic wrenched his arm away and instead drove his fist into a nearby tethering post. The timber—most likely a section taken from a long-broken mast—was evidently still sound enough, because it did not splinter. Fitz-Godebert winced. He let out the breath he had been holding, exchanged a rueful glance with Adam, and rubbed his own abused muscles.

"Why in the name of God did you let her do it?"

The words were hissed from between clenched teeth as Dominic cradled the cracked and bruised knuckles of one hand in the palm of the other.

"He let her do it because there was no choice." It was stating the obvious, and all three men knew it, but the Fleming continued, regardless. "She judged that her life was in no danger, but the lives of two good men were. Would you have done any differently?"

Dominic did not answer, and Fitz-Godebert sighed, regarding him with an air of mild irritation. He jerked his head in the direction of an old wine cask that had found new employment as a water butt—clearly the landlord of the Rose was a master at the art of salvage. "If I were you," he remarked dispassionately, "I'd go and stick my hand in there."

With another fulminating glare at Adam, Dominic stalked across the inn yard.

"Christ, I did not *want* to leave her, Dominic, surely you must know that?" Adam protested vehemently. "But it is as Richard says—there was no choice, and Bel insisted. She said..." He paused, trying to recall the exact words his sister had used.

"Yes?" Dominic spoke tersely, removing his hand from the water to examine the damage.

Adam's brow furrowed slightly. "She said I was to tell you it was 'a necessary risk'—and that you would understand."

Dominic gave a short mirthless laugh and muttered something under his breath. In the same instant, he looked up, caught the flash of hesitation in Adam's eyes, and knew there was more. "Well, go on, then, let's hear it. What else did she say?"

Adam swallowed hard. "I am to remind you that you are the king's man, bought and paid for, and that you are to do what you must."

Dominic swore colourfully. "Christ *Jesu*! I'll bloody kill her myself when I get her back. Of all the stupid, headstrong, wilful..." He stopped abruptly. "Where's Williams?"

"He took an arrow in his shoulder," Adam admitted

uncomfortably. "A stray shot, loosed by one of de Bracy's men before Montierre ordered them to leave us and go after Isobel."

"Is it serious?"

Adam shook his head. "Just a flesh wound. The arrow was almost spent by the time it struck, and it bled cleanly. The innkeeper's wife is seeing to it."

"He will take her to Penllan, of course," Fitz-Godebert mused.

Adam's face twisted in an expression of pure disgust. "He'd flaunt her openly under the nose of his pregnant wife?"

The Fleming laughed. "Of course he would. Don't make the mistake of crediting de Bracy with your fine sensibilities, lad. Besides, do you think Lady Aleyne would care? It's my belief she would welcome an entire troupe of dancing girls into her home if she thought they would keep her husband out of her bed."

Dominic was regarding Adam with narrowed eyes. "I did not know that Aleyne de Bracy was with child—how came you by *that* information?"

Adam floundered. He had not told Dominic about the manner of his meeting with de Bracy's wife earlier in the day. For reasons he did not care to examine too closely, Aleyne de Bracy's condition was something upon which he preferred not to dwell.

"From me, of course." Fitz-Godebert came to his rescue once again. "Even though he was the one who found her alone on the quayside, puking her guts up, the boy's such a sweet innocent himself, I doubt he'd have guessed the reason for her sickness had I not told him."

Adam flashed the Fleming a grateful look and received a wink in return.

"He didn't waste any time, did he?" Dominic observed bitterly.

His brother-in-law, about as far from being a "sweet innocent" as Dominic was himself, wisely chose to remain silent, sensing this would not be a good moment to apprise Dominic of his suspicions and point out that if Aleyne de Bracy was already *enceinte* then it was entirely possible that Isobel, too, could be expecting by now. They had enough to worry about without adding a further measure of anxiety to the brew.

Fitz-Godebert snorted. "I doubt he even waited for a priest's blessing. If the gossip at Penllan is to be believed, he'd made sure of the girl long before Sir Roger gasped his last."

He was intrigued to note that his words had Adam de Lescaux thrusting the knuckles of his right hand hard against his lips, almost as if he was suppressing the urge to vomit. Recalling the younger man's reaction when he first learned the likely nature of Aleyne de Bracy's "illness," Fitz-Godebert was struck by the realisation that Dominic's brother-in-law seemed uncommonly disturbed by the plight of de Bracy's wife, and the notion once formed seemed difficult to dismiss.

"You'll need to get back to Pyr, Dominic." To Fitz-Godebert's ears, Adam sounded uneasy about the turn the conversation had taken, and eager to change the subject. "And they're bound to have set a watch on the gates."

"Hmm." Dominic pursed his lips. "How well do you know Penllan?"

Fitz-Godebert responded with a wolfish grin.

"As well as you would yourself, if you'd seen it."

"His defences?" Dominic probed.

"In a poor state of repair when he inherited them," Fitz-Godebert answered promptly. "Allyngton had been ill for a long time, and de Bracy's been far too busy arse-licking in recent weeks to have done much to better their condition."

"I could take it, then, without too much difficulty?"

"He's probably effected temporary renovations to the weakest spots, in anticipation of such action on your part," the Fleming allowed. "But why waste time and energy forcing your way in when you could just get a friend on the other side to open the door?"

Dominic's head came up. "You think there may be one such amongst de Bracy's company?"

Fitz-Godebert made a derogatory gesture with his hand. "From what I've seen of the men he brought with him, I would imagine most of them would sell their own mothers if they thought there was a decent profit to be had from the transaction. That was not, however, quite what I had in mind."

He took a swig of wine from the jug Adam offered him, and his face twisted in an appalled grimace.

"Bloody hell, du Bois, it's obvious you frequent this place for something other than the quality of its vintage!" He shook his head reproachfully. "I waste my time pouring expensive Anjou down your miserable throat, and what do I get from you in return? Goat's piss."

"Stick to the ale next time," Adam advised him helpfully, proffering a sturdy stave-built tankard instead.

Fitz-Godebert sniffed suspiciously, raised it to his lips, and took a cautious swallow.

"*Jesu*, I've half a mind to leave you to stew, you pair of misbegotten whelps!" He wiped the sleeve of his tunic across his mouth and shuddered. "As things stand, I have a dozen of my men at large in Pembroke…"

At Dominic's raised brows, the Fleming shrugged.

"I wanted to see which way the wind was blowing before I made any obvious show of support for de Clare—can you blame me?"

As neither Dominic nor Adam seemed inclined to argue, he continued. "They're under the command of Dieter Parle." He paused, seeing a flicker of recognition in Dominic's eyes at the mention of the name. "He's waiting out there somewhere, probably wondering where the hell I've got to and mentally consigning my worthless carcass to the devil. Nevertheless, I would trust him with my life—and yours."

"And Isobel's?" Adam asked pointedly.

Fitz-Godebert ignored him. "It's late in the day, and de Bracy's keep is a deal closer than mine. Quite apart from the distance, I'd have to ford the Cleddau in order to get back to Roch. Since de Bracy has not the slightest idea at the moment that he and I are no longer dancing the same jig, what more natural than that I ask him for a night's lodging within his walls? In all likelihood he will be only too happy to oblige, because once my men are inside Penllan he will be able to put them to good use guarding the walls against your inevitable attempt to rescue your wife."

"And just where, precisely, do you plan to be, whilst all this is going on?" Dominic wanted to know.

Fitz-Godebert afforded him a longsuffering look.

"I shall be back in Pembroke, doing what you asked me to do, trying to talk some sense into de

Clare—a task for which, incidentally, I intend to enlist the aid of Hervey de Montmorency, who I feel may at least be counted upon to see reason, even if his nephew cannot."

Adam snorted. "I think you'll find that's already been tried. What makes you think you can succeed where Henry and Fitz-Harding failed?"

Fitz-Godebert gave him an incorrigible grin. "Because I shall be at pains to point out to de Clare that most of his support is still firmly on the other side of the Irish Sea—and that our friend de Bracy's private war with Dominic here has put us at something of a disadvantage, since both my men and his will be holed up inside Penllan, defending it from yours."

"My men are stuck inside Pyr," Dominic reminded him.

Fitz-Godebert raised one brow in sardonic amusement. "I know that on the evidence of this afternoon you might be forgiven for thinking that your second in command has rather lost his touch, but surely you and he between you may be counted upon to take care of whatever lackwits de Bracy has posted to keep watch on your gates?"

"If they can't, then I can." Matt Williams spoke quietly from the shadow of kitchen door.

"You're injured, Williams," Dominic stated flatly.

Matt sniffed. "It was one arrow, my lord, and that with its force well spent. I reckon I'm still more than a match for any man under Piers de Bracy's command."

"It's settled, then," said the Fleming with a nod of satisfaction. He stabbed a finger in Dominic's direction. "And when we come out the other side of this little fiasco, du Bois, you are going to owe me a cask of *decent* wine."

"If we come safely through this," Dominic promised him, "I'll have Archie MacPherson fill his entire hold with the vintage of your choice."

Fitz-Godebert beamed in happy anticipation. "I'll drink to that!"

Chapter Thirty

Roisin was tiring. Isobel could feel the tension against her hands lessening a little more with every stride. Very soon the mare's pace would begin to slacken correspondingly. She risked a glance behind her and saw with a sinking heart that the men intent on taking her were well-mounted, astride light-boned coursers bred for the chase. Roisin, spirited as she might be, was still a lady's palfrey and no match for them over any great distance. Isobel counted rapidly. There were at least a dozen of them, and they were already gaining on her.

Deciding that her capture was inevitable and that there was nothing to be gained from riding her own horse to exhaustion, Isobel eased her weight back into the saddle and gradually relaxed her grip on the reins. She began turning the mare in a wide arc and heard a shout go up from her pursuers. Despite the gravity of her situation, she could not resist smiling as she saw three riders detach themselves from the main group and cut across the open ground towards her, with the obvious intention of heading her off. Evidently it had not occurred to them that she herself had already decided to call an end to the game.

She ran one hand down Roisin's sweating neck and murmured soothing words until the mare responded by falling into a shambling walk. Her flanks were heaving, and with a pang of guilt Isobel swiftly dismounted and loosened the girth.

Louis Montierre had evidently decided to lead by example, as he was at least a length and a half ahead of his companions. With little thought for the mouth of his unfortunate mount, he hauled hard on the reins, forcing the horse back onto its hocks. There was a deal of squealing, snorting protest, accompanied by flying divots of turf and a string of impressive guardroom epithets, as De Bracy's squire fought the animal to a standstill before swinging his leg over the pommel and affecting a seemingly nonchalant dismount.

"Lady du Bois," he greeted, the very proper inclination of his head completely at odds with the arrogant insolence of his manner. "You appear to be alone and in some difficulty. Allow me to assist you."

Isobel raised her chin and gave him a haughty look that anyone acquainted with her Aunt Rohese would have recognised instantly.

"And if I choose to decline your offer?"

Montierre's full lips curved upwards, and he gestured at the remainder of his men, by whom he and Isobel had now been efficiently surrounded. "I fear that would be unwise, my lady."

Isobel pursed her lips thoughtfully and surveyed the circle of grinning faces, as though considering the matter. "Then it seems I must perforce accept."

Louis nodded, satisfied that the woman recognised her predicament and was going to be sensible. "See to the mare," he rapped, taking Roisin's reins from Isobel's hand and tossing them to one of the waiting soldiers. "The lady rides with me."

Isobel sniffed disdainfully, ignoring the knowing

looks his words had provoked, and turned her attention to the squire's lathered courser. It rolled its eyes nervously at her approach and jerked its head, sending flecks of foam spraying from the corners of its mouth.

"I would not advise it, my lady."

Louis had moved close enough for Isobel to feel the warmth of his breath against her ear, and the sensation made her skin crawl. She regarded him coolly, having already decided it would avail her nothing to take the animal in its present state.

"Doubtless you would not," she allowed. "But then, I am not yours to command—and you would do well to remember that."

Ugly colour stained Montierre's prominent cheekbones, and one powerful arm shot out. The fingers of his right hand closed around Isobel's slender wrist and tightened. She bit down hard on her lower lip to keep from crying out, and his eyes narrowed with speculative interest. By slow degrees he increased the pressure of his grip until the force was such that Isobel was unable to prevent her breath from escaping in a hiss of pain. Immediately Louis relaxed his hold, lightly caressing the marks left by his fingers with the ball of his thumb. He felt the shudder that ran through her and laughed.

"It would appear that we have reached an understanding, *ma dame*."

Abruptly he withdrew his hand and used it to administer an ungentle shove in the small of her back, sending her forward with such impetus she was forced to grab hold of his mount's stirrup leather in order to keep her balance. The already nervous horse shied violently, almost dragging Isobel off her feet. She shot

Louis a furious glare but said nothing.

"Very good, my lady," Louis nodded approvingly. "I shall be able to tell Lord Piers that you learn quickly—but now let us test the strength of our accord. Do you get on the horse of your own free will, or would you have me put you there?"

For answer Isobel tossed her head and set her foot in the stirrup, settling herself at the front of the saddle. She arranged the skirts of her riding dress as decorously as she could and tensed herself against the feel of Montierre's body as he sprang up behind her. Taking the reins in one hand, he snaked his other arm about her waist, holding her securely.

"You should relax a little, *petite*," he admonished in mocking tones. "After all, I would not want you to fall and hurt yourself."

"Go to hell!" Isobel snapped, goaded beyond bearing.

Montierre threw back his head and laughed. "Oh, I intend to, my lady—but I'd be willing to wager you'll arrive there ahead of me. I should warn you that my lord may not be so forgiving towards your intemperate tongue as my good self." He touched his heels to the courser's flanks, and the horse shot forward. "*Ȁ* Penllan!" Montierre shouted, eliciting a raucous cheer from the rest of the company as they thundered in his wake. Isobel buried her fingers in the animal's wiry mane and prayed he would not kill them both with his recklessness.

Chapter Thirty-One

Adam slipped silently through the copse and sank to his haunches behind the uprooted trunk of a once-substantial oak. He was immediately assailed by the unmistakable aroma of rotting wood and leaf mould.

"Well?" Dominic hissed.

"There are two men watching the main entrance," Adam supplied in equally hushed tones. "No mail and lightly armed, by the look of them—both wearing swords and in all likelihood poniards, as well. I couldn't see any bows." He frowned and shook his head slightly. "My guess is that Matt will find at least two more watching the postern gate."

Dominic nodded. "De Bracy may be showing a marked lack of discernment at present," he agreed, "but, unfortunately for us, he's not that stupid." He flicked a critical glance at the crenellations above the gatehouse. "Do you think Sim knows they're here?"

Adam followed the direction of his gaze. "Depends who he's got on guard duty. If Robert and Stephen are up there together, there's a good chance they'll sense something amiss." He shook his head and smiled slightly in response to Dominic's sceptical expression. "Don't ask me *how*, but they just seem to know…" He broke off abruptly, the fingers of his right hand closing on the hilt of the dagger thrust in his boot.

"Christ, you two are jumpy as a pair of old hens

sitting on a clutch of eggs!"

"I'm glad you seem to find our situation amusing, Williams," Dominic snapped, as Matt dropped down beside them.

The soldier opened his mouth as if to defend himself, but Adam sent him a warning glance, accompanied by a slight negative movement of his head.

"How many men did you see?"

"Just the two watching the drawbridge…"

"The other two are presently sampling the hospitality of your dungeons, my lord."

Adam's mouth dropped open.

"*Jesu*, where did you spring from?" he demanded crossly, as a familiar figure emerged from the lengthening shadows.

"Robert?" Dominic hazarded a greeting.

The newcomer favoured him with a wounded look and sighed as he shouldered the longbow he was carrying. "It's Stephen, actually, not that it really matters, I suppose."

"Whichever you are, you're a welcome sight," Dominic assured him with an answering smile. "I take it you came out through the postern gate?"

His youngest brother-in-law nodded.

"Scared the bloody shit out of me!" Matt offered, aiming an affectionate cuff at Stephen's head.

"Serves you right," the younger man riposted cheekily as he ducked the blow with practised ease. "You were making enough noise to wake the dead."

Dominic shook his head reprovingly. "Getting sloppy, Williams," he chastised, taking revenge for Matt's remark about old hens.

Matt rubbed his ribs. “Not my fault the southern slope of your defences is thick with gorse bushes, my lord,” he opined pithily.

Dominic frowned ominously. “I thought I left instructions for that underbrush to be cleared?”

Stephen shrugged. “With three victims to its credit already, I’d say it’s proved itself as good as a line of sharpened stakes any day—nature’s very own *chevaux-de-frise*.”

Dominic shook his head at this blatant impudence but could not help smiling. Stephen’s good humour was infectious, and his own spirits had been considerably lifted by it.

“You’ll not get out of it that easily,” he vowed. “When all this is over, you and your twin will find yourselves out there with a pair of thick leather gauntlets and a billhook each—and that’s a promise.”

Stephen saluted very properly, but the merriment in his eyes remained.

“Where is Robert?” Adam asked, looking about him suspiciously.

“Sulking inside because Sim sent me instead of him,” Stephen supplied promptly, with more than a hint of smugness. “How soon do you wish us to leave, my lord?”

Dominic’s mouth twisted wryly. “I see Matt has lost no time in apprising you of the facts. The men are ready?”

Stephen nodded. “Sim turned out the entire troop as soon as we got wind of our uninvited visitors.” He sniffed disparagingly. “De Bracy’s men have evidently not learned that cleanliness is next to godliness.”

“Maybe they just don’t have free access to the well

house?" Adam teased.

"We leave as soon as we have dealt with the last two lookouts," Dominic decided. "Providing, of course, you are satisfied that they are all that remain."

Adam turned to Matt. "How's the shoulder, Williams? Are you up to accompanying me, or shall I be forced to make do with the assistance of my insufferably cocky little brother on this occasion?"

"Oh, I reckon we could manage, sir," Matt replied, with a wink in Stephen's direction. "Mind you, there'd be no harm in our taking your squire, as well, to my way of thinking."

Adam gave an exaggerated sigh. "Oh, very well, then. Come along, stripling—let's see if you can't learn something from all this."

"Yes, my lord." Stephen flourished an exaggerated bow. "Will this be like the time you offered to teach me the secrets of tracking, my lord?" he enquired innocently.

Adam grabbed his unrepentant brother by the scruff of the neck. "One of these days I'm going to silence you permanently, brat."

"But not today," Stephen told him with maddening certainty. He jerked his head towards Dominic and Matt. "For one thing, there are too many witnesses, and for another, we're wasting time."

He unslung the bow and reached over his shoulder to withdraw one of the barbed and fletched shafts from the quiver on his back. His three companions watched as he competently nocked the arrow.

"I'll take one, you two get the other—I know," he said as Adam drew breath to speak, "don't kill him; just bring him down."

Without waiting for a response, he set off at a run, crouching low so as to avoid being silhouetted against the skyline in the encroaching dusk. Dominic shook his head ruefully.

"Dear God, what I would give now for a quarter of his confidence. I take it his faith is not misplaced?"

"Oh, he's good," Adam admitted. He flicked a glance at Dominic, as if trying to gauge whether he should say any more.

"And…?"

"I've only ever seen him bested once," Adam allowed grudgingly. He waited as realisation dawned.

"Isobel." Dominic swore. "Christ, I should have known better than to ask!"

Chapter Thirty-Two

With mounting fury, Piers de Bracy studied the chalk-white countenance of the unconscious woman whose body had just been laid on a convenient trestle.

"I thought I said she was not to be harmed?"

His squire shrugged carelessly.

"She fell from the horse."

"You graceless whelp!" de Bracy struck the youth across his face. "Could you not have taken her *before* she galloped off?"

An unerring instinct for self-preservation told Louis that it would be imprudent to admit that the lady's fall had occurred not as a result of her own folly but of his subsequent negligence.

"She had an escort, my lord," he ground out, with a belligerent glance at the other men who had been with him, as if daring any of them to contradict his version of events.

"Really? You do surprise me," de Bracy responded with smooth sarcasm. His gaze wandered briefly over the recumbent form on the board before coming back to rest on the truculent Montierre. "How many?" he barked.

Louis shot another look at his fellow soldiers. Their guarded expressions told him little, but he suspected they were unlikely to support him in any further deception, and it was not a risk he cared to take.

“Two,” he muttered, the colour mounting in his cheeks.

De Bracy swung round. “Two?” He echoed incredulously, looking askance at the assembled soldiers. “There were just two of them, and you could not take the girl without mishap?”

One or two of the men shifted uncomfortably, but no one said anything, leaving it to their leader to tender an adequate explanation. Louis scowled and kicked moodily at the soiled rushes, stirring them with the toe of a scarred leather boot.

“One of them was Adam de Lescaux,” he offered sullenly.

“Really?” De Bracy’s interest was piqued. “And where is the noble de Lescaux now—crows’ meat, I hope?”

“He ran away, my lord—they both did.”

De Bracy’s lips curled away from his teeth. “So your precious brother ran off and left you to your fate, *doucette*?” He addressed his oblivious captive. “I wonder how you will you feel about that when you awaken.”

“I would not have thought you needed her conscious for what you want to do with her anyway,” Louis said, greatly daring.

Piers threw back his head and laughed. He beckoned Louis closer, tucking one arm about the squire’s shoulders and drawing his head down so as to whisper menacingly, “Oh, but I do, boy,” he breathed, his voice heavy with lustful intent. “I want her to remember every moment of my possession. When I have finished with her, she’ll wear her shame and humiliation like a brand—for as long as it pleases me to keep her alive."

He swung away abruptly, unbalancing Montierre and sending him staggering drunkenly towards the wall. "Summon my wife," he commanded. "It's time she stopped cowering in her chamber and did something to earn her keep."

The cool touch against her forehead was soothing. Isobel forced her eyes open, frowning at the unfamiliar surroundings. The movement sent shafts of pain lancing through her head, and she swore as she tried to sit up.

"Lie still." The admonishment was delivered softly. Unable to argue, Isobel subsided meekly against the bolster. She raised one hand and cautiously explored her right temple. Her fingers were caught, held, and guided by those of another, allowing her to feel the swelling.

"Fool! I swear I will kill him for this."

"If by 'him' you mean my husband's squire, then you may have to stand in line," the voice advised dryly. "By all accounts Piers was most wroth with him, and he's not inclined to be merciful at the best of times."

Isobel studied Aleyne de Bracy's averted profile. Their one previous meeting had been brief, to say the least, and so charged with the hostility between their respective escorts that there had been no opportunity for either of them to do more than stiffly acknowledge the presence of the other.

Here in her own domain Aleyne had discarded the obligatory head covering worn by all respectable women. A thick braid of hair, the colour of sun-ripened wheat, swung over one shoulder as she bent forwards to wring out the cloth she had been using to bathe Isobel's forehead. She pushed the braid back impatiently and faced her unsolicited guest with a mild look of enquiry.

"It would be no more than he deserves," Isobel muttered as she pushed herself upright. Her stomach lurched with unmistakable intent. "Oh, *Jesu*, I am going to be sick!"

Aleyne thrust a basin against her chest, and she obliged by retching miserably into it. The basin was removed, and Aleyne returned with a horn beaker which she held to Isobel's lips.

The unwilling occupant of the bed swallowed obediently and slumped back against the pillows.

"You do know why I am here?"

Aleyne said nothing.

"It is none of my doing, I assure you," Isobel snapped angrily. "I have never given your husband cause to believe I would welcome his attentions."

Slate-grey eyes regarded her pityingly.

"You do not need to convince me, Lady du Bois. Piers takes whatever he wants, whenever he wants it. Who should know that better than I?"

Her words filled Isobel was remorse.

"Forgive me," she murmured. "You did not deserve that."

Her sympathy was almost Aleyne's undoing.

"It was a long time ago," she said abruptly.

Isobel was looking at her with undisguised curiosity, and Aleyne sighed. Her carefully constructed wall of indifference was crumbling around her, undermined by the simple compassion of another human being.

"Piers is a distant cousin, on my mother's side of the family," she began haltingly. "He was a frequent visitor to Penllan when I was small, and he never arrived without bringing me a gift of some sort—sweetmeats, ribbons for my hair—pretty trinkets. He lavished attention on me, and naturally I adored him, just as he intended I should. He was very clever. He knew my mother was in poor health and was unlikely to bear my father any more children.

"Near my eleventh year-day, Piers came to visit as usual. Mama was already failing, and I spent much of my time just sitting with her. One afternoon, Piers sought me out while she was resting. He had guessed that Mama was dying, and I think he feared Papa might marry again. He held me so tightly I could not breathe. I told him he was hurting me, and I remember him smiling. He apologised very prettily, of course, and swore he would wait until I was older, but he begged me to let him speak to my father so that we might be betrothed immediately."

Aleyne shook her head sadly. "Child that I was, I could not think of anything beyond my desire to be rid of him in that very moment, so I agreed. He laughed and called me his poppet. He wasted no time in going to my father, and the betrothal contract was made that same evening. Shortly afterwards he left, and all I knew was that I was glad to see him go.

"I was never sure whether Papa sent for Piers when Mama died or whether he had his own spies within Penllan who told him. Either way, he returned with flattering speed and immediately took charge of everything. By the time he had finished, no one thought to question his claim to me—or Penllan."

Aleyne paused, and Isobel saw that she was trembling.

"You do not have to speak of it, if you do not want

to," she said. "I am not so lacking in imagination that I cannot guess the rest."

"Please." Aleyne's voice shook. "I think that I must, and until now there has never been anyone I felt I could tell."

Isobel smiled weakly. "My brother Adam would say it is because we are companions in adversity."

The corners of Aleyne's own mouth lifted a fraction. "It would seem that your brother is a man of sound wisdom as well as uncommon courtesy."

Isobel's eyes narrowed. "I did not know you were acquainted with Adam."

Aleyne coloured.

"I am not, not really, but he happened upon me by chance, earlier today. I was unwell, and he came to my assistance." Her tone was distinctly wistful. "I envy you your family."

Isobel grunted. "They are a mixed blessing, I can assure you, especially the twins."

Aleyne sighed and sat down on the bed beside her.

"Do you wish to hear the rest of my sorry tale?"

"Only if you can bear the telling," Isobel assured her.

Aleyne nodded and set herself to continue.

"After we had buried my mother, Piers encouraged my father to drink himself into a stupor. He poured wine for me too, and urged me to accept it. He said it would take away the pain and make me feel better. It tasted unusually sweet, and I did not really want it, so I do not think I swallowed above two or three mouthfuls before I began to feel lightheaded."

"Poppy syrup," Isobel surmised. "It would seem to be a favourite with your husband and his minions."

Aleyne inclined her head in acknowledgement. "I believe you may well be right. At any rate, Piers simply told everyone I was overcome with grief, and no one questioned him. Once we were away from the hall, of course, he abandoned all pretence of caring for me. He took me to his chamber and dropped me on the floor. Then he dashed cold water in my face. When I cried out, he laughed. He said that I was drunk, and swore he would have me conscious again before he took his pleasure. Even an innocent such as I was could not mistake his intent. I managed to scream just once before he placed his hands around my throat and began squeezing. The pressure increased, little by little, until I could barely breathe—and all the time, I remember, he was smiling…" Aleyne shuddered, and one hand crept unconsciously to her neck.

"When he stopped, I think I would have collapsed, had he not gripped my shoulders and forced me upright. He pulled me against him and held me there, stroking my hair and murmuring soft words, telling me it was my own fault and I should not have made him angry. He spoke so convincingly, so reasonably, that I could scarce believe it—and then he offered me a choice."

"He offered you a choice?" Isobel echoed. "What kind of choice?"

Aleyne's voice was bitter. "His kind, of course. He said I could either submit willingly to him, alone and in the privacy of his chamber, or unwillingly, in the stables, with half a dozen of his men watching and waiting to take their turn."

Isobel felt the bile rise in her throat, and she pressed her fingers to her lips. "*Jesu*," she whispered.

"I was twelve years old," Aleyne said dully, "alone

and terrified. I could see no escape, so I chose what I saw to be the lesser of two evils. I gave myself to Piers de Bracy."

"But surely you told your father the truth of the matter?" Isobel murmured.

"Yes, I told him," Aleyne agreed, "but he chose not to believe me. Piers managed to convince him that I had been more than willing, and we were, after all, betrothed."

"But…"

"It was not difficult," Aleyne told her with a helpless shrug. "I had made it easy for him. I see that now. Everyone in Penllan knew how I had worshipped Piers as I grew up. My father told me I should consider myself fortunate he was an honourable man, and be thankful he still wished to marry me." Aleyne shook her head. "Nothing I could have said would have made any difference. He had quite made up his mind, and indeed, why should it be otherwise? Did he not rid himself of the need to worry about my future, or that of Penllan, with one simple stroke of his quill? That is one reason I envy you your family," she said softly. "They would never have stood by and watched you married against your will."

Remembering the circumstances of her own marriage, Isobel grimaced.

"You might be surprised."

"But they love you," Aleyne said unequivocally. "So does your husband—and they will come for you."

"When Dominic married me, his willingness was proportionate to what he stood to gain," Isobel corrected her firmly, "and the price of the wealth and position I brought him was his loyalty to the crown.

Whatever feelings he may have for me now, he will put his duty ahead of them."

Aleyne was clearly dismayed.

"*Jesu*! Then it would seem that *I* must think of a way to get you safely away from here—and if I am to do that, then I will need time to think. It would not do for Piers to find out you have recovered your senses."

She jumped to her feet and crossed the room, sweeping aside one of the woven hangings to reveal a deep recess in the wall. Producing a key from the ring at her girdle, Aleyne placed it in the lock of a stout oak coffer. The mechanism was stiff, and she wrestled with it for a few moments before it yielded. A variety of garments were heedlessly thrust aside as she groped within, and when she emerged there was a small glass vial in her hand, in which a tiny amount of liquid remained. Isobel regarded it with deep suspicion.

"I kept it for Mama," Aleyne offered by way of explanation. "Had you not made mention of poppy syrup earlier, I might never have remembered it was there." She brought the flask to Isobel and held it out for inspection. "Two drops will be enough to render you unconscious again."

"And how does that help me?" Isobel was mystified, and Aleyne gave her another of those pitying looks.

"He will not touch you while you are *unconscious*," she explained patiently. "Piers derives his pleasure from seeing his victims suffer. This"—she gestured at the vial—"will give us the time I need to arrange your escape."

Isobel looked unconvinced. "Could I not just pretend?" she asked hopefully. "I might be able to take him by surprise—I have done it once before."

"Then you will not do it again," came the uncompromising response. Aleyne unstoppered the vial and held it out. "The lesser of two evils," she reminded, with a bitter twist of her lips. "Would to God he had used enough of it that night to render me senseless."

Still Isobel hesitated, and Aleyne glanced towards the door.

"Trust me," she urged softly.

She fetched a flagon of wine and poured a small measure into a delicate glass cup. Isobel's hand tilted, and two beads of clear liquid dropped from the neck of the vial, to be immediately swallowed in the ruby depths. With a grimace she tossed back the wine and settled herself against the bolster.

Aleyne smoothed the linens around her.

"Had our circumstances been different," she mused, "we might have been friends. I think I should have liked to have had you for a friend, Isobel du Bois."

"We are not enemies." Isobel struggled to form the words as the white poppy began to do its work. "Your husband's misdeeds are not yours. There is no reason why friendship should not grow between us."

"No reason at all," Aleyne whispered sadly, as she retreated to the cushioned seat in the window embrasure, "save that Piers would never permit it."

She watched the regular rise and fall of Isobel's chest for a moment before redirecting her gaze through the opening. Men, some mounted, others on foot, were approaching from the Pembroke road, raising a swirling cloud of dust as they kicked up the dry, sandy soil. For a moment Aleyne's heart raced, until she realised they were too few in number—perhaps no more than a dozen—to be a credible force, and as they drew closer she recognised the colours of Richard Fitz-Godebert at their head. She frowned thoughtfully. Since Piers had taken possession of Penllan it was already more heavily garrisoned than ever it had been in her father's day. The added presence of even a small contingent of the Fleming's men must mean that Piers was expecting Dominic du Bois to come against him with considerable strength. Her gaze flicked back to the serene occupant of the great curtained bed. "So your husband will follow the dictates of his duty and abandon you to your fate, will he, Lady Isobel? I think not."

With a sigh she shifted her back against the cool stonework, seeking a more comfortable position. The day already seemed endless, and instinct warned her it was far from over yet. Smoothing one hand down over her gown, she tried to imagine what she would look like a few months from now. On reaching home that afternoon, she had hastened to her chamber, intending to take to her bed until this awful malaise left her body. A call for someone to attend her had elicited a visit from one of her husband's more sympathetic bedmates, who had, after asking Aleyne a few pertinent questions, enlightened her as to the reason for her affliction.

Although naturally apprehensive, she was surprised to find that the prospect of bearing Piers' child did not dismay her, partly because the obligingly informative Heledd had intimated that in all likelihood Piers would make no further demands on his wife until she was safely delivered, and this in itself was a blessing that should not be discounted.

Aleyne listened to the gate sergeant hail the arrival of Fitz-Godebert's men. With a clatter of hooves the half dozen or so mounted soldiers swarmed into the bailey, closely followed by their comrades on foot. The portcullis rattled down and the drawbridge thudded into place, closing Penllan off from the outside world. She chewed anxiously at the tip of her thumb and returned her gaze to the Pembroke road, realising there was nothing for her to do now but wait and pray. Quite what she should pray for was another matter entirely, and one which vexed her greatly.

Chapter Thirty-Three

With barely a whisper of warning, the arrow found its mark. In the brief moment of numbness following impact, before the pain had time to scream along his nerves and register in his brain, the victim blinked and stared uncomprehendingly at the fletched wooden shaft protruding from the back of his hand. He watched, helpless, as the fingers of his right hand convulsed and his plain but serviceable sword fell from their disabled grip. In the split second he opened his mouth to cry out, the body of his assailant slammed against him, crushing the air from his lungs; the only sound that emerged was a choked gasp.

"Nothing personal," Stephen de Lescaux assured, working swiftly to complete the task of gagging and binding his prisoner before turning to examine the injury he had inflicted. "Clean entry," he pronounced with an air of evident satisfaction, "and very little blood. Lucky you didn't move after I'd loosed, or it might've been a great deal worse." He gestured at the offending arrow. "Our surgeon will remove it for you. It will hurt like the very devil, and may take a while to heal, but hopefully the damage will not be irreparable."

The wounded man emitted an unintelligible grunt, but it was clear from the expression on his face that he did not share the optimism of his youthful attacker. Unconcerned, Stephen shrugged and turned away, emitting a low whistle as he did so. The call was immediately answered, and within seconds Adam appeared by his side.

"When you've quite finished…" he said with more than a hint of sarcasm.

His squire sighed theatrically. " *'Don't kill him; just bring him down.'* " He nodded in the direction of the fallen man. "I think you can say I did as I was told."

"Hmm, well, they do say there's a first time for everything," Adam commented dryly. "Hurry up, Stephen. Dominic is on edge enough as it is, without you keeping him waiting still further."

"And he's patently not the only one," Stephen muttered.

His brother's head whipped round, and for a moment Stephen seemed to hesitate.

"Matt told me what happened, Adam." His face was serious in the pale light.

A muscle worked in Adam's jaw. He moved forward to check the bonds securing the prisoner's wrists, and when he spoke it was with difficulty.

"Believe me, you cannot blame me any more than I blame myself."

The bitterness in his tone was impossible to ignore, and Stephen reached out to touch him lightly on the arm.

"I do not blame you for anything. Bel was right to do what she did, and you had no choice but to let them take her. It was the only way—you know that."

When Adam did not respond, he tried again.

"Bel knows how to look after herself, Adam. She's quick-witted, and she's strong-willed. Like as not, de Bracy will be wishing he'd never set eyes on her."

Adam sighed and ran a hand through his already disordered hair. "*Jesu*, but I hope you're right. I doubt Dominic is ever going to forgive me for my part in this."

"I'd worry more about Robert, if I were you," Stephen advised him, as he assisted their prisoner to rise.

"Robert?" Adam seemed genuinely surprised.

Stephen gave him a pained look. "We may look alike, Adam, but, contrary to popular opinion, that does not mean we always think alike. Robert's a hothead…"

Adam snorted. "And you're not?"

His brother chose to ignore the interruption. "Particularly where our sister is concerned. Remember how he reacted to Alain at Vaillant?"

Adam groaned. "Christ, as if I hadn't got enough on my trencher already!"

"I'll talk to him," Stephen promised. "Hopefully, I'll get my version of events in before anyone else tells him theirs, and he'll see reason." He gave de Bracy's man a gentle push in the small of his back, indicating that he should move forward. "But until you know that I have, give him a wide berth, just in case…"

"You think I'm scared of him?" Adam asked in mild disbelief, as he fell into step beside his brother.

"You should be," Stephen affirmed solemnly. "I am."

Adam's jaw dropped; then he realised his brother was laughing. He swore volubly. "You little shit! I almost fell for that, didn't I? I ought to tan your hide for you."

"You're welcome to try," his sibling conceded cheerfully, "but I think Dominic would probably rather you waited until after we have Isobel back safe and sound."

"Dominic most certainly would." Their commander's voice cut across any further response from Adam. From habit, he too checked the bindings on the man Stephen and Adam had brought in. With a nod of satisfaction, he jerked his head in the direction of Matt, who was standing guard over the unconscious form of the remaining lookout. "Since this one's still capable of walking, you'd best help Williams take care of his companion over there, Adam. Stephen, since I have no desire to be fired upon by my own men, you get back inside and tell Sim to get that drawbridge down—and I want the troop ready to leave within the hour."

Chapter Thirty-Four

Richard de Clare had dined alone with his uncle, whose company he had found far from diverting. Now that the dishes had been removed, Hervey's monosyllabic responses seemed to have dried up altogether, and he had sunk into morose contemplation of the wine in his cup. Strongbow frowned, and his long fingers drummed an impatient tattoo on the edge of the linen-draped board.

"My lord?" A young page bowed low in front of him. "Richard Fitz-Godebert is here."

De Clare smiled expansively.

"Then, by all means, show him in, boy."

The page bowed again and held the door wide to admit the Fleming before retreating and closing it quietly behind him. Fitz-Godebert had taken time to bathe, and his chin showed signs of having been recently barbered. De Clare raised his eyebrows in a gesture of mild enquiry.

"Well?"

Fitz-Godebert glanced in the direction of Hervey de Montmorency, slumped in his chair, and realised with a sinking heart that he could expect little support from that quarter.

"My lord, I have received intelligence that the king is on his way to Pembroke."

De Clare toyed with the stem of the exquisitely

formed Venetian glass goblet on the table in front of him, seemingly absorbing the information without any outward show of surprise. He nodded at Fitz-Godebert, indicating that he should be seated. "I see. And the source of this intelligence?"

Fitz-Godebert gritted his teeth and tensed himself against the explosion of rage. "Dominic du Bois, my lord."

He was not disappointed.

There was a splintering sound as the fragile glass stalk snapped. Another attendant stepped forward smartly, intending to stanch the crimson tide spreading across the pristine white tablecloth, but de Clare intercepted him, snatching the clean napkin from his hand and waving him away. With a coarse oath he examined his palm and extracted the small sliver of glass he found there, wadding the fabric against the cut to stem the flow of blood from the wound.

"God's bollocks, Fitz-Godebert," de Clare blasphemed, his temper not improved by the self-inflicted injury. "I thought I had made it clear that du Bois was to be removed from the field." His fury was almost tangible. "Yet here you are, apparently consorting openly with the enemy!"

"Du Bois is not my enemy," Fitz-Godebert reminded him, with a patience he was far from feeling.

"But he is undoubtedly mine," de Clare snapped, "and since you are in my pay, I might be forgiven for thinking that makes him yours, too."

Fitz-Godebert sighed inwardly. This was going to be even more difficult than he had anticipated.

"He would make a much better friend, my lord."

De Clare favoured him with a look he usually

reserved for men he regarded as complete simpletons.

"If du Bois is privy to information about the king's current whereabouts, then his allegiance is of a certainty given to the crown. That being the case, I hardly think he is likely to extend the hand of friendship in my direction, unless"—his eyes gleamed ferally—"you are saying you think he can be bought?"

"On this occasion, regrettably not, my lord."

"And your point is?"

"My lord, I think it is time to make your intentions known."

De Clare's eyes narrowed. "Meaning what, exactly?"

Fitz-Godebert drew a deep breath and metaphorically grasped the nettle.

"Meaning, my lord, that it should be made widely understood that you have returned to these shores to report to the king in person and to discuss how he would like you to proceed in *his* campaign against the Irish."

"Man's right, Rishart," de Montmorency slurred, struggling to raise his head. "'Swhat I've been tryin' to tell you ever sinch Dublin." He belched and squinted blearily at his nephew.

De Clare shot him a look of intense dislike before returning his gaze to the Flemish mercenary. His mind was working furiously, and he chose his next words with care. "The king has not misunderstood my intentions?"

"No, indeed, my lord." The response was as oblique as the question, but Fitz-Godebert needed to make sure his point had been taken. "How could he, when you have returned with only a handful of your retinue, whilst your forces remain in Ireland, safeguarding his interests?"

De Clare chewed on his thumbnail. "What about you?" he asked abruptly. "Does the king know that you are in my service?"

Fitz-Godebert leant a little closer, sensing victory. "I have no doubt he is aware of the position, my lord. It is no secret that I have served you well in the past. What more natural occurrence than that you should engage my services again on your return to these shores? These are dangerous times, my lord, and no man of rank is expected to travel any distance without an armed escort."

"Hmm." De Clare nodded, seemingly satisfied. Then a thought struck him. "And de Bracy?"

Fitz-Godebert smiled serenely. "You cannot have failed to notice, my lord, that there is little love lost between him and Dominic du Bois, and the situation is hardly likely to have improved in the last few hours, since I have it on good authority that our rather impetuous acquaintance has taken it upon himself to abduct du Bois' wife."

"Dear me, how very unchivalrous of him," de Clare commented urbanely.

"Just so, my lord," Fitz-Godebert agreed. "I think we may therefore safely leave his fate in the hands of Dominic du Bois, ably assisted by the lady's brothers. I believe them to be mounting an assault on Penllan as we speak."

He pulled the wine jug towards him, inspected the contents, and was gratified to see that a good quantity remained. Reaching for two fresh goblets, he poured a measure into each. De Clare took the proffered cup and drank deeply.

"What makes you so sure they will win?"

Fitz-Godebert grinned. "Because I know Dominic du Bois," he replied promptly. "And I've already taken the precaution of sending a few of my men to assist. At the moment, they are on de Bracy's side, but I can confidently predict they will have a sudden change of heart, round about the time du Bois' troops arrive outside de Bracy's front gate, which, by happy coincidence, my men will be guarding for him."

De Clare regarded him broodingly over the rim of his cup. "You're a devious bastard, Fitz-Godebert, I'll give you that. Did your *friend* du Bois also tell you when the king is expected to get here?"

"Tomorrow, or possibly Friday. And before you ask, I don't know what kind of force he's bringing with him—even du Bois himself is not privy to that information."

Fitz-Godebert rolled the wine against his palate and gave a deep sigh of satisfaction before he pronounced, "To your true—and unmistakably honourable—intentions, my lord."

Chapter Thirty-Five

Piers de Bracy regarded his wife suspiciously.

"I thought you said she was not seriously injured."

"I am not a physician, my lord. I have very limited knowledge of such matters, but her breathing is steady, and her colour is good. I am sure it is only a matter of time."

Aleyne watched covertly through downcast lashes as Piers stalked over to the bed. He glared down at the unconscious form, as if willing Isobel to betray herself, but he had to admit that the object of his desire seemed genuinely beyond his reach—for the moment.

"I am to be informed as soon as she stirs, do you understand?"

"Yes, my lord."

His wife's voice was little more than a whisper. Nothing out of the ordinary, but Piers found that it irritated him even more than usual. Abruptly he turned away from the bed and crossed to the window embrasure. Aleyne's needlework lay on the velvet cushion where she had left it when the last of the sun's rays had faded and she could no longer see to set the stitches properly. Piers stared at the neatly hemmed linen strips.

"They are swaddling bands, my lord."

She made no attempt to close the distance between them, merely standing there, patiently, as she always did, a pretty doll with a vacant expression. His top lip curled contemptuously.

"Well, well, well! So my little Aleyne has finally worked out why she's been casting up her accounts on such a regular basis?"

"One of your whor…" Aleyne coloured and bit her lip. "One of the women explained it to me," she amended hastily.

Piers laughed. He reached for her and drew her unresisting into his embrace. Tipping her chin on his forefinger, he studied the smooth, perfect oval of her face.

"I'd have told you myself, sweeting, if you'd but thought to ask. I am to be congratulated, you know—it's not easy to get a child on a plaster saint."

He kissed her savagely, grinding his mouth against hers, before thrusting her away. To him she was nothing more than the means to an end—an end that was now tantalisingly within his grasp, providing she bore him a son. Once the child was safely delivered, he'd have no more need of her.

"The moment she stirs," he reiterated.

Not trusting herself to speak, Aleyne merely inclined her head in dutiful obeisance. She listened to his footfall fading as he descended the stairs, and once she was sure he had gone she raised her fingers to her bruised lips.

"I will not cry." She spoke the words out loud, but her voice trembled, and the defiance sounded hollow in her own ears.

Piers, his mood considerably improved by the prospect of ridding himself of his pallid and unresponsive wife in the not-too-distant future, entered the hall with a smile on his face. It disappeared quickly when he saw his squire lounging with a group of his cronies against one of the trestles still bearing the remains of the evening meal. He crooked his finger and thought for one moment that the sulky-faced youth was actually going to ignore his summons, but just as he had begun contemplating his revenge for such insolence, Louis stepped forward. De Bracy almost sighed his disappointment.

"You've checked the defences?" he demanded without preamble.

"Yes, my lord. Front and postern gates secured, archers on the wall, and Fitz-Godebert's rabble guarding the main entrance."

"Lookouts?"

"Both towers, my lord."

"Very good, Louis. We'll make a soldier of you yet."

Montierre's cheeks reddened. "I don't want to be a common soldier. I want to be a knight," he muttered sullenly. "Anyway, I don't think he's coming—maybe you overestimated the lady's value."

It was an unwise taunt. Swift as a snake striking, Piers pinned him up against the wall.

"*You* don't think he's coming?" he snarled. "Your problem is you don't think at all. Of course he'll come—for the sake of his pride, if nothing else—and then there are the rest of the de Lescauxs. Do you honestly imagine they will allow such a slur on their precious family honour to go unavenged? Of course, we might have had one less of them to worry about had you done your job properly earlier."

"You told me to get the girl," Louis gasped

desperately. "You didn't say anything about Adam de Lescaux."

"Because, you halfwit, I did not know he would be part of her escort—although perhaps I should have guessed," he conceded, "since the other two whelps were nowhere to be seen."

He released his grip on the neck of Louis' leather jerkin and flexed his fingers.

"Get out of my sight, before I choose to remember it's your fault the girl's in no fit state to be of any use to me either."

"My lord?" The newcomer bowed deferentially. Piers recognised him as Dieter Parle, one of Fitz-Godebert's men. He grinned mockingly at his squire.

"Ah, a proper soldier. How refreshing!"

"My lord." Parle received the compliment with another bow. "They've been sighted, my lord. Four mounted men, and a sizeable contingent of infantry."

"Four mounted men." De Bracy favoured his squire with a sarcastic sneer. "Did you hear that, Louis? That will be Dominic du Bois, accompanied by three of his brothers-in-law, no less—and you didn't think he would come," he taunted, turning back to Dieter.

"You know what to do."

Fitz-Godebert's fellow countryman bowed yet again. "Yes, my lord."

It was, after all, the truth.

Robert de Lescaux pressed his mount closer to his brother's as they completed their circuit of Penllan's walls.

"*Jesu*, the old man would have a fit if he could see the state of these defences. I doubt anyone's ordered a single repair in at least a decade."

His twin nodded agreement. “Mind you,” he observed, “it will be so much easier if we can just use the front entrance, like the courteous visitors we are.”

“Left,” Robert said idly.

Stephen responded instantly, crouching low over the neck of his mount so the arrow spun harmlessly over his head. He twisted round, took aim, loosed, and waited. A single piercing scream split the night.

“Lucky,” Robert told him. Stephen grinned back at him, his teeth white in the darkness.

“Bet you’d rather hunt with me than him, though.”

They cantered back to where Dominic and Adam stood with the rest of the men, still out of range of de Bracy’s archers.

“Heavily garrisoned,” Stephen reported, “but it’s quantity; not quality. If for any reason Dieter is unable to oblige us, we should be able to scale the wall close to their postern gate. The moat is fairly revolting round there, though—probably counting on the stench to help keep people out.” He pulled a face.

Dominic turned in his saddle to address Adam.

“Take Stephen and half the men round to the postern side. Make them think we’ve decided that’s our best option. Whilst you distract them, Robert, Sim, and I will try to scale the moat and get underneath the walls, although if Dieter’s where he should be, then we’ll get the gate open and we’ll be in.”

Adam nodded and wheeled away, motioning Stephen to follow.

“Robert, *à moi*—and stay close. I’ll need you to protect my back,” Dominic barked.

His squire grinned incorrigibly. “I get all the best jobs!”

Inside Penllan, a shout went up as Adam and his men were sighted. There was a rush of activity as soldiers hastened across the bailey to reinforce and defend the threatened section of wall. Taking advantage of the moment, Dieter glanced upwards at the man stationed on the walk immediately above the gate. An infinitesimal inclination of the head told him that it was time. Gesturing silently to two of his comrades Dieter indicated they should draw back the bar securing the gate. In his own opinion, the timber was so rotten Dominic's men could easily have broken through without his assistance, but, as he had assured Piers de Bracy, he knew what was expected of him. He decided to let down the drawbridge and raise the portcullis, for good measure.

It was, Dominic acknowledged, one of the smoothest operations he had ever undertaken, and he could not help wondering at the ease with which it had been accomplished. Within minutes his men, aided by the dozen well-trained soldiers planted inside Penllan by Fitz-Godebert, were hand to hand with those fighting for de Bracy. The cries of the wounded soon alerted those who had initially gone over to the postern, and they now began running back in alarm. Simultaneously, Adam had discovered that the mortar in the crumbling south wall was so badly decayed that many of the stones could simply be kicked out. Joined by the group of men under his command, he and Stephen swarmed over the tumbled wall and into Penllan. Panic ensued, as de Bracy's men began to realise they were effectively trapped between the two contingents of Dominic's force. The intensity of the fighting increased, and the level of noise rose concomitantly as the attackers pressed closer to the keep. De Bracy, distracted from his idle contemplation of Isobel de Lescaux's flawless countenance, crossed to the window and looked down.

"God rot you, du Bois!" Piers swore, his complacency deserting him. He swung round, wrenching at the hoop of keys which hung from his belt and thrusting them at Aleyne.

"Lock this door after me, woman, and don't open it for anyone until I tell you to myself."

Then he was gone. With a sigh of relief Aleyne turned the key in the lock as she had been bidden, then leant against the door for support since her knees were threatening to give way beneath her. Isobel sat up, the effects of Aleyne's minute dose of poppy syrup having largely worn off about an hour since.

"What's happening?" she demanded. Aleyne shook her head.

"I don't know, but whatever Piers saw just now displeased him greatly, so I think that we can safely assume that matters are not going his way."

"Dominic?"

Aleyne smiled. "Evidently still very much alive, judging by my husband's reaction."

Isobel swung her legs over the edge of the bed.

"Keep away from the window," Aleyne warned. "If Piers should look up and see you there…" She fetched Isobel's overdress from the coffer on which it lay, neatly folded. "Here, you'd better put this on, so you can be ready."

Isobel struggled into the garment, and Aleyne laced it for her. Unlocking the door, she opened it a fraction and peered out onto the landing.

"Where are you going?" Isobel hissed.

Aleyne put a finger to her lips. "I need to find your husband, so he can come for you—there is no one else who would tell him where you are being held."

"He may not believe you," Isobel cautioned. "He may think it is a trap."

"Is there something I can say that will convince him?"

Isobel thought for a moment, then inspiration struck, and the corners of her mouth lifted in a small smile.

"You may tell him I said that trusting you is 'a necessary risk.' "

She saw Aleyne's lips shape the words as she memorised them, then she shrugged. "If that is what it takes."

Isobel frowned. "Piers told you to stay here," she reminded.

"I know," Aleyne admitted. "I'll be careful, but if I do run into him, I'll tell him that I thought to help with the wounded."

"Won't he be angry that you have disobeyed him?"

"Yes," Aleyne acknowledged, "but I do not think he will beat me for it this time."

Isobel looked uncertain.

"How can you be so sure?"

"Because I am carrying his child," Aleyne said simply, "and Piers will not do anything to endanger his son and heir." She managed a watery smile. "God alone knows what he will do if I should bear a girl—I don't suppose that possibility has occurred to him yet." She detached the key from the iron ring and pressed it into Isobel's hand. "Now it is your turn to lock the door, and do not open it until *your* husband bids you do so."

Then, with a flurry of skirts, she was gone.

Chapter Thirty-Six

Louis Montierre faced up to the unpleasant fact that, for the second time in a matter of hours, his back was, quite literally, against the wall. A fist connected with his face, and he came close to vomiting as he felt the soft nasal cartilage tear.

"Where is she?"

It was Robert de Lescaux asking the questions, with his twin apparently no more than an interested bystander, not that it made any difference to Louis. He sleeved his streaming nose and spat blood and a fragment of tooth at his tormentor.

"Go swive yourself, de Lescaux!"

"Wrong answer," Robert advised.

Bunched knuckles slammed into Louis' gut, and he doubled over, retching, only to find himself grabbed by the hair and forced upright once again.

"I've tried asking nicely," Robert said mildly, "but now I think you should know you're really beginning to try my patience."

He addressed himself conversationally to his twin.

"I should imagine it's quite hard to pursue a career as a professional soldier when you've had both your arms broken," he commented.

"Oh, undoubtedly," Stephen agreed.

"And I have heard it said," Robert continued, "that such old injuries can plague you like the very devil on cold winter nights when you're forced to bed down on hard ground."

"He might be lucky," Stephen observed judicially, "if the breaks are clean and they heal well."

"Of course, it would not be very chivalrous of us to break both his arms," Robert demurred.

"True. But then, we're not knights yet, are we—and neither is he," Stephen pointed out. "So we don't really need to worry about such niceties of behaviour."

Robert shrugged. "If you say so."

He wrenched back Louis' sword hand and slammed it with calculated force into the wall. There was an unmistakable snap, and the youth's face whitened as he crumpled helplessly against the stonework.

"Only the one arm, after all," a voice purred in his ear. "It seems my brother's just naturally more chivalrous than I am. By the way, Montierre, I hope you've still got a little supply of white poppy hidden away somewhere, because I'd say you're going to need it."

With a satisfied nod, Robert got to his feet, only to find Adam and Dominic staring at him in horrified fascination.

"I can't believe you just did that." Adam shook his head.

Robert shrugged. "He wasn't going to tell us anything, and we had an old score to settle."

"*Jesu*, you're brutal," said Adam in disgust.

"Oh, and you're not, I suppose?" Robert looked askance at him. "Wasn't it you who once told me that half the secret of being successful in this business is carving a reputation for yourself?" He jerked his head in the direction of de Bracy's now unconscious squire. "Well, there's at least one man who'll think twice before he crosses our paths again."

Dominic regarded Adam's shocked expression and grimaced ruefully.

"I think it's time to face the fact that your little brothers have come of age, my friend." He leaned towards Robert and gestured surreptitiously at Adam. "For Christ's sake, make sure your sister doesn't get to hear about this—she hasn't forgiven me for what she thinks I've done to *him*, yet."

He poked experimentally at Montierre's body with the toe of his boot. "Ah, well, since de Bracy's squire is not going to oblige us, then I suppose we'd best seek out someone who will."

"Looking for something, du Bois? Or should I say, some*one*?"

Dominic spun round. De Bracy was standing at the top of the stone steps in the entrance to his keep, silhouetted in the open doorway by the yellow light from the torches in the hall behind him. He grinned like a gargoyle and spread his arms invitingly.

"Why don't you come on up, and I'll see what I can do to help?"

With an oath, Dominic started forward, but Adam's hand closed on his arm, holding him back.

"Let me," he said. "Take Robert and Stephen with you and find Bel. I'll take care of De Bracy."

Stephen exchanged a look with his twin. "Adam," he admonished severely. "Please tell me you're not about to do something *brutal*?"

"I'll do something brutal to you one of these days," Adam promised menacingly.

Stephen grinned and nodded in de Bracy's general direction. "You have my full permission to be as brutal as you like where he's concerned. Just be careful, big brother."

Dominic regarded them with mounting exasperation. "I swear, if I live to be a hundred—which I know seems unlikely in our present circumstances—I will never understand you de Lescauxs. Now, if you've quite finished making sport of one another, perhaps we could get down to business?"

"What's he doing?" Robert wondered aloud, glancing back at where de Bracy still stood in the open doorway. "No one in his right mind would just stand there and invite us in."

"It's more than likely a trap," Dominic agreed, "although the arrogance of the gesture is in keeping with his character."

"We'll need to take the steps together, and at a run," Adam decided. "Once we get to the top, I'll engage de Bracy. Remember, Isobel is our priority—we have to get Dominic clear inside."

"Need a hand, sir?" Sim Walters' grizzled face appeared at Adam's shoulder. Close behind him was Giles le Blanc, accompanied by at least another two dozen men.

"You're a welcome sight," Dominic greeted them, then paused searchingly. "Where's Williams?"

"We've left him rounding up the stragglers, my lord, with the aid of Dieter and the rest of Fitz-Godebert's men."

"Any losses?"

Le Blanc grinned. "Not on our side, my lord."

Dominic nodded his approval. "Wounded?"

“A few, my lord, but none serious.” Giles gave a contemptuous sniff. “If you ask me, de Bracy needs to choose his men more carefully—either that or he should pay them better. There weren’t many who were prepared to lay down their lives for him.”

“Hmm. It may be that his best fighters are yet inside.”

“There’s only one way to find out.” Adam drew his sword. “Shall we?”

“On three,” Dominic commanded.

De Bracy saw the body of men start up the steps and realised that in the darkness he had seriously underestimated the size of the force Dominic had brought against him—either that, or he had been purposely misinformed. Assessing the situation, he rapidly concluded there was no way the few men who had remained inside the keep with him were going to be able to hold the door. Cursing his ill luck, he took the only sensible option and retreated.

****

Aleyne emerged hesitantly from behind the colourful woven curtain that screened the doorway between the hall and the stairs leading to the east turret. Aghast, she stared at the wreckage of her home. There were armed men everywhere, a few still engaged in desultory hand-to-hand combat but the majority simply milling around amidst the overturned tables, spilt wine, scattered food debris, and torn hangings. A cold, hard knot formed in her chest as she surveyed the damage to her mother’s treasured tapestries, and she forgot the need for caution. She started forward, only to be pulled back almost immediately by a strong arm that curled about her waist, bringing her up hard against a solid, unyielding wall of muscle. Instinctively Aleyne panicked and began to struggle.

"Oh, no, little one." The voice was gentle but firm. "Believe me, you do not want to go in there. It is no place for a pretty child like you."

Stephen de Lescaux turned the girl round, intending to send her swiftly back up the dark stairwell to where he judged the women of de Bracy's keep might sensibly have taken refuge. It was only then he discovered his error.

"Lady de Bracy?" There was a hint of uncertainty in the question.

She inclined her head in the barest gesture of acknowledgement. "You are correct, my lord. And you, I believe, are one of Lady du Bois' remarkable twin brothers." Her lips twitched as she surveyed his face. "Although I own I could not begin to say which. You see, I recognise you from that day in the market also."

Hazel eyes swept over her in swift appraisal.

"I am Stephen de Lescaux," he informed her coolly, "and most people remember me and my brother, lady, but few can tell us apart."

Aleyne sighed, an unmistakably wistful sound. "I've no doubt your sister can. She loves you both so very much."

That surprised him. "You have seen Isobel? Spoken with her?"

"She was injured when they brought her here. Piers bade me care for her."

Finely shaped brows quirked in evident disbelief.

"My husband is a man of few sensibilities," Aleyne supplied dryly.

Stephen frowned. "How came she to be hurt?"

"I believe it was the fault of my husband's squire."

"*Jesu*, I should have broken his other arm after all!" Stephen swore.

Aleyne's eyes rounded. "You broke Louis' arm?"

"Robert did," he confirmed dismissively. "But I'd not waste any sympathy on Montierre, if I were you. Where is my sister now? Is she recovered?"

Aleyne nodded in the direction of the stairs. "She is much recovered, my lord, although I should imagine she is a little tired—and she is safe in my chamber."

Stephen's eyes narrowed. "And what of your husband, lady?"

Aleyne shrugged. "Not with your sister. Other than that, I am afraid I cannot tell you."

He made no comment, but she knew what he was thinking.

"Naturally you are suspicious. It is only to be expected. Your sister gave me a message for her husband, so that he might know he can trust me."

"And the message?"

"I doubt it will make much sense to you. I think it is something he alone will understand. She said to tell him that trusting me was '*a necessary risk.*' "

Stephen pursed his lips as he considered the words. He shook his head. "You're right. I am none the wiser. Let us hope it will mean something to Dominic."

He reached for her hand, intending to guide her into the hall, but Aleyne evaded his touch.

"I will wait here," she said. "Please hurry, for I would see your sister reunited with her husband and all of you safely away from Penllan."

Stephen hesitated and turned back to her.

"And why is that, lady? Does your willingness to

help stem from a simple desire to thwart your husband's plans, or perhaps it is that you want revenge against him for daring to bring another woman under your roof?"

Aleyne laughed, but the sound held no warmth. When she raised her eyes to his, the pain in them pierced him like an arrow.

"I know perhaps better than anyone exactly what Piers intended to do to your sister," she said softly, "and no woman deserves that, Stephen de Lescaux, least of all her."

She watched him cross the hall to his twin and the tall, dark-haired man who stood beside him. Of Adam de Lescaux there was no sign, and she felt an irrational stab of disappointment.

Stephen spoke urgently, in hushed tones, and immediately both his companions raised their heads to look in her direction. There was another rapid conversation, and within seconds they had arrived at her side. They surrounded her, and Aleyne felt the familiar sensation of panic rising. She willed herself to stay calm, telling herself that these men were not like her husband.

"You have a message for me, I believe?" Dominic du Bois addressed her without preamble.

"Yes, my lord."

She repeated the words Isobel had told her to say, and saw some of the tension leave Dominic's body. Robert and Stephen were looking questioningly at him.

"Your sister's idea of a joke," he said with an apologetic shrug. "She has a strange sense of humour."

"It is the room at the very top of the tower, my lord," Aleyne spoke quietly. "The door is locked, and your lady has the key, but she will not use it until you tell her to do so yourself."

Dominic took her hand and raised it to his lips. "Lady Aleyne, I am in your debt. Robert—come with me. Stephen—stay here at the foot of the stairs. No one comes up, you understand?"

Stephen saluted Dominic and made a rude gesture at his brother, who responded with one of his own.

"Ah, he's so childish," he said with a grin. He sat down on the bottom stair, stretching his long legs out in front of him, and looked up at Aleyne, but her attention was clearly elsewhere, and her eyes were scanning the faces of the men grouped around the hall.

"Are you looking for anyone in particular, Lady de Bracy? Your husband, perhaps?"

Aleyne started. "Oh, no, I…"

He raised one curious brow.

"I was just wondering where your other brother might be," she admitted haltingly.

Stephen favoured her with a shrewdly assessing look, and she coloured under his interested scrutiny.

"I believe, madam, that Adam *does* seek your husband."

The bloom left Aleyne's cheeks abruptly. "But he must not!" she exclaimed. "Sweet *Jesu*, he will kill him."

Stephen laughed. "I am sure my brother would be flattered to learn of your faith in his abilities. Do not fret, Lady Aleyne. He will prove himself a worthy champion."

"I cannot let this happen."

"Why?" Stephen reasoned with calculated coldness. "Surely you would find widowhood infinitely preferable to wifehood?"

"You do not understand," Aleyne said with a little shake of her head. "I must find him."

"Lady, wait! Lady Aleyne!" Stephen was startled into using her given name. "Surely you do not intend to…"

But she was already gone, and Stephen, bound by Dominic's command to remain where he was, allowed himself an oath that would not have disgraced his father. "Women!" he muttered disgustedly, aiming a vicious kick at the wall.

Chapter Thirty-Seven

"Isobel." Dominic's voice was low and urgent. "Are you there?"

A single torch flickered desultorily in a bracket halfway along the passage. It did little to dispel the creeping darkness.

"For Christ's sake, Bel, open the door!" Robert added his own exhortation for good measure, glancing anxiously back down the stairwell.

A dull scraping sound told them a key was being inserted into the lock. The mechanism clicked, and Dominic threw himself to one side of the door, motioning Robert to remain on the other. As soon as it swung open, he was into the room. He blinked rapidly, dazzled by the light from a dozen candles, and only just had time to drop his sword before Isobel flung herself at him.

"You idiot woman," he rasped the words against her hair even as his arms closed around her. "Don't you know better than to hurl yourself at an armed man like that?"

Isobel pulled free of his embrace and scowled at him. "Yes, thank you, Dominic, I am perfectly fine, and I'm delighted to see you, too. What took you so long?"

"Ah, *Jesu*, can't we just leave her here?" Robert suggested hopefully. Dominic glared at him.

"Wait outside," he ordered.

His squire gave an exaggerated bow and retreated to the landing, with a knowing smirk.

Dominic drew a deep breath, released it, and ran his hands through his sweat-dampened hair. "One of these days…" he began.

"You'll have to get behind the rest of us," Isobel promised him.

He reached out and drew her back into his arms. Their lips met in a butterfly caress, and her fingertips traced the line of his jaw.

"*Jesu*, Bel, if you only knew how frightened I have been."

"I'm sorry, Dominic, truly I am, but you must see that I had no choice. Forcing them to pursue me was the only way to give Adam and Matt a chance." Her lips curved. "I calculated the odds, my lord, and decided that it was a necessary risk."

Dominic groaned and, for one brief, blissful moment, gave himself up to her kiss before reluctantly pushing her away from him.

"Enough, you witch! There is a time and a place for seduction, and this is neither." He held her at arms' length and studied her anxiously. "You are all right, Bel? He did not…?"

She shook her head emphatically. "No, Dominic. He never touched me—and for that I must thank his lady wife."

Dominic looked as if he would know more, but she raised her index finger and pressed it gently against his lips. "Later," she said. "Where's Adam?"

****

Aleyne edged her way along the cold, stone-flagged passageway, her heart thumping against her ribs. This was the oldest part of Penllan, riddled with dark corners and small storerooms. On the floor above were the original family rooms. Once as familiar and welcoming to her as her mother's warm embrace, now all they held were bitter memories, and she seldom came here. As she groped her way along the wall, her hand slid on something faintly sticky. The metallic tang of blood assailed her senses, and she almost lost her footing on the wet patch beneath her. Aleyne moaned aloud, "Oh, please, God, no!"

****

Adam had taken the steps two at a time and pinned his enemy against the solid oak door through which he'd been hoping to escape. De Bracy swore, fumbling one-handed for the latch whilst struggling to keep up his guard and parry the attack. It gave suddenly, taking both men by surprise, and they tumbled into the room together.

Piers risked a downward glance. He was bleeding heavily now, and even the thickness of his padded gambeson could not disguise the severity of the wound that de Lescaux had managed to inflict when they had clashed on the floor below. He saw Adam's eyes follow the direction of his own and knew immediately that he too recognised the significance of that rapidly blossoming stain.

Adam renewed his attack, concentrating his efforts on de Bracy's damaged left side, and the force of the blows sent his opponent staggering backwards. Through sheer strength of will Piers righted himself and parried again, but his laboured breathing throbbed in his own ears, and he knew without doubt he was nearing the limit of his endurance. Sweat dripped from his hair into his eyes, blurring his vision. He shook his head, hoping to clear it, but he had reckoned without the heavy blood-loss he had already sustained, and the action sent him reeling dizzily into the wall. His sword fell from his limp fingers. Slumped against the painted plasterwork, he watched helplessly as Adam's booted foot kicked it beyond his reach. A slow smile spread across his pain-distorted face.

"You're too late, de Lescaux. I've already had your precious sister."

He closed his eyes, crossed himself, and waited.

"No."

Adam felt the weight that dragged down on his arm, and with a bellow of rage he thrust his elbow back sharply, intent on dislodging it, but the tenacity of the grip surprised him.

"No!" The single word was uttered again, even more forcefully than before. "He is lying, my lord."

Piers opened his eyes and swore. "Stop your mouth, you witless bitch, unless you'd have me do it for you."

Aleyne afforded one quick glance in her husband's direction, and having reassured herself that he was at present in no condition to enforce the threat, she returned her attention to Adam de Lescaux.

"He lies," she repeated firmly. "Your sister is unharmed."

Adam faltered.

"Congratulations, sweetheart. You are most convincing."

With a supreme effort of will, Piers inched his back up the wall and managed to right himself. Leaning against it for support, and with one hand clutching at the jagged tear across his ribs, he leered in Adam's direction.

"What can I say? Such is her fondness for me, it appears she would say almost anything to have you spare my miserable life." He switched his gaze to Aleyne, and his eyes narrowed. "A word of warning for you, though, my poppet. The protection afforded by your interesting condition has limited duration, and you would do well not to store up trouble for yourself."

Cold hazel eyes raked de Bracy in swift, professional assessment. Despite the show of bravado, he was clearly incapable of any further engagement, and Adam lowered his sword. Deliberately he swung his arm forward with sufficient force to jerk Aleyne off her feet. She stumbled, and he watched her hands fly unconsciously to her stomach as she instinctively shielded the child within. His own innards cramped, and his mind screamed denial.

Aleyne recoiled from the look in his eyes. It seemed he was barely able to conceal his disgust for her, and she was surprised to discover how much the knowledge hurt. As the fingers of his right hand flexed and tightened their grip on the hilt of his sword, she steeled herself to beg.

"Please," she entreated. "Do not do this."

Adam regarded her impassively, allowing his gaze to travel from the crown of her impossibly fair hair to the bloodstained toes of the deer-hide shoes visible just below the hem of her gown.

"Give me one good reason why I should not?"

Aleyne swallowed hard, not daring to look at her husband. "I can think of none, my lord, save that I ask it of you."

In the corner of the room, De Bracy moaned with pain. His eyes had closed again.

With some surprise, Adam realised the killing rage had left him. He drew a great shuddering breath and forced himself to relax. It was over, for now, and Aleyne de Bracy was urging him towards the door.

"In God's name, go."

Adam stared at the slender fingers clamped once more about his arm, and his feet seemed to obey with a will all their own. The door closed behind him, and he heard the sound of the bar dropping into place. Cautiously he set one hand on the wall and began slowly to descend the wedge-shaped stairs to the hall below. His whole body ached, and his mind was weary beyond belief.

****

Aleyne examined the deep gash made by Adam de Lescaux's sword. Although it still bled copiously, the blood ran rather than pumped. Provided it healed cleanly, she would continue to be a wife rather than a widow. Distantly she wondered what Stephen de Lescaux would say when he heard that his brother had not finished the job after all.

As she began stitching, Piers uttered a curse that made her ears burn. Instinctively she flinched back, and the thread pulled tight against his torn flesh.

"God damn you, woman, get on with it!"

Murmuring an apology, she completed the task as swiftly as she could and made to stand, but as she did so Piers caught her chin with his good hand, forcing her to remain on her knees and look at him.

"You should have let him kill me, sweetheart," he mocked. "You could have been free."

She resisted the urge to pull away from him, knowing that to do so would only make matters worse.

"At what price," she queried stiffly, "a man's immortal soul?"

He laughed, then cursed again, as the action sent tongues of fire streaking down his ribs to pool, throbbing, in the newly-closed wound. He released her, and she got to her feet, a trifle unsteadily.

" 'A man's immortal soul,' " he echoed derisively. "It pains me to shatter your childish illusions, *ma chere*, but I can assure you the soul of a man like Adam de Lescaux is at least thrice damned already."

Aleyne busied herself disposing of the basin of bloodied water and soiled linens, concentrating on recovering her composure before turning to face her husband once more.

"Perhaps it is," she said quietly, "but not on my account."

"My virtuous little wife," he sneered.

"I will find someone to assist you, my lord."

Her tone was polite, neutral, and impossibly distant. Had it not been for his physical limitations, Piers knew he would have shaken her until her teeth rattled, regardless of the fact that she was carrying his heir.

Chapter Thirty-Eight

"Christ, what happened to you?" Stephen stared at his brother in dismay.

"De Bracy," Adam admitted grudgingly, through gritted teeth. "Where's Bel?"

"Safe," Stephen assured him, "and in a better case than you, by the look of it."

Adam managed a weak smile.

"Wouldn't be difficult," he allowed with a painful grimace. "Lend me your shoulder, will you, brat?"

Stephen obliged.

"Is he dead?"

"No, but he would be, had his wife not come between us."

A cup was thrust into his hand, and he drained it in one swallow, not caring what it contained. He closed his eyes and groaned.

"Is she…all right?" Stephen asked hesitantly.

Adam opened one eye and squinted up at him.

"I don't make war on women, Stephen," he said sourly. "I'm not *that* brutal."

"Maybe not," Stephen acknowledged stiffly, "but I doubt the same could be said of her husband, and as we are in the lady's debt, I fancy we have a duty of care towards her."

"Well, you're like to have a hard time fulfilling it," Adam snapped back at him. He did not want to think about Aleyne de Bracy.

Stephen opened his mouth to reply, but whatever he had planned to say was lost in the arrival of his sister and her husband.

"*Jesu*, Adam, sit down before you fall down," Isobel ordered, pushing him into a vacant curule chair and proceeding to examine him critically. "Congratulations," she observed caustically. "When this lot heals, I think you may have almost as many scars as Dominic."

"I wasn't aware we were in competition," Adam told her, arching with pain as her questing fingers found a particularly sensitive spot. "They're scratches," he dismissed, catching hold of her hands and pushing them away, "and maybe a rib or two. What about you?"

"*I* can take care myself," she told him smartly. "Where is Aleyne?"

"How the devil should I know?" Adam scowled at her. "I imagine she's still with her husband. His injuries are a great deal worse than mine, I assure you."

He flinched again beneath her touch, and Isobel arched her brows in evident disbelief.

"Enough, Bel. Let me be," Adam snarled with uncharacteristic irritability. "There's nothing wrong with me that a bath and a good night's sleep will not cure—and it's Stephen's job to tend me, not yours. For God's sake, help me up, will you?" he barked at his hovering squire. "The sooner we are away from this miserable place, the better."

Isobel looked as if she might be about to argue with him, and Dominic, sensing Adam was close to the breaking point, decided it was time to intervene.

"Amen to that," he concurred vehemently, shooting

a warning look at his wife. "I'll speak to Dieter. He and Fitz-Godebert's men can stay behind and sort out this mess."

****

Dominic closed the door softly and crossed the room on silent feet. It was almost dawn, and he fully expected his wife to be asleep, so it was with some surprise that he saw she was not only still awake but sitting up in their bed apparently waiting for him. He settled himself beside her and reached for one of her hands. Turning it palm upwards, he smoothed the ball of his thumb over the faint calluses he saw there.

"It happened when I was trying to lead Montierre and the others away from Matt and Adam," Isobel said, following the direction of his gaze. "I was so heavy handed that poor Roisin will need saltwater washes for a week for her mouth to heal. Sim has promised me he will see to it."

Dominic raised her fingers to his mouth and brushed his lips over their tips. He felt the shudder that ran through her and was instantly contrite.

"I am sorry, *ma* Bel. You must be tired, and I am a thoughtless idiot."

She scowled at him. "Stop treating me as if I were some precious, fragile piece of Rhenish glass."

He leant over and kissed her thoroughly.

"Better?"

"Maybe," she allowed, grudgingly. "Dominic, did you know that Aleyne de Bracy is with child?"

He regarded her warily. "Yes, I knew. What of it?"

"She said that Piers would not punish her for helping me until after the child was born—because he would not want to risk harming his son."

"Sweetheart." Dominic planted another, altogether gentler, kiss on her brow. "Whatever the so-called wise women may have promised her, she cannot know that the child will be a boy."

"I know." Isobel bit her lip. "So does she—and I am afraid for her."

From the little his wife had told him of Aleyne's sorry history, Dominic could not disagree. He shook his head regretfully.

"Adam should have finished the bastard while he had the chance."

"But Aleyne stopped him, didn't she?" Isobel reminded him. She frowned. "Why wouldn't she let Adam kill Piers, Dominic? Unless…" Her fingers flew to her mouth, and her eyes widened. "Oh, *Jesu*," she whispered. "She is in love with him."

Dominic's jaw dropped. "You cannot be serious, Bel."

Isobel picked up the bolster and threw it at him.

"Not Piers, you oaf. With Adam. Aleyne de Bracy has fallen in love with my brother."

Dominic caught the bolster and held it in front of him like a shield.

"Did she tell you that?" he demanded.

Isobel shot him a scornful look. "Of course not, but it makes no difference."

"It doesn't?"

Not for the first time, Dominic found himself struggling to follow his wife's train of thought.

"I should have guessed it from the look on her face when she spoke of meeting him in Pembroke," Isobel continued thoughtfully. "When Stephen told us how she had left him in such haste at the foot of the tower, none of us thought other than that she sought to protect her husband. Aleyne *did* want to stop Adam from killing Piers, but not for reasons any of us might have imagined."

"But why?" Dominic argued perplexedly. "If she had let Adam kill de Bracy, then she would have been free."

A shadow crossed Isobel's face. "If I am right, then I doubt you would understand her reasoning. I'm not sure I do myself. I think Aleyne may have prevented Adam from killing Piers because to stand by and do nothing would have been murder, in her eyes, and she could not bear the thought of Adam paying the price for that sin."

She fell silent, and Dominic was left contemplating the enormity of what she had said. Hesitantly Isobel touched her fingers to his cheek.

"Dominic?"

"Hmm?"

"What will happen now?"

"To Aleyne de Bracy?" Dominic shook his head. "God knows. But one thing is certain. Adam was right. Whilst her husband lives, there is nothing we can do to aid her, however great our debt."

"I suppose we could pray that he has the decency to die from his wounds," Isobel offered uncharitably. "What about de Clare and the king?"

"Ah, now, that is an easier question for me to answer." Dominic smiled at her, capturing her hand in his. "As I was otherwise engaged at the time, the unhappy task of trying to persuade Strongbow to see sense fell to my good friend Richard Fitz-Godebert—to whom, incidentally, I also find myself indebted for what promises to be an extremely expensive shipment of wine. Fortunately, he appears to have been successful, although I suspect it was probably Hervey de Montmorency who actually came up with the solution.

"Strongbow is to return to Ireland, with orders to finish what he started. In a few months' time, Henry will follow. When the king steps ashore, de Clare will make a very public display of offering him everything that *he* has taken from the Irish, including Dublin, Waterford, and Wexford, and the lordship of Leinster—all of which Henry will, of course, graciously accept before promptly granting the whole lot back to de Clare, to be held and administered in his name. You have to admit, it's a diplomatic masterpiece—neat, effective, and above all face-saving."

"Providing the king agrees," Isobel felt bound to point out.

"Oh, he'll agree," Dominic assured her. "Fitz-Harding will see to that. He'll make sure Henry understands that a civil war with de Clare would be ruinous to the treasury—always a winner with the Angevins, that one. Besides which, Henry's got more than enough trouble on his hands already. By now, he'll be well aware of the mischief Eleanor's been fermenting over in Aquitaine, and if she's successful in stirring their unholy brood into open rebellion against him, Strongbow will be the least of his problems."

"So de Clare is going back to Ireland now?"

Dominic nodded. "Henry is never going to grant him the formal right to Pembroke—the best he can hope for in his lifetime will be a tacit acknowledgment of his family's claim."

Her fingers tensed under his light caress.

"If he is going back to Ireland, does that mean you will be going, too?"

"It might."

He could not resist the impulse to tease her a little. Her disappointment was immensely flattering, and he grinned engagingly at her as she tried unsuccessfully to hide it.

"On the other hand, I could just offer Henry three of my best men, in lieu of my own service." His eyes danced. "You have to agree it would be a most effective means of ridding myself of your incredibly tiresome brothers."

"But however would you manage without them?" Isobel teased him in return.

"Better than I would without you, sweetheart," Dominic promised as he tumbled her beneath him. "Far better than I would without you!"

Historical Note

Anyone familiar with the history of the period—and in particular with the history of the Fitz-Hardings of Berkeley—will be quick to point out that Robert Fitz-Harding actually died in 1170, some months before the action of this book takes place, and I freely admit to bending the timeframe a little in order to accommodate Dominic and Isobel's story.

Robert was an accomplished political figure who rendered important services both with arms and money to the Empress Maud and to her son Henry. When he became king, Henry rewarded Fitz-Harding's loyalty with the Manor and Barony of Berkeley, previously held from the crown by Roger de Berkeley, Lord of Dursley. Roger, however, proved unwilling to hand over his inheritance, and the ensuing dispute was resolved, as so often happened, through expedient marriages between the two families, with Robert's eldest son Maurice marrying Alice, the daughter of the Lord of Dursley, whilst Roger's son espoused one of the daughters of Robert Fitz-Harding.

Fitz-Harding commissioned and endowed the monastery of St. Augustine at Bristol (now the Cathedral), where he was eventually laid to rest.

Any other anachronisms or historical errors are entirely unintentional, and the blame for them lies solely with me.

Emily Ross
21 November 2014

A word about the author...

Emily Ross lives in West Wales with her longsuffering husband, two allegedly grown-up children, one very spoiled dog, and a completely neurotic but much-loved horse.

A passion for history initially led to a degree in archaeology, but in the years since graduation and bringing up her family she has done a variety of jobs and currently works full-time in the family department of a busy local law firm.

A Necessary Risk is Emily's first full-length novel, and a sequel is in progress.

Emily loves to hear from readers and can be contacted at:

emilyross2405@yahoo.co.uk

Thank you for purchasing
this publication of The Wild Rose Press, Inc.

If you enjoyed the story, we would appreciate your letting others know by leaving a review.

For other wonderful stories,
please visit our on-line bookstore at
www.thewildrosepress.com.

For questions or more information
contact us at
info@thewildrosepress.com.

The Wild Rose Press, Inc.
www.thewildrosepress.com

Stay current with The Wild Rose Press, Inc.

Like us on Facebook

https://www.facebook.com/TheWildRosePress

And Follow us on Twitter
https://twitter.com/WildRosePress